SIX
AND A HALF
DEADLY
SINS

ALSO BY COLIN COTTERILL

SIX AND A HALF DEADLY SINS

COLIN COTTERILL

SOHO
CRIME

Published by
Soho Press, Inc.
853 Broadway
New York, NY 10003

Library of Congress Cataloging-in-Publication Data

Cotterill, Colin.
Six and a half deadly sins / Colin Cotterill.
1. Paiboun, Siri, Doctor (Fictitious character)—Fiction.
2. Coroners—Fiction. 3. Laos—Fiction. I. Title.
PR6053.O778S56 2015
823'.914—dc23   2014033790

ISBN 978-1-61695-558-8
PB ISBN 978-1-61695-638-7
eISBN 978-1-61695-559-5

Printed in the United States of America

10 9 8 7 6 5 4 3 2 1

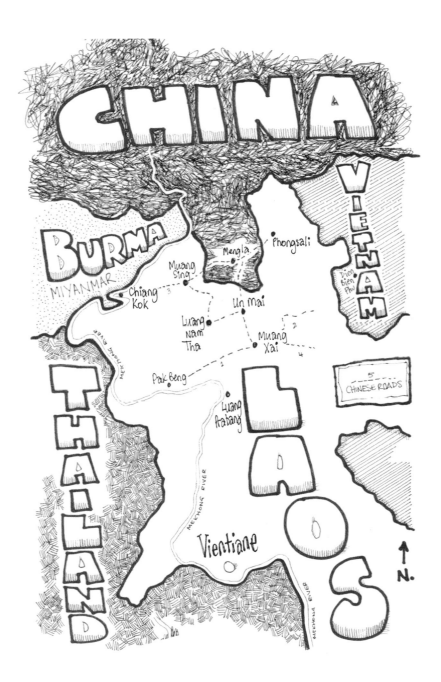

TABLE OF CONTENTS

1

The First Deadly Sin

On December 25, 1978, the concrete public-address system pole in South That Luang's Area Six unexpectedly blew itself up, a Lao skirt with a severed finger sewn into the hem passed through the national postal system unchallenged and Vietnam invaded Cambodia. A few weeks had passed since then, but the two old men sitting on a log beside the milk chocolate–colored Mekhong River hadn't yet exhausted their opinions on the three events. Dr. Siri Paiboun—ex-national coroner for the Lao People's Democratic Republic—had been responsible for the first of them. Comrade Civilai Song-sawat—ex-politburo member—had predicted the latter, and nobody had listened to him. But the finger? Well, neither man could make heads or tails of that.

"Do you suppose it might have belonged to the weaver?" asked Civilai. "Some loom accident?"

"What?" said Siri. "You mean she was so engrossed in her skirt-making that she didn't notice she'd sewn her own finger into the hem? Got home that evening, and her husband says, 'Hey, where's your finger?' And she looks down to find it gone and says, 'Hm. I must have inadvertently sewn it into one of the skirts'?"

There followed a brief silence while the old boys worked on their baguette lunches. They'd noticed how much more difficult it had become to chew the crusty beasts since reaching their mid-seventies. Siri surmised that just as the rice whiskey distiller had added ingredients that increased the odds of a raging hangover, and the bicycle manufacturers had removed the gears that allowed one to climb hills without becoming winded, so the baker had changed to a more leathery dough recipe. All were signs of the declining standards of modernization.

Civilai took a mouthful of tamarind juice and swirled it around his mouth before swallowing. "Sarcasm," he said, "is like throwing a stick at your enemy when you've run out of bullets."

Siri nodded and smiled at his oldest friend. "Lenin?"

"Civilai."

"You don't say? Well, in that case, it was very good."

"Thank you. And I stand by my hunch. An illiterate young woman enslaved in a sweatshop sends a last-gasp plea for help by snipping off her finger and sending it out with the day's batch of *pha sin* skirts."

Siri nodded again. His nods were rarely those of agreement. "That's even sillier, Old Brother," he said. "I mean, how would we trace her on the strength of a lopped finger?"

"Fingerprints."

"Fingerprints? Right. Well, that pretty much sums up the difference between a medical man and a politician."

"How so?"

"A medical man—a man of science—would look at the relative values of a fingerprint. He would consider the options available. Should he go to a central databank of fingerprints like the one we don't have in Laos? Should he compare it with similar fingerprints found at the absent scene of the crime? Or should he travel door to door like Prince Charming until he found a Cinderella whose stump matched the discarded finger?"

Civilai smiled. "And the politician?"

"He would make a statement promising great things to come, get elected, then blame the scientists when they failed to come up with the goods."

They returned to their baguettes.

Nearby, a frail woman in yellow wellington boots tossed a huge mushroom net into the river. The weights sank below the grimy surface, and the fisherlady yanked at the ropes. It was her seventh or eighth cast, and like its predecessors, it yielded nothing.

"Like attempting to lasso a fly," said Siri. "If only she—"

"Then what do you make of the finger?" asked Civilai, not at all interested in fish unless they were steamed in lemon juice.

"I think perhaps it's a clue."

"And it was pointing toward the next clue?"

"I'm assuming that the finger was merely a part of the puzzle. There was no letter enclosed and no return address on the wrapping paper. I admit it's not inconceivable that the letter censors at the Ministry of Disbelief and Paranoia confiscated a note. But I believe the skirt itself has something to tell us."

"A talking skirt?"

"Very much so. The *pha sin* weave is very distinctive, quite colorful. Madame Daeng informs me it's likely to have originated in the north. She's taken it to the ladies at the morning market who specialize in such things. A Lao *sin* is every bit as useful as a fingerprint for tracing its origin."

"The frank stamp on the parcel didn't help in that regard?"

"It was so faint it was illegible."

"I'm surprised the people at the post office didn't notice the finger."

"It was rather spindly. I didn't notice it myself at first. It was only the other day when Ugly the dog started staring at it and salivating that I took another look. He's rather good with body parts."

"And how are his climbing skills?"

"Quite average as dogs go. But how is that relevant?"

"Just wondered whether you'd taught him to shimmy up a public-address pole."

"Oh, Civilai. Not you too? Why is it that whenever a lump of shoddy Soviet technology blows itself up, the blame lands on my shoulders?"

"Oh, I don't know. Perhaps the two previous arrests for chopping down wooden loudspeaker poles."

"I was acquitted both times."

They watched an aerial skirmish as a hundred or so swallows darted back and forth above the river, picking crunchy dung beetles out of the warm air.

"I'm reasonably certain it's because of you they switched to concrete," said Civilai.

"And you're suggesting a frail seventy-four-year-old with dodgy lungs, a semi-crippled hand and a missing left earlobe could climb four meters, unlock the control box, insert a hand grenade and climb rapidly down before the thing exploded? . . . If, indeed, it *was* a hand grenade. I confess I could sympathize with the person responsible. Nobody enjoys being woken at the crack of dawn with jaunty Party songs and advice on what percentage of urine to water in the soil produces the best papayas. Although, goodness knows, I was getting fond of those endless lists of names of this month's Most Productive Socialist Men and Women and reports on cooperative farming yields. And so clear too with the speaker pointing directly into my . . . I mean, *his* bedroom window. Yes, I have to admit I admire the scoundrel."

"They'll get you, you know."

"Innocent until proven otherwise, Brother Civilai. And

what's all the fuss? A little bit of melted soldering? It's not like I invaded Cambodia, is it now?"

"The smaller the incident, the easier it is to penalize. You know that. And given your run-in with Brother Number One, I doubt you even consider the liberation of what's left of Cambodia to be a crime at all."

"No, you're right. More power to the heroic Vietnamese. They created the Pol Pot dynasty and watched while he murdered two million people. Their crime isn't that they're invading; it's that they're invading four years too late."

On her eighth cast of the net, the woman in the yellow boots brought in a fish harvest that would feed her family for a week. She could barely drag the net up the bank. The old boys went down to give her a hand. Siri missed his step at the bottom and slid down into the river. He swallowed some but laughed it off.

"You know, the Chinese aren't going to be at all pleased about this," said Civilai.

"Catching fish?"

"Vietnam. China's supported the Khmer Rouge all through the genocide. Even now they're pumping in aid."

By the time they reached the top of the bank, all three collapsed onto the grass to catch their breaths. There followed a fit of coughing and laughter. The fisherwoman handed them each a malnourished thick-lipped barb as a tip and loaded her catch onto her bicycle sidecar.

"I see major repercussions," said Civilai, lying back on the grass.

"From the fish?"

"The Chinese."

"What can they do?" Siri asked. "Declare war on Vietnam?"

As Chinese troops began their deployment to the northern border of Vietnam, Siri was sitting at the outdoor table behind his government-allocated house near That Luang Temple. Opposite was his comparatively new wife, Madame Daeng. Beside her sat a spindly but attractive old lady in clothes some might have considered too large for her. Siri, however, could see that Madame Chanta of the Lao Women's Union was merely in the process of shrinking. He too had trousers that had mysteriously grown too long in the leg. Madame Chanta had fine dentures that were neater than the synthetic Chinese sets on sale behind the morning market. Her hair was dyed black, all but for a small crown of white that girded her scalp. She told them she had decided to stop the battle. If her hair so desperately wished to be white, she would let it.

"And pray," she said, "that it looks as stunning as yours, Madame Daeng."

Siri's wife—recently turned sixty-seven—wore her hair gray, wild and short, a style that complemented her handsome face. And on this day it was a face that sported a smile as bright as Venus. Siri often found himself gazing at his woman with great pride even on days when he knew the smile was a vestige of a buzz from her opium tea. It had been many years since Madame Daeng last walked with grace, not since the rheumatism first started to knot her ankles, then to bind the muscles and tissues of her legs into an excruciating macramé. Some days she could hardly get out of bed. Unlike morphine, opium didn't make the pain fade into the background; it allowed you to face it in a mellow battle and conquer it, to feel less like a victim. The victories of late had become shorter and less convincing.

"It's Thai Lu," said Chanta. "Unmistakably."

"How can you tell?" Siri asked, looking down at the old *pha sin* stretched across the table between them.

"Well, one reason is that most Lao *sin*s have the pattern band at the bottom, a *tin sin*. A decoration around the hem.

The Lu prefer their brocade high up and leave the hem plain. That's the first indication. Although different Lu groups have their own styles, there are one or two regional peculiarities. You'll notice that the weft here is vertical. The Lu often weave the front and back horizonally then cut and sew them at the sides so the design matches. It's also longer than most. The Lu traditionally wore their skirts high below the breasts, what we call an empire waist. That . . ."

As Chanta went into more detail, Daeng looked into her husband's eyes and saw a familiar glazing. "Sister," she said, "this is what you explained to me earlier. I think the doctor would prefer you to just tell him where you believe this *pha sin* came from. He has a short attention span."

"Doctor," said Chanta, "this is a very heavy handspun cotton designed for cold weather the type of which we have in the north. As I'm sure you know, the Lu settled in several provinces in the north but never very far from their roots in China. The Lu are more likely to have black or indigo hems. But I've seen other samples with green in the north. I'm quite certain this *sin* comes from Luang Nam Tha."

"Luang Nam Tha?" said Siri.

"I believe so."

"Then that is where we shall go."

Siri took Madame Chanta home on the back of his Triumph. He had opted not to ask whether a severed finger was a feature of the Luang Nam Tha *sin*. Due to her lack of bulk and her billowy clothes, his passenger had almost blown off the saddle twice, so he'd slowed the motorcycle to a crawl. This in turn led to her picking up a cough from the exhaust fumes. She thanked him and suggested that fate would draw them back together very soon.

When Siri returned home, Madame Daeng was still seated

at the backyard table. She'd been joined by four of their housemates: Comrade Noo, the Thai forest monk, currently incognito in a singlet and Bermuda shorts; Mr. Inthanet, the puppet master; the silent wandering woman whose name and background they still hadn't learned, even after three months of cohabitation; and Crazy Rajhid, the Indian street person. Rajhid had joined the household, which now comprised eleven vagabonds and exiles, just a week before. He'd arrived at the ever-open front door with a perfectly fine suitcase and asked in perfectly fine Lao, "Where do I sleep?"

This from a man who had not spoken for two years. So shocked were they all to hear words come from his mouth, Siri and Daeng pointed to a corner of the large living room, where he chalked an outline of himself on the decorative green tiles and hadn't spoken again. They decided that this technically meant Rajhid was no longer homeless. Siri and Daeng would never refuse a person in trouble, but if the truth were to be told, they'd never expected to be living together with this menagerie of waifs and strays.

Until a few months earlier, the couple had lived above Daeng's famous noodle shop down by the river. Siri had reveled in the intimacy and privacy, rare commodities in a city where families were crammed together in single rooms in the old French villas. Above the shop, he would read from his illegal library of classics and spend blissful hours in uninterrupted conversation with his wife. There they could retire to the bedroom without stepping over sleeping bodies or allowing frightened children to curl up between them.

All those privileges had been taken from them by a homicidal maniac with two cans of benzene and a Bic lighter. The walls still stood, but the books and the privacy were charred memories. Siri's previous accommodation had fared little better—blown to smithereens by mortars—and he was developing a reputation of being a clumsy householder. Some would say it served him right—that his personality attracted disasters. Men his age shouldn't get into so much trouble. They believed if he just toed the line and did as he was told, he could enjoy his retirement in peace. But he was bored to hell and back. Without his library he had no vicarious lives to live. Without his morgue he had no exercise for his overactive brain. Without a vacant room he could no longer prove to his wife that he was a remarkable man in many ways. He'd begun to doubt himself.

And that was exactly why the finger in the *pha sin* had come as such a blessing.

He sat on the bench beside Daeng and shuffled her along with his bottom to make space for himself. He squeezed her knee, wondering whether she could feel it.

"So let's go," he said.

"Where?" asked his wife.

"To Luang Nam Tha," said Siri. "Nice scenery. Cool weather . . ."

"Drug warlords and violence," added Inthanet, who had the house franchise for pessimism. The old puppet master bore more than a passing resemblance to Dr. Siri and had, on one or two occasions, doubled for the doctor to get him out of scrapes. He felt he'd earned the right to be ornery.

"Ah, old fellow, you're thinking about the old days," said Siri. "Of the Hor Chinese bandits and the French opium riots. We're a socialist state now. The far north's as safe as a stroll down Samsenthai Avenue on a balmy evening. What do you say, my wife?"

"How do we get there?" she asked.

"That's the spirit."

"No, I mean, how, practically, would we go there? It's not like we have functioning public transport. We can't just wander down to the airport, buy a ticket and hop on a plane. Not that we've got any money to afford it. Just getting the *laissez-passers* could take six months."

"I know that," said Siri. "But don't forget I'm acquainted with a lot of influential people."

"That's true," said Inthanet, "but none of them likes you."

"Blackmail," said Noo, the monk.

"See?" said Siri. "There's always a way."

"I think you've exhausted all your resources for dishonest leverage," said Daeng.

"Nonsense," said Siri. "There's always Judge Haeng. Need I remind you the seedy little man is firmly in my pocket? He can ever be trusted to do something untrustworthy."

He smiled as he thought about a letter that was rolled safely in the shaft of his Burmese shooting stick. Were it to be shown around to the powers that be at the Ministry of Justice, it would signal the end of the young judge's career and, almost certainly, of his life. Blackmail indeed. The ultimate persuasion.

"Hmm, you won't get much luck there," said Inthanet.

"Why not?"

"You haven't heard what happened?"

"No."

"He's out of Justice. They've got him running a training course at the Ministry of Foreign Affairs pending an inquiry."

"What did he do?" asked Daeng. "He was head of Public Prosecution last time I saw him."

"There were rumors," said Inthanet.

"About what?"

"Suggestions he had a stable of young women cached around Vientiane."

"Well, he does," said Siri.

"Turns out he beat some of them up, and they went to the Women's Union. They put pressure on Justice to investigate. Justice had no choice but to move him to an inactive post."

"Who's he training?" asked Daeng.

"Domestic staff."

Siri and Daeng both laughed. The silent woman's eyes twinkled.

"What on earth does Haeng know about domestic service?" asked Siri. "And what's it got to do with Foreign Affairs?"

"It's a spy school," said Inthanet. "Anyone working for foreigners in Vientiane has to attend. All the maids, the gardeners, the cooks—they're all highly trained undercover operatives."

"Nonsense," said Siri.

"All right, perhaps they don't get down to the microcameras and the phone bugging and the James Bond level of spying, but they do have classes on eavesdropping and personal document browsing. They have to file a weekly report on all visitors to the house, car registrations, names."

"Good grief," said Siri. "What has our world come to? How do you know all this?"

"My fiancée," said Inthanet. "She's a cook. She's had to take the course to get her license."

"I thought your fiancée was a basket weaver," said Daeng.

"No, that was my previous fiancée. This is a more serious engagement."

"You do know you don't have to propose to every woman you go out with?"

"Madame Daeng, you'd be surprised how grateful women can be when a man even mentions marriage. They develop an ability to see beyond his flaccid muscles and wrinkled demeanor."

"You're a dirty old man, Comrade Inthanet."

The dirty old man smiled at the silent woman, who smiled back briefly.

"We have to rescue Judge Haeng," said Siri. "Get him back at Justice where he belongs."

"He's a woman beater," Daeng reminded him.

"He has flaws," said Siri, "but I don't see him beating any-one up, do you? He might hire someone else to do it, but he wouldn't get his own hands bloody."

"Am I right in thinking this new campaign has little to do with your respect for the judge and the pursuance of fair play?" asked Daeng.

"You're absolutely right, Daeng. We have to get ourselves to Luang Nam Tha, and he's the man who can get us there."

The next day, Siri rode the old Pigeon bicycle along a dusty lane to the Lao Women's Union. Ugly the dog trotted beside. The low grey building lay shrouded in well-cared-for vegeta-tion. The fine weather that had begun sometime around August was now into its sixth month. This was something of a disappointment to the government. The floods and droughts of the previous three years had provided timely excuses for things going wrong. Now the only disasters were those they created themselves. Currently, as an excuse for the shortages around Vientiane, the authorities were blam-ing the Cambodian invasion and the humanitarian aid Laos was pumping into that country. In fact, their one-off aid package came to a paltry million dollars, and that had been borrowed from Vietnam. The markets were empty because the farmers had stopped producing more than they needed to survive.

The cool, sunny days of January were kind to the garden. In spite of the Party directive that all available space should be planted with vegetables and fruit, the Auntie's Tendon, the Pulling-Down Elephant and the Farting Spirit flowers all vied for prominence in the front yard; the Maiden's Breasts were resplendent in their yellow tassels. Clearly, the women of the union were aware that in hard times, the sight of a beautiful garden had a most energizing effect. Siri took some time to sniff on his way into the reception area.

"Hello, Dr. Siri," said the happy, hoppy young woman who came to meet him. She bounced from foot to foot and held out her hand. Handshakes had entered Laos with the French and been consolidated by Communism, but this new phenomenon of women offering their hand was hard for an old man to get used to. He never knew what to do with it. He tickled her fingertips.

"Hello, Boun," he said. "Is your boss in?"

"She's in a meeting," said the girl.

"You know, if this country just allowed a couple of hours between meetings, we might actually have time to achieve something."

"Are you still whinging, Dr. Siri?" came a voice from behind him.

He turned to see Dr. Porn heading a small posse of women out of the meeting room. As always, she looked neat but flustered. Sweat glistened on her hairless brow.

"Still no luck with the eyebrows?" Siri smiled.

"I was thinking of starting steroid injections," she said. "But I couldn't picture myself with a beard. Get in here."

She took his arm and led him into her office. There was no door. For the next fifteen minutes, over a cup of tea, she told him all the details of Judge Haeng's violent attacks on two young women. The evidence against the judge was overwhelming. He had arrived at their rooms in the dark while they were sleeping. He had spoken to them; then, with no provocation, he had beaten them. She showed him the photographs they'd taken of the two victims. Two days after the attack, the bruises were still prominent.

"What did the judge say?" Siri asked.

"He's denied it, of course. Said he'd been set up."

"Did the girls say he'd done anything like this before?"

"No. It appeared to be one insane night of frenzied violence. We weren't in a position to have him tested for drugs or alcohol, but all the indications are that he was high on something."

Siri shook his head.

Siri rode his old Pigeon over the hill to the Ministry of Foreign Affairs. Ugly the dog continued to trot happily beside him. The day ran hot and cool in spasms as the air currents wrestled for dominance in the dusty city. The sun glided from cloud to cloud, and some flocks of birds headed south while others headed north. These were uncertain times.

The guard at the ungated entrance to the ministry was overweight. Siri recalled a health department memo circulated during his first year in Vientiane. It suggested that overweight people were not to be trusted. They symbolized overindulgence, a lamentable capitalist trait. To the doctor's mind, the young man in unmatching fatigues was more a symbol of a glandular disorder and intolerance.

The guard yelled at Siri. "Hey, you! You can't leave that bicycle propped up against the gatepost like that. And where do you think you're going with that mangy dog? You're not entering this building with that thing."

It was a bold effort from an unarmed man whose inner thighs rubbed together as he walked, but Siri and Ugly ignored him. The guard took a step toward them, and Ugly snarled. The guard took a step back. "I'll be reporting this," he shouted.

Siri nodded.

The class for domestics was being conducted out of a bunker-like room to one side of the dirty two-story ministry. There was a small glassless window on either side of the doorway, and both shutters and the door were thrown open as if gasping for air. Some forty servants of assorted ages, sizes and genders were squashed onto small benches behind squat desks. Each person held a pencil over a sheet of paper, but nobody was writing, and as far as Siri could see, the papers were untouched. Judge Haeng wore a grey safari shirt with darker grey sweat circles at the armpits, and he had violently inflamed acne around the gills. He was attempting to teach the art of gleaning relevant information from householders who spoke in foreign languages. This lesson might have been effective in French, as there were ex-nannies of French children still in domestic service. It might have even worked in English for the ex-employees of the Americans at Kilometer Six. But the vast majority of foreign experts now were from the Soviet Bloc, some two thousand Russians, and the Soviets, anxious to hang on to their humble per diems, were reluctant to take on local staff. And those who did, like the ambassador and the head of the cultural center, found themselves speaking French or English when dealing with servants. So to Siri, the listening comprehension exercise—a chalk sentence written in Russian, and transcribed and translated in Lao, WE ARE PLANNING TO OVERTHROW THE LAO GOVERNMENT—was somewhat overambitious.

Siri and Ugly sat at a bench outside the classroom and enjoyed another twenty minutes of Judge Haeng's suffering.

"Serves him right," came a voice from inside Siri's head. Only Siri could hear it. Very few living people shared the secrets of the comings and goings between his ears. It was all a little complicated. Dr. Siri, you see, was a carrier. His chief passenger was Yeh Ming, a thousand-year-old Hmong shaman. Yeh Ming had made a number of dangerous enemies in the spirit world and was currently holed up inside the doctor. He made no comments at all, and Siri had no direct contact with him, but those with abilities could sense the shaman's spirit. Then there were several personal ghosts, like the mother he couldn't remember and his ex-dog. And some-where off in the distance, there were the hushed breaths of several thousand troubled Khmer who'd stowed away when he left Cambodia.

But now, as if the afterlife wasn't crowded enough, he heard the voice of Auntie Bpoo, the transvestite fortune teller. She'd died a few months earlier and stepped rudely into his subconscious. He'd hoped she might act as a guide to make sense of all the madness in his head, but although he could hear her voice, they had yet to hit on a two-way method of communication. It was as if someone had left the microphone on and the background noise was constantly audible. Every now and then Bpoo would step up to the mike and make a comment such as, "Serves him right." Siri still believed everything was learnable, but for now he had to live with dead people in his head and no control whatsoever over when or how they communicated with him.

Finally, the judge dismissed the students with the motto, "A good socialist is like a motorcar. At the pump of life, he is filled with valuable information which he uses to complete his journey. And any information that is contradictory or anticommunist he allows to blow out of his exhaust pipe." The students fled like a group stirred by an air-raid siren. Siri walked into the classroom to find the judge seated at the teacher's table with his head cupped in his hands. He may have been crying.

"Developed a soft spot for any of your housemaids yet?" Siri asked.

The judge looked up with the expression of a drowning man now handed a heavy rock. "Siri," he said, and buried his face back into his hands.

"You have very nice handwriting," said Siri. It was probably the first compliment he had ever paid the judge. Undoubt-edly the last.

"What do you want?" the judge asked through his fingers.

"My wife and I would like to go to Luang Nam Tha."

The judge looked up again and laughed. "Siri, do you not see where I am?"

"I see it."

"Then?"

"I can get you out."

"If I, as the head of Public Prosecution, can't get myself out, how could somebody like you expect to?"

"Well, Judge, you have to remember that I am much cannier than you. I thought you would have learned that by now. All we need is an agreement. I get you back in your old job, and you send Daeng and me up north."

The judge drummed his overly long fingernails on the desktop. He looked beyond Siri as if addressing someone standing at the back of the room. "Why would anyone want to go to Luang Nam Tha?" he asked.

"Tourism. Is it a deal?"

"There's no possible way you—"

"Is it a deal?"

The judge selected a sarcastic smirk from his repertoire of annoying expressions. "If by some miracle you were able to re-establish me in my previous position, yes. I give you my word."

"Good, but I don't put much faith in your word, which is why I brought this." Siri reached into his shoulder bag and produced a sheet of paper.

"What is that?" the judge asked.

"It's a copy of a letter you wrote applying for immunity in the USA."

The judge turned the color of sand. "You told me you . . . You said you'd destroyed it."

"I did, didn't I?" Siri smiled. "It would appear my word is no more tangible than yours."

"Siri, you have to know this. I was framed," said the judge with a sincere expression on his insincere face.

"You mean the women set themselves up in love nests around the town and coerced you to sleep with them?"

"No, look. I might have done that."

"Might have?"

"All right. Yes. I did it. Come on, Siri. You're a man. You know what it's like. It's hard to turn down some of these girls. I am, after all, very attractive."

Siri was surprised the man had been able to say that with a straight yet pockmarked face.

"And I'm single," the judge continued. "Single men have liaisons. It's nature's calling card. All the species do it."

"Not too many tortoises use government-allocated housing with box-spring mattresses smuggled in from Thailand," said Siri, citing information Auntie Bpoo had passed along before she passed away. As well as being a very effective psychic, the old transvestite had been inordinately nosy. The temptation to rummage through the minds of important people had proved irresistible to her.

"How do . . . ?"

"I have sources."

"Siri, I merely found accommodation for a few poor homeless girls. The rooms were empty. With all the red tape, it takes a year, sometimes two, to match families with appropriate accommodation. And all that time the places remain vacant. I was merely utilizing resources. Our President encouraged us to do so. A good socialist can—"

"Don't."

"I swear I did not lay a hand on those women . . . in a violent way."

"Then why would they claim you had? And two of them, no less."

"I really don't understand it. One of them I hadn't seen

for a month, and suddenly she arrives at the Women's Union with bruises."

Siri, it must be remembered, had no positive feelings toward Judge Haeng. There had been no bonding between them on any level. From experience he knew that the judge was a cheat and a liar. But he wasn't a particularly good one, and this current routine would have been far beyond the little man's acting ability. But what would the girls have to gain by inventing such a story? With the judge ousted from his position or, worse, incarcerated, their small comparatively luxurious lifestyles would dissolve. They'd be back in the fields.

Siri took down the addresses of the judge's concubines and said he would pay them a visit.

2

The Chicken Autopsy

On the next leg of his Vientiane bicycle tour, Siri leaned the
Pigeon against a recently decapitated tree in front of the Mahosot morgue. Several other trees had been similarly butchered
in his absence, yet the grounds remained neglected and sad.
Grass grew on the footpaths but not on the old lawn. Weeds
had taken over the flower beds. The laboratory goats who
reluctantly donated their blood once a week in the interests
of medical science looked gaunt and in need of transfusions
themselves.

Siri and Ugly wiped their feet on a new plastic mat that had
replaced Siri's old "Welcome" rug and walked inside. The
morgue felt devoid of life. Mr. Geung was no longer there.
The morgue assistant during Siri's entire tenure had been
a man blessed with the innocence of Down syndrome. For
many years he had swept and dusted the building, changed
the broken louvers and the burned-out lightbulbs. But with
Siri's retirement, Mr. Geung had been removed from hospital
service. Until the blaze, he had worked at Daeng's restaurant.
Then, twice unemployed, he had headed off to the village of
his fiancée, Tukta, to spend time on her family farm—now
part of one more disastrous cooperative.

The morgue was largely unused these days, but Siri had arranged to meet Nurse Dtui for a little nostalgic slab work. Dtui had been the third member of his highly successful team. Together they had solved cases that had left the police baffled. They'd received no official kudos for their work, but 1978 Laos wasn't known for its compliments.

Siri entered the cutting room to discover Dtui hacking away at a plucked chicken with a number-seven cleaver. Her large frame rocked back and forth to an unheard rhythm. Her daughter, Malee, lay in a hammock suspended between the freezer door and a concrete pillar.

Siri stood beside Dtui and admired her work. "Accident?" he asked.

"Murder," said Dtui. "A wrung neck. See the ecchymosis to the clavicle and the lateral neck abrasions and bruising?"

"Do you have enough forensic evidence to put the killer away?"

"No need. It was me. I confess."

"Motive?"

"Dinner."

"Fair enough. I don't suppose you'd let me make a Y incision just for old times' sake?"

"Are you bored, Doc?"

"To death. How are classes going at the old Lido?"

"Excruciating. Nursing students so young and so countrified, they still giggle whenever I refer to sexual organs. 'Penis' brings the house down. And the ministry hasn't paid us teachers since October. They must think I'm there for the fun of it. This was the last chicken standing. We're on yams and dirt when this is gone. Phosy's police pig bank dried up at the end of last year, so no pork. The markets are empty. The farmers are so against all that cooperative nonsense, they've stopped breeding. I mean, the animals. Not amongst themselves."

"I gathered that."

"I mean, I can see their point. What good does it do if you have to give most of your livestock away to your layabout neighbors? The government pays so little, the breeders prefer to hide their animals in the forest when the chicken counters come around." Dtui looked at the doctor's glazed expression.

"My classes?" she said. "They're going fine."

"That's good to hear," he said. "You know, I think I can see signs of tobacco addiction in this chicken. Lungs are a little sooty. Nicotine stains on the claws. I'd say if you hadn't strangled her, she'd have died of lung cancer within the week."

"Then I can fry her with a clear conscience," she said. "Why did you want me here, Doc?"

"I thought you'd never ask."

He coughed, reached into his shoulder pouch and produced a plastic bag. He opened it on the stainless steel mortuary table, removed the *pha sin* and told her the story of how it had come into his possession. Once he had done so, he dramatically reached into the section of hem that had been unstitched and produced the severed finger.

"Yuck," said Dtui.

"Yuck, indeed," Siri agreed. "This is the reason I wanted to meet you here."

"To repulse me?"

"To solve the mystery of why I was sent a finger. I have learned that the skirt itself probably originated in the north. Now we need to ascertain the fate of the finger owner."

"You're the coroner."

"Ex-coroner. You are the coroner-elect."

"I'm unqualified."

"But not untrained. You have drained every last milliliter of knowledge from me, digested numerous books in languages I could never read, and you have an uncanny instinct. The only reason you aren't the national coroner is that the cheapskates up at Parliament House can't afford to send you to the Soviet Union to get a certificate."

"Well, plus I have a one-year-old daughter and a husband who expects food on the table when he comes home from a busy day of policing."

"And where is our brave Inspector Phosy these days?"

"Luang Nam Tha."

"No? Huh! See?" Siri shuffled around the slab with his arms aloft.

"See what?" asked Dtui.

"There is no such thing as a coincidence, Nurse Dtui. Here I receive a parcel from Luang Nam Tha, and there he is in Luang Nam Tha. Tell me there's not something suspicious about that. What's he doing there?"

"Something top secret."

"What?"

"How could I know? It's top secret." She blushed and turned away.

"Dtui, your husband discusses all his cases with you. He'd be a fool not to. And given my wealth of experience, you'd be a fool not to tell me."

"I'm not supposed to."

"Of course you're not."

She rolled her eyes. "Two important village headmen died mysteriously within a few minutes of each other. He's up there to avert an international incident."

"Fascinating. Which nation are we placating?"

"China. You know things are a little difficult up there now."

"As ever."

"Well, the two villages are on the route of Chinese Road Number Two. The Chinese laborers are camped nearby. There are rumors that the headmen were killed by the workers."

"Cause of death?"

"Multiple stab wounds."

"Weapon?"

"Sharpened bamboo poles."

"Ouch."

"If it turns out the Chinese are responsible, there'd be enough pressure from Hanoi to have the road project shut down. The Chinese have been laying roads up there for twelve years already. The Thais and the Viets are certain there are motives beyond international aid. Some of those roads are getting perilously close to their borders."

"That sounds like a remarkably patient invasion to me."

"It took them two thousand years to build a wall."

"Good point. What they need up there is a forensic investigator and his wife."

"Don't bother. Phosy tried that one. The police department doesn't want an in-depth investigation. They want a senior policeman to go up there to make a statement that the Chinese couldn't possibly have been responsible. The government wants to keep the road program going for as long as it can."

"My thought is that they didn't select the right man for the job. He's hardly going to fabricate a report just to please the government. He's far too conscientious for that."

"Phosy's Phosy. He'll go there and discover the truth and submit his report, and if it suits them, they'll announce it. And if it doesn't, they'll rewrite it. He just needs to be seen up there."

"He needs me."

"You'll have to find another way of getting there. The police won't fly you up. What about Justice?"

"I'm working on that. But first, the finger. I doubt I'll be able to analyze it in Luang Nam Tha."

Dtui looked around at the morgue lab. At the peeling paint and the grumbling air conditioner. At the open cupboards that had once contained equipment. At the flickering strip light and the unswept floor. "I doubt you'll be able to here."

"We have the books. We have Teacher Ou at the *lycée* with her chemistry set. We have experience. We are a highly professional crew."

"Then you would have heard there are protocols about not contaminating evidence."

"I've heard that. Your point?"

"You just put the finger in your shirt pocket with the pens."

He hurriedly removed the finger and held it up between his thumb and forefinger like a cigar. There was an ink stain along one side. He hadn't noticed the pen was leaking because his peasant shirt was the same color as the ink.

"Let's just say that if we were in a country that accepted evidence based on trace elements," said Dtui, "our finger here would be thrown out of court."

"I most certainly would not allow anyone to throw my finger out of anything. We've become quite attached over the past month."

"You've had it for a month?"

"I only recently found it in the hem."

"It's just . . ." She took the finger from Siri and held it to her nose.

"Ah, an insight," said Siri.

"There's not much deterioration," said Dtui. "You didn't have it in formaldehyde, did you?"

"It's been in the fridge with the soy milk for the past week, but the freezer doesn't work."

"And if you assume it was in the post office for the usual couple of weeks, you'd expect it to stink by now."

"Odd, isn't it?"

"I don't smell any preservatives, but there is a strange . . . I don't know, pervasive odor of something I should be able to recognize." She took up the *pha sin* and sniffed at the hem.

"It's stronger here . . . something chemical," she decided, "but it's as if there are several scents combined."

"Teacher Ou might be able to isolate the compounds," said Siri.

"I'll take it over to her after."

"What about the finger itself?"

"Well, it's quite well preserved, so I imagine there hasn't been much shrinkage. It belonged to a male."

"What makes you think so?"

At sessions such as this, Dtui always assumed her boss had already arrived at his conclusions and was merely seeking a second opinion. "Hairs," she said. "We girls don't generally have hairy knuckles."

"I've dated a few who did."

Dtui laughed.

"So if it is male," she said, "its size suggests it's a pinky. Callused pad. This is the finger of a laborer, not a clerk or a rice planter submerged in water all day."

"Any chance he's still living?"

"Don't know. There's no congealed blood at the base, so no evidence it was cut off when he was alive."

"How was it cut?"

"Scissors."

Siri raised his bushy white eyebrows.

Dtui smiled. "Or more likely shears of some kind," she said. "With a knife or machete, you get an even cut. But look here. There's a step. You get that when two blades meet at different levels."

"You do realize you're wasted teaching basic bed-wetting?"

"Yes."

"Anything else?"

She took up the magnifying glass and rotated the finger. "Dirt," she said. "Clay, perhaps, under the fingernail."

"Laterite."

"How do you know that?"

"I took a sample to an ex-patient at the public works department."

"And he recognized the color?"

"The taste. It's particularly—"

"But the nail's still dirty."

"Yes, I put it back."

"For me? How sweet."

"But don't you see, Dtui? Another connection. Phosy's headmen were allegedly killed by Chinese road workers. And here we have a severed finger with laterite under the nail. A road builder."

"Or somebody climbing out of a pit. Or a brickmaker. Or the center forward of a football team who fell over in the penalty area. Laterite's everywhere, Doc."

Siri diverted his look of disappointment into an inquisitive gaze at the missing louvers.

"Regardless," he said, "I believe the answer to all our quests lies to the north. At the Chinese border. The sooner Daeng and I can get there, the better."

"You do realize that even though the *sin* originates from the north, it could have been sent from anywhere?"

"Never mind. Daeng's never been to Luang Nam Tha. We're attempting to see every province before we pass away. And we really want to get out of our noisy house."

"How can I help?"

Siri took the scissors from the equipment cabinet and cut the *sin* lengthwise into two halves. "I'll keep half of this in case we find ourselves suddenly jetting off to Luang Nam Tha. You take the other half to Teacher Ou and see if she can identify the conflicting compounds we can smell. I'll leave the finger with you. Do your Dtui magic on it."

"You know, it's strange," she said. "The digital pulp is

callused, but the skin is surprisingly pale. You'd assume a laborer to show the ravages of the sun."

"An albino, perhaps?"

"Hm. Not impossible."

"What fun Simenon would have with this one." Siri laughed. *"The Case of the Finger of the White-Skinned Chinese Laborer."*

With that, his laugh broke into a coughing fit. Flu—European-style, more damned annoying than lethal—seemed to be going around the capital, and Siri was afraid he'd caught it.

Before leaving the hospital grounds, Siri looked at the piece of paper that contained the addresses of Judge Haeng's mistresses. He triangulated them in his mind and decided he only had the lung capacity that day for one visit. His choice was mistress number three, Miss Singxay, the one who hadn't claimed abuse. In battle it often proved just as valuable to analyze those targets not attacked by the enemy as those that were.

Miss Singxay lived in a small apartment above a hairdresser's on Pangkham. Ugly guarded the bike. There was a steep private staircase to the rear. Siri had to catch his breath before knocking. The moderate force of his knock opened the door. It swung on uneven hinges, affording him a view of the room partly blocked by the small shower alcove inside the door. He could see cheap plastic furniture. Snoopy drapes that filtered in more sunlight than they blocked. Three burning incense sticks in a jar of sand with wispy smoke curling up to the ceiling and filling the room with a sweet musk. And two sets of naked legs on a thin mattress.

Politeness dictated he should turn and leave, but being the curious type, Siri kicked off his sandals and stepped inside.

Once beyond the bathroom wall, he had a full view of the two naked sleepers. Empty beer bottles on the floor partly explained why they hadn't been roused by the knock. On the window side slept a rather plump but not unpleasant-looking girl who couldn't have been much older then eighteen. On the door side, also naked and rather hideous, lay the permanent secretary of the Ministry of Education and Sport.

You never have a camera when you could most use one, thought Siri.

He stifled a cough, reversed out of the room, retrieved his sandals and went downstairs. There he sat at a roadside stall and nursed a cup of truly awful coffee for almost an hour. Just as he was about to call it a day, a shiny black ZIL limousine turned into the lane, drove past the hairdresser's shop, honked its horn once and pulled up twenty meters away. A rather pathetic attempt at subterfuge, thought Siri. In under a minute, a portly elderly comrade in a floppy hat and glassless spectacles appeared from the alleyway beside the salon. He went to the car and climbed in the backseat. In a wheel spin of dust the car headed off.

Siri paid for his coffee, albeit reluctantly, re-climbed the stairs, recollected his breath and reprodded the door. As before, it fell free from the broken hasp and swung open. To his right the plastic curtain was pulled across the shower stall, and he could hear the splashing of water behind it. He entered the room and sat at the foot of the bed. There were no pictures on the walls, no calendar, no signs of ownership. The only personal touch was a suitcase that stood against the back wall of the shower stall. It acted as an altar for assorted plaster deities and photographs of ancestors on curling paper. There were two unlit yellow candles.

There was no closet in the room, just a cardboard box piled with clothes beside the bed. He reached down into it but found nothing but polyester. His legs creaked as he sank to his knees and checked beneath the bed. He saw nothing but balls of dust and dead cockroaches. Thus he decided there was only one hiding place in the room. The splashing sounds continued. Miss Singxay was either very dirty or was attempting to drown herself. He heard the clearing of her throat and the spit of whatever had lodged there. One by one, Siri removed the cheap idols from atop the suitcase. It had to be said he had no legal right to be in that room and no suspicions at all that anything incriminating was hidden there. But Singxay had once belonged to a judge. Now she was entertaining a permanent secretary. Judge Haeng hadn't hinted at a time-share agreement, so Siri was interested to know when and how the girl had changed ownership.

The suitcase was full. Occupying most of the space was a tape recorder that looked old enough to predate the invention of sound recording. There were numerous tapes, many labeled with the names of popular Thai singers. But one small pile held together with a thick rubber band carried just the one word, HAENG. Beside the name were heart stickers—1, 2, 3—which appeared to signify the order of the tapes. There was a framed photograph without glass that contained an impressively touched-up photograph of Judge Haeng. The words TO MY LOVE were written across the bottom. And there were objects: a Party tie, a black comb, a wad of official-looking documents, a clip of dark hair in a small plastic bag. And then, to Siri's utter surprise, a diary. There was a vast population of illiterate girls in Laos, any one of whom would fit the role a wealthy man might have in mind. But Judge Haeng had a great ego, and the stimulation for such a man would be that he could attract a female who had spent time in school. A knowledgeable girl who could engage his intellect, but not so smart that she might surpass it.

When Miss Singxay finally emerged from the bathroom,

she was wearing a paper-thin *pha kow ma* cloth. Her first move was toward the open front door. She swore and pushed it shut, using her hip to force it back into its frame. She turned, walked a few steps and noticed the open suitcase before she saw the elderly gentleman leaning against the wall beside it. Her diary was open on his lap. To her credit, she didn't scream or reach for a weapon. Perhaps she was pleased to find someone interested enough in her to read her thoughts. Or perhaps she was no longer shocked at the sight of old men in her bedroom.

Siri parked his Pigeon inside the front gate of his allocated house and stepped beneath the badminton net strung across the path. From it hung various articles of clothing. These included one or two ladies' garments that could only be described as brief. He wondered naughtily whether Madame Daeng had bought them for their next honeymoon up north. He entered the hallway and nodded at blind Pao, who nodded back. It always gave Siri the willies when that happened. He stepped around a large metal bowl and the four women who knelt there peeling turnips. Forest monk Noo and Mr. Inthanet were sitting cross-legged in one of the side rooms playing cards. They invited the doctor to join them. He told them he'd be there anon. He passed three other characters in the kitchen, only one of whom he recognized, and emerged into the small backyard feeling he'd just passed through a busy bus terminal.

At the back of the yard, Crazy Rajhid stood behind a bush. He was apparently naked. Madame Daeng sat at the garden table while five children ran rings around her firing invisible Kalashnikovs. From the step it appeared she had a cigar between her lips, but on closer inspection, it turned out to be a wedge of wood. She was biting down on it.

Siri smiled and sat opposite her. "Have a good day, dear?" he asked.

"I'm torn between chronic boredom and insanity," she told him, allowing the wood to drop onto the table. "You?"

"I have a story to tell you," he said. "The wheels are in motion. Or, as Judge Haeng might say, 'A good socialist does not smash a snowman with a hammer because he knows that when things warm up, the snowman will be a small puddle of water, and buying the hammer would have been an unnecessary expense.'"

"It had better start melting soon, Siri," said Daeng. "The old fellow who sells grass brooms came by today, and I was tempted to throw myself at him—to beg him to take me away."

"You made the right choice to stay, my beloved." And he told her about his adventure at the room of young Miss Singxay. "It's only a matter of time before our judge is free to abuse his position again."

"Time we haven't got. Why don't we just jump on the Triumph and head north?"

"We used up our petrol allowance riding back from the pump."

"Wasn't Communism supposed to make poverty bearable?"

"I kept telling you, 'Charge more for the noodles, Daeng.' Did I not say that? But no. We had the restaurant full every day and barely broke even. With a bit of commercial tweaking, we could have had our own Lear jet by now. I could fly you north."

"If we had a jet, I'm starting to think I'd sooner go in the opposite direction."

"Shock and horror," said Siri. "Not to evil capitalist Thailand? You don't mean that, surely? You spent the greater part of your life fighting for the socialist revolution."

"And what do we have to show for it, Siri? Membership to

an empty co-op, shoddy Soviet appliances and no say at all
in how the place is run. We've watched the officials siphon
off a little bit here and a little bit there to feather their nests
just like it used to be in the old days. Just like it always will be.
Rajhid!" she yelled, causing her husband to jump. "You step
back behind that bush, or I'll bring the ax out."

The children fled in horror at the sound of her voice and
the sight of the Indian's nakedness. Rajhid grabbed a flower
pot to mask his organ and retreated inside the house, causing
a long-overdue moment of mirth for Siri and Daeng. Siri lost
control of his cough again.

"What you need is some cough linctus," said Daeng.

"What you need is a romantic stroll," Siri said at last.

"If only," replied Daeng. "I've had my mobility allowance
for the day."

"I wasn't suggesting you use your legs."

"How else would I stroll?"

"Your bottom looks in good shape to me."

It was five kilometers to the river, and Fa Ngum Road was
already dark and deserted by the time they got there. The
Pigeon had footrests for a passenger to stand astride the rear
wheel and hold the rider's shoulders, but only the snazzy Thai
bikes had a spare seat at the back. So Siri had put Daeng on
the saddle and wheeled her the entire way. Ugly trotted ahead
as scout. The road was in poor repair, so a good deal of the
effort went into avoiding potholes. Normally Siri's wife would
have insisted on pedaling part of the way, but this evening
she held on to the handlebars and enjoyed the ride. She was
in a bad way.

They stopped in front of the burned-out remains of their
restaurant. The charred beams were lit only by a moon smile.
They turned to the river upon which the lights of Thailand
flitted and flickered. Sri Chiang Mai opposite was hardly even
a town, but still it shone brightly like a diamante necklace on

a velvet cloth. Tourists on the far bank might have been asking what had happened to Vientiane. "It's so dark over there," they'd say. "That's a city?"

Siri and Daeng sat on their recliners still embedded on the riverbank. It was the time of the evening they enjoyed most: the bats swooping, the bloodthirsty mosquitoes departed, the night jasmine giving off its scent and the road empty. This was the time they swore they could still feel the beating heart of a grand city underfoot.

"You wouldn't really want to live over there, would you?" Siri asked.

"I'd like to see it, just once."

"You didn't bring your spectacles?"

"You know what I mean. Not just this. All of it: Bangkok, Chiang Mai, Phuket and its sea. Cinemas and vast restaurants where the waiters need roller skates just to get from the table to the kitchen. The Emerald Buddha they stole from us. I'd like to see it all with my own eyes."

"Then I'll take you."

"Thank you."

"We might need a windfall. I suppose I could swim over and get some lottery tickets."

"They say there are still four hundred people crossing every day to get away from Laos."

"There are midnight ferry services," Siri told her. "They pay off the Thai sentries."

"That's why it feels so empty here."

"They'll come back," said Siri, squeezing her hand. "They'll go to the West and get rich and come back and hire people like you and me as domestic servants."

"We're destined to be poor, Siri."

"But lucky, Daeng. Poor but lucky."

*   *   *

Inspector Phosy's hindquarters were numb. He'd been on
and off the road for two and a half days. The blacktop had
ended about fourteen kilometers out of Vientiane, and he
saw little evidence of paving thereafter. He'd taken one of
the police headquarters's jeeps, but there was a new policy of sharing and brotherhood between ministries. The
announcement that a vehicle with a supply of petrol would
be heading north yielded passage for the new head of the
teaching college in Thangon, the next governor of Udomxai,
and two engineers trained in Bonne who were being posted
in Luang Prabang to stop the erosion of the river.

From Luang Prabang to Luang Nam Tha, apart from a few
hitchhikers, Phosy had been on his own. He used to love the
life of an adventurer, the freedom of making his own deci-
sions and living on his wits. But of late he'd begun to relish
the domestic life. He enjoyed being at home with his wife,
Nurse Dtui, and Malee, their daughter. Simple things like
growing beans and repairing bicycle punctures had become
so important. As a revolutionary and a spy, he'd had all the
excitement he needed. Now, as head of Police Intelligence,
he had reached a position that involved a good deal of sitting
and writing and eating coconut macaroons. He'd become
used to going home at five and spending all day Sunday with
his family—even when they were engaged in gratuitous acts
of socialist group activity. He'd learned that weeding footpaths with a baby strapped to one's back and a wife cracking
jokes at one's side could be surprisingly enjoyable.

He loved his wife but he would never tell her so. He'd
made that mistake with his first family, and they'd fled
to America without a trace. That experience had left him
with a feeling that admitting to love was the kiss of death
to a relationship. Like mistakenly calling the spirit of the
rains by name and watching the clouds vanish above your
head. Driving alone on bad roads gave a man far too much

time to weigh the good against the bad. Bad invariably won through.

So there he was in Luang Nam Tha. Another cowboy town. He'd been to so many. Big dusty villages dotted along the roadside. Chickens and ducks cohabiting as if they had no idea they were different species. Babies with plump bottoms. Old women with saggy tops. Cobwebbed motorcycles. No paint. The Lao countryside always gave him a feeling of reluctant attempts to restart. Of bombed-out villages being rebuilt without enthusiasm. Of people who had seen enough resurgences to know they'd be short-lived. The early inhabitants of Luang Nam Tha had settled on a river that flooded regularly. The villagers considered flooding to be their karma. So when the new authorities told them to relocate ten kilometers to higher ground, most did not. Thus, Luang Nam Tha became a place of two extremes—one underwater, one deserted. In the latter, buildings were built and roads were laid, and government offices were erected, but nobody lived there.

And it was into this ghostly quiet place that Phosy drove at 10 p.m. His headlights were the only illumination. He had a map with the town police station clearly marked, but nothing around him resembled the lines on the paper. There was nobody on the street to ask, but there was a black sky salted with stars from one horizon to the other. There was far more action in that sky than there was on the ground, meteoroids shooting back and forth like drunken fireflies. So he unfastened the canvas roof of his jeep, lay on the rear seat wrapped in a blanket and allowed the universe to lull him to sleep.

He was awoken rudely by a scruffy-bearded man in a wool cap poking him with a stick. The sun had began to rise somewhere behind an eerie lilac mist. There was barely enough light to make out the toothless features on the face of his assailant.

"You Phosy?" said the man.

"Inspector Phosy."

The man continued to poke. "The rank doesn't make you any more of a Phosy, does it?" he said.

Phosy thought of mornings gently woken by Nurse Dtui's fingers on his cheek and the words, "I've made coffee." This compared poorly to those awakenings.

"If you don't stop poking me with that stick, I'll break your arm," said Phosy, not sure how he might go about it shrouded in a blanket as he was.

The man glared at him, then his mouth opened into a ghastly gash of a smile. There wasn't so much as a stub of a tooth. "Yeah," he said. "That's more like it. Move your arse. We're waiting for you at the police station."

The stench of the man's breath wafted over Phosy. "And who are you?" Phosy asked, peeling himself from the blanket and taking in his surroundings. He'd parked badly a few meters from the edge of the road where a footpath might someday appear. There was no likelihood he'd be blocking traffic. The town was silent. A few buildings along the main street had opened their shutters but didn't appear to have anything on sale.

"None of your business," said the man. "Call me one more person who doesn't want you here."

Phosy smiled, then glared back at him. The man's hair crawled from beneath his hat like that of some hippie artist, and apart from a good pair of boots, his clothes were well used and unwashed. There was nothing new or fresh or tasteful about him. Phosy guessed him to be around fifty, although his drawn cheekbones and cavernous mouth made him look older. His Lao was accented.

"You work for the tourist board?" Phosy asked.

"Listen, smartarse," said the man. "You get this all wrong and you'll know who I am soon enough."

"What?"

"Up here, your rank and your lifelong commitment to the socialist cause don't mean shit. You're in no-man's-land. There's a statement waiting for you at the police station. You walk in. You sign it. You turn your jeep around, and you go home. Easy job. When it's done, you might even find an envelope stuffed with banknotes under the dash. But you do anything more or less than that, and you won't go home at all. Never."

"Are you . . . ?"

"Or you go home wrapped in tobacco leaves, and Dtui meets your corpse at the airport."

A chill wind seemed to blow through Phosy's body as if he were ripped and holed and hung out on a line. His head filled with the sort of fury that banged drums and imploded the skull. He made a lunge at the man, who merely stepped to one side to expose a second man standing behind him with an AK-47 aimed at the jeep. This one was built like the side of a mountain.

Phosy had a natural tendency toward revenge, but tangled with his rage were questions: *How does this freak know about Dtui? Who is he and why is he so confident?*

"There I go again," said the toothless man. "I didn't plan to go on to part two of the program quite so soon. But you didn't show up last night when you were supposed to. That pissed me off. I would have bought you a few drinks and got into the financial side of things on a social level. Money's no object, you see? I'd much sooner not have to resort to, you know, having your relatives killed. But time's pressing."

Phosy's fingernails cut deep into his palms until blood ran down his fingers. He had no choice. His face didn't betray the horror in his heart. Neither did his voice. "Brother," he said, "I'm a public servant. I get nineteen dollars a month and stale rice. You know I have a family to support. Nothing about this crap job is important enough to put my wife and child at risk. Let's talk money."

The toothless man's jaundiced eyes stared at Phosy. He looked up at the sky as if everything he ever suspected was confirmed: *Police. Corrupt, every last one of them.*

"Glad to hear that, Inspector," he said. "You sign the statement, and we'll talk money. You can trust me."

"All right. Where's the police station?"

"Follow us."

"So how did Judge Haeng avoid the guillotine?" Civilai asked.

"Well, he was innocent."

"History has proven time and time again that innocence does not preclude having your head severed, Little Brother."

"Well, in this case, there was empirical evidence in written and audio formats. We have tapes."

"Heaven help us. Technology arrives in the People's Democratic Republic. We're doomed. You do know the tape will have drooped from the heat and become inaudible long before the trial?"

"There won't be a trial. Everything was settled amicably out of court. Too much embarrassment all round to go public."

The old gentlemen were back on their favorite log, studying the sand bank rising from the water like a friendly whale. They'd given baguettes a rest and were enjoying some of Madame Daeng's number two noodles instead. She had provided them several choices in a tiffin that had fit neatly in the basket of the Pigeon. Ugly waited patiently for leftovers.

"So how did she do it, and why?" Civilai asked.

"I suppose the most mysterious aspect of the case was why the girl was madly in love with Judge Haeng," said Siri.

"Even the Phantom of the Opera found love," Civilai reminded him.

"She obviously could see beyond his looks and his personality," Siri agreed.

"Rich family. Influence."

"You had a rich family and influence, brother, but you didn't get a date till you were forty."

"But what a date that was. Now, back to the story."

"So Judge Haeng decides she's getting a little too clingy for him and passes her on like an Olympic baton. One day he announces she'll now be the minor wife of a married government official. She's shocked and suddenly realizes that all the promises and plans had just been part of Haeng's politicking to keep her happy. Miss Singxay plots revenge. She is given to snooping. She finds the addresses of Haeng's two other concubines and decides that all of the players in the drama deserve to suffer."

"See what happens when you educate a woman?"

"Miss Singxay had been secretly taping her trysts with the judge on her cassette recorder. All their intimate moments. I doubt the objective was blackmail. Just a young girl's infatuation. At one point she had the judge saying, 'I've got a surprise for you, darling. You can expect this on a regular basis.'"

"I dread to think what he was referring to."

"Miss Singxay has a younger suitor, a less-than-brilliant boy who'd do anything for her. At one stage she'd stolen Haeng's key ring and sent it off to make copies. The judge is apparently particularly clumsy when it comes to security. I imagine at that time she'd had no concrete plan as to what she'd do with the keys. She just collected memorabilia from her darling. But now she has a purpose. With her young paramour in tow, she goes to the rooms of the two other women in the dead of night. Unlocks the doors. Clicks PLAY on her cassette recorder. 'I've got a surprise for you, darling. You can expect this on a regular basis.' Her boy, drenched in Judge Haeng's favorite aftershave, runs in and beats the girls unconscious. When they come to, all they can recall is the darkness, the judge's voice, the aftershave and the beating. One of them finds the address of the other suspiciously dropped at the scene of the crime. They contact each other and compare notes. The Lao Women's Union had been campaigning for abused women to come forward, so the two women tell their tale. And voilà. The Union has a ready-made case against an influential man. With so many wives of ministers on the committee enthused by the supposed equal-opportunity policies of our grand politburo, this was their chance to show how much power they wielded.

"The police interviews concluded that the two witnesses hadn't actually seen the face of their attacker. After a little more investigation, the judge's story that he had been at home with chronic diarrhea on the night of the attacks was substantiated by his private physician, who had been dragged from his bed to attend to the drainage problem."

"He has a private physician?"

"I accepted the fictitious role retrospectively when I discovered that on the afternoon of the attacks he had been sent a box of sweets by Singxay. A simple microscopic sample confirmed that the Thai strawberry teardrops contained a particularly high concentration of intestinal parasites. The gift was obviously intended to keep him home while she went about her wicked business that night. She naturally didn't want the actual judge turning up at any of his nighttime love nests."

"She sounds like my type of girl."

"So all that remains is for Judge Haeng to be reinstated

and send Daeng and me to Luang Nam Tha to assist Inspector Phosy in his case."

"There are those who might consider your assistance to the judge mercenary."

"I doubt I made any friends at the Women's Union, but there's a sizeable difference between philandering and grievous bodily harm."

The men gave the noodles a little of the silent respect they deserved, but soon the clatter of spoons on stainless steel could be heard across the river. Ugly was devastated.

"Another masterpiece," said Civilai. "Have I mentioned that your wife is wasted on you?"

"Ad nauseam. And how is your otherwise boring life progressing?"

"This Vietnam/Cambodia thing is creating such a lot of paperwork."

"Yes, I've heard invasions can be administrative nightmares. I'm sure that's the reason half the world's incursions fail to take off—not nearly enough clerks. But what's that got to do with you?"

"I've been named Chairman of the Ad Hoc Committee on Lao/Chinese relations."

"You're retired."

"It's a hobby."

"You hate the Chinese."

"I didn't say Lao/Chinese 'good' relations, did I? With the Chinese still backing Pol Pot, there's a lot of vitriol being spat back and forth between Peking and Hanoi. The Chinese had supported Ho Chi Minh to the tune of twenty billion dollars over twenty years leading up to the war with America. They somehow thought they'd bought themselves a little bit of respect. They're miffed that Hanoi's still acting like an independent nation rather than a colony. The Vietnamese were instructed not to interfere in Cambodian internal affairs, but when the Khmer started stretching their bloody empire across the Vietnamese border, Hanoi decided they'd had enough. Wallop! Three weeks down, and they're already in control of all the major cities apart from Pailin. We only saw the tip of the bloodberg when we were over there, Siri. There are unconfirmed reports that two and a half million people have been annihilated."

"And China doesn't have a problem with that?"

"The numbers wouldn't worry them so much. A million's a *dim sum* queue in Peking. They win wars by sending in wave after wave of expendable militia until the enemy runs out of bullets. It's like Stalin said, 'One death is a tragedy. A million deaths is a statistic.' No, it's a matter of principle. Ho was rude. Pol Pot was polite. He sent thank-you notes."

"And we get stuck in the middle again," said Siri.

"It's not like we're completely innocent," Civilai reminded him. "We have four hundred thousand Vietnamese troops stationed here. We let them launch offensives into Cambodia. We've aided and abetted. Vietnam doesn't have that many friends. They're pressuring us to tell the world we love them. I'm afraid our senile leaders are going to do something silly."

"Like?"

"Declare war on China."

Siri slapped his knee and let out a hoarse laugh. "Well, that's one war that wouldn't last long," he said. "We'd be out of bullets shortly after morning tea on the first day. We'd be forced to throw sticks. And they might interpret that as sarcasm. No war was ever won on sarcasm."

"You're a peculiar man, Dr. Siri."

"So you agreed to host this think tank to come up with alternatives to being overrun by angry Chinese?"

"In a way."

"Any luck so far?"

"We've convinced the Khao San Phathet Lao newsletter to

print a photograph of our illustrious president eating dinner in the Chinese restaurant on Samsenthai. It's symbolic."

"It would have to be. It certainly isn't edible."

"It doesn't matter. The Chinese will see the photograph as surreptitiously siding with them."

"While simultaneously contracting food poisoning."

"You really have no aptitude for diplomacy."

Inspector Phosy had followed slowly behind the Chinese truck driven by Toothless and the man-mountain, who were leading him to the police station. He'd needed time to think. Luang Nam Tha was a remote province. The police office had a staff of four. The real policemen from the old regime had fled the country, been sent for re-education in the north or had taken on new lives denying any links to law enforcement. They hadn't been any more honest, but they were disciplined and subtle in their indiscretions. The senior sergeant here by the name of Teyp had gone to Vientiane a year earlier to learn skills. Phosy had met him there and attempted to convert Teyp from a battle-hardened soldier to a logical, law-abiding policeman. It had been a daunting task, and given the lack of qualified candidates across the country, Teyp had been plucked from the tree long before he was ripe.

Phosy knew Teyp and his constables would yield to any authority. Money, power and threats would leave a no-hope public official very little choice. Out here in the wilds, these country policemen were easy pickings. Taken for a drink here. Bought a new tape player for New Year. And suddenly there were obligations. They had to live side by side with villains, and everyone knew where your house was. The inspector was on his own.

He'd really only had one choice. According to his map,

Luang Nam Tha's new town was laid out like a grid. The main road was the eastern-most axis. The Chinese truck had been about to turn left a hundred meters ahead. It had slowed down to wait for him to catch up. Instead, Phosy had slammed his foot on the accelerator, swung into the next small lane on two wheels and gunned the motor.

And here he was twenty minutes later, heading back in the direction he'd come from the previous day, south and away from Dodge City.

3

Counting Ghosts

Hours passed, as they often did in the PDR Laos where, apparently, nothing happened. Where no announcements were made. No changes evident. No signs of time having served any purpose at all. Yet during that apparently non-moving period, China had been able to amass a quarter of its available ground troops on the Vietnamese border. On the day the Lao Prime Minister was on the radio announcing projections that two-thirds of the nation's farms would be collectives by mid-1980, China invaded Laos's number-one ally—Vietnam. As there was no announcement of this on Lao bulletins, and the news had apparently not reached the Thai media, Siri and Daeng had no reason to reconsider their vacation to the northern border.

The only trip they'd taken in all that non-moving time was a visit to the shrine of the people they'd killed. It was a monthly pilgrimage. The Party would have frowned on such foolishness—the shrine, not the killings. That was why Siri and Daeng had found a place remote from the city. They'd selected a tree many times older then themselves and decorated it in ribbons and spun cotton. They'd asked its spirits to accept the souls of the men and women who currently resided only in their consciences.

The old couple had fought for independence from the French, then fought again against a Lao royalist army pumped up with US aid dollars. Being a guerilla for three decades had made it impossible to avoid death. Daeng's kills had been too numerous to recall names. So apart from one or two particularly satisfying homicides, she'd opted for a sort of blanket forgiveness; a package apology to the relatives of everyone who'd died at her hand. She'd killed in battle, in self-defense and in the interests of the Party. There was nothing she regretted, but her victims deserved respect.

Siri could count his ghosts. His business had always been the preservation of life. There had been unavoidable deaths in battlefront surgery tents, and he had his own way of dealing with those. The victims came to see him often and bore no grudges. He had killed four human beings deliberately, three with his own hand in do-or-die situations. One, a woman—a royalist spy they called The Lizard—had been put to death as a result of his evidence. Not murder, perhaps, but culpable homicide once removed. Though he'd fully expected a visit from The Lizard's tormented spirit, there had been no contact. It was impossible to put a soul to rest unless she showed herself.

Like Daeng, Siri felt no compunction but often wondered what might have happened if he'd joined the other side. His victims then would have been his erstwhile comrades, his friends. And so he felt no hatred and believed they deserved a small suburb in the spirit world where they might graduate to another life. It never hurt to mix beliefs. Siri and Daeng left an open bottle of soy milk and a mango at the base of the tree, along with two burning jossticks, and Siri dropped in a hushed Hail Mary for good measure.

There had been no news from Judge Haeng, the Lao Women's Union or Dtui. The past twenty-four hours had been thicker and slower than any twenty-four hours Siri and Daeng could recall. They were reaching their brick wall of desperation. Madame Daeng's opium tea was becoming more of a sedative against life than against pain. Siri was rashly betting and losing more cups of husked rice in his late-night poker games. Ugly was snapping at everyone.

Then at last, the world began to rotate again. It was kickstarted by a postcard with the stamp stuck to the photo and a large smiley face on the reverse. At the bottom was one of Mr. Geung's hearts, which resembled a suet pudding. Obviously, their lab assistant's romance was progressing well.

Within minutes, Nurse Dtui stopped by. Her cold was thick, and it made her sound like a heavy-smoking gangster. She'd come to return the finger and to tell Siri that the half *pha sin* was with Ou at the *lycée*. The lab teacher was working through the basic color tests to identify the chemicals they could smell on the material. Ou's sense of smell was phenomenal, but she too had come down with the dreaded flu and could no longer trust her nose. They'd tested the finger and had indeed found evidence of formaldehyde. Somebody had gone to the trouble of preserving the severed digit. But the formaldehyde wasn't alone there. It was one of Dtui's hunches that led to the discovery of the second compound. She had noticed how the ink stain from Siri's leaky pen had faded rapidly overnight. This anomaly, combined with the ashen pallor of the skin, had caused her to suggest they test for bleach. And sure enough, there were high concentrations.

More worrying was a telegram message Dtui had received from Phosy. It had been brief, and in his usual uncompromising style said for her and Malee to move out of the police dormitory for a few days and take the rest of the week off work. He would explain when he got back. It was important not to tell anyone but her closest friends where she was staying and to remain incognito until further notice. Phosy emphasized that he was in no danger himself, that this was just a precaution. Dtui was angry but knew Phosy wouldn't have insisted on such a thing if he wasn't afraid for his family's safety.

Dtui stayed just long enough to pass on this message and arrange temporary accommodation, but not so long as to pass on her cold. She left the mystery of the bleach to Siri, admitting she had no idea as to its purpose.

The annual flu bug took hold of Vientiane at the slightest excuse and spread like a bean fart. Changes in temperature. Heavy rain. Non-conditioning air conditioners. They all helped. As soon as Dtui had gone, Daeng and Siri ate half a bag of oranges, but Daeng could feel the tickle in her throat. Siri already had the cough. Vitamin C was probably too little and too late.

The doctor was out front putting the orange peel in the mulch bucket when the messenger arrived. Siri heard him call out, "This Dr. Siri Paiboun's house?"

Siri walked to the open gate and saw a teenager on a moped just about to drive on. "The street number and the name plaque would suggest so," said Siri.

"Message from Justice," said the boy and held up the envelope as if expecting Siri to walk to the curb to receive it.

"I have neuroabstroperosis," said Siri.

"What?"

"It's a nerve problem. I can't walk."

"You just walked to the gate."

"I had somebody at the house push me. Once I had the momentum it was fine. Now that I've stopped, I can't start up again. It's a bugger being old."

The boy looked bewildered. He hesitated, then climbed down from his bike, walked the two meters to the gate and handed Siri the note.

"Thank you, son," said Siri.

They stood staring at each other.

"Should I give you a push?" asked the boy.

"That would be splendid."

Siri arrived at the backyard table where Madame Daeng spent most of her time.

"Siri, why are you walking backward?" she asked.

"Neuroabstroperosis," he said.

"It sounds made up."

He sat.

"What's that?" she asked.

"A note from Justice."

"Are you going to open it?"

"I'm nervous."

"Why?"

"They might ask us to leave our beloved home and head off to excitingly fearsome places."

"Open it."

Siri deliberately took his time. He pulled a tissuey sheet of paper from the envelope and unfolded it. "And the winner for best cinematography goes to . . ."

"Siri!"

"It's from Haeng."

"Ha! He's back. Well done, my husband. Does he send his love and gratitude?"

"Even better." He read, "For the attention of Dr. Siri Paiboun. The ministry appreciates that you are now retired, but we have a matter of grave importance with which we hope you can help us. Inspector Phosy is currently in Luang Nam Tha investigating a highly sensitive case. He has requested the assistance of a forensic pathologist. If you and one assistant are available to travel north, we have a cargo flight leaving for Luang Prabang at five tomorrow morning.

From Luang Prabang you should be able to find connecting transportation to Luang Nam Tha. I emphasize that we have a budget for no more than one other staff member. You may not bring your entire entourage on this mission. Haeng Somboun, Head of Public Prosecution and Justice Related Internal Affairs."

Siri and Daeng had learned to low-five from the American MIA team in Xiang Kwang. They had perfected their own version, which involved just the index fingers. It was far more dignified.

"Free!" said Daeng with such enthusiasm they both started into a coughing fit.

"We should start packing," said Siri.

"Packing takes us ten minutes," she reminded him. "In fact, I don't believe we ever got around to unpacking from our last trip. We're always prepared."

"Like Superman," said Siri. "I just rip off my shirt, and everyone can see my big S."

"You keep your big S covered, Siri Paiboun," said Daeng with a smile.

The three officers on duty in the Luang Nam Tha police office were surprised to hear a vehicle in the late afternoon. Only the military and the Chinese road teams had petrol allowances, and there was precious little reason for either to be in town that day. The officers were already outside on the sidewalk beside the dirt road when Phosy's jeep pulled up in front. He had two passengers with him: one tall, thin man in an ill-fitting Mao jacket and a middle-aged woman with greasy cheeks who looked like a low-budget version of Imelda Marcos. Senior Sergeant Teyp recognized Phosy and appeared to consider running back inside to put on his shirt. But he changed his mind and gave a slapdash salute instead. There was a look of surprise on his dark shiny face.

"Are you well?" Phosy asked.

"We . . . we were expecting you this morning," said Teyp. "Last night, even. We thought you'd left without . . . we heard you'd gone."

"Why would I go without doing the job I've been sent here by the government to do?" Phosy smiled. "But I decided it would be inappropriate to conduct an investigation into a crime that might or might not involve Chinese nationals without inviting observers from China. Allow me to introduce Comrade Xiu Long from the Chinese/Lao trade commission."

"Observers," said Comrade Xiu Long, stepping down from the jeep. He had apparently picked up a number of words during his tenure as surrogate consul in Phongsali but not the ability to put them together to make sentences, hence the accompaniment of Mrs. Loo, his interpreter. Phosy had no knowledge of the Chinese language, but it had already occurred to him that Mrs. Loo was somewhat sparing with the amount of information she chose to pass on to her boss.

Phosy explained to the sergeant, "Unfortunately, the letter we sent to Comrade Xiu Long from Police Headquarters in Vientiane didn't arrive. But regardless, he was kind enough to drop everything in order to be involved here."

Phosy looked at Mrs. Loo, and she reluctantly translated a few words. Her boss nodded and smiled. "Involved," he said.

Phosy walked past the policemen in their less-than-white T-shirts and entered the small, open-fronted building. The hand-painted sign over the entrance claimed that this was the Luang Nam Tha Police Headquarters.

"So," said Phosy, kicking off his shoes and making himself comfortable in a cane rocking chair. "Who's going to brief me about the case?"

The Chinese sat on a wooden bench opposite, leaving the three policemen outside looking uncomfortable.

"We thought . . . er . . . we thought you'd just be signing the document," said Teyp, joining them inside.

"Really? And what document would that be?" Phosy asked.

"The doc . . . the document we have to send to Vientiane."

"Well, let me see it."

"It's . . . I . . . I can't, really . . ."

"Look, man, you either have a document to sign or you don't. Which is it?"

"It's already signed."

"Is that so? And who signed it?"

"We thought you'd left and . . . and forgotten to sign it."

"I could hardly have forgotten something I didn't know about, could I now? So who signed it?"

"Comrade Goi."

"He sounds important. Who is he, the governor of the province?"

"No."

"Then . . . ?"

"He's the senior foreman of the Chinese road project."

"Really? So show me the document."

"I . . ."

"That's an order."

Teyp went to his desk and removed a banana that was acting as a paperweight for a brown envelope. The banana reminded Phosy he hadn't eaten for twenty hours. He instructed the smallest of the constables to organize food for himself and his guests as soon as possible. In the meantime, they'd settle for tea. The little officer ran off.

Teyp brought over the envelope. Phosy smiled. It was sealed. He hooked his little finger into the flap and ripped it open. It contained one sheet of greying paper with a rather brief typed letter on one side. It said that, following a thorough investigation, Inspector Phosy had come to the conclusion that there was no Chinese involvement in the incident that led to the deaths of the two village headmen.

Phosy looked up at the sergeant, who was staring at his own bare feet. "It appears that not only am I a poor speller," said Phosy, "but that I've already signed this crock of shit, and it's all addressed and ready to go off. Now how do you account for that?"

Sergeant Teyp could say nothing.

"Well, I'll tell you what we'll do," said Phosy, ripping the letter into smaller and smaller pieces. "We'll assume that you didn't know your Comrade Goi signed my name on this letter instead of his own. We'll assume you believed he was authorized to communicate directly with the ministry. We'll assume that the eight regulations and two laws you and your men have already broken will not be written up in my report and that you are able to start again with a clean sheet. And we'll assume that you, rather than the Chinese road builders, are in charge up here. How does that grab you?"

Sergeant Teyp nodded and said quietly, "Thank you, sir."

Phosy didn't feel nearly as confident as he sounded, but he needed the sergeant and his men to have faith in him. "We have a system. Laws. Everything that happens here is reported to and acted on in Vientiane. You are members of the Lao police force. Never forget that. If we don't investigate a crime, we don't issue documents to say we did. Now brief me on the case."

There were no laws as such. The ministry had drawn up a list of crimes and suitable punishments, but the judicial system was in its infancy and justice was being meted out by old military officers and headmen who interpreted the ambiguous lists however they saw fit. Even so, Phosy's serious talk seemed to have penetrated, as a brief expression of pride shone in the sergeant's face. Phosy was suddenly aware of the bruises where the stick had been poked repeatedly into his ribs that morning.

Before going to the filing cabinet, Teyp took his shirt from the back of his chair and put it on. He opened a drawer and started to finger through the files. There was a sudden flurry of language from the previously silent Mrs. Loo.

"Here," said the sergeant, holding the file aloft.

"Read it to me," said Phosy.

"Yes, sir."

Teyp sat at his desk and gave the date of the crime and the names of the police involved in the investigation. "As we don't have any working phones up here, we were alerted to the crime by a villager who got a ride in on an army vehicle," Teyp read. "We were led to a clearing down the gully from the village of Muang Se. It's a Yao village, and not many of the residents speak Lao, but our own constable Buri does. There we found the two corpses of Headman Mao, the Yao, and Headman Panpan, the Akha, both lying facedown in the dirt. Both had sustained multiple wounds. Both were shirtless and barefooted and wearing only football shorts. To all appearances it seemed that the two men had been overpowered by unknown assailants. Two sharpened bamboo poles covered in blood were left at the crime scene. Signed, Sergeant Teyp Bounyamate."

There was a pause.

"Wait," said Phosy. "That's all?"

"Yes, sir."

"No witnesses?"

"No."

"Nobody saw anything unusual? No idea why the two men were together and shirtless?"

"We assumed they'd been cutting trees or collecting fruit."

"And did you find any collected wood or produce?"

"No, sir. We assumed the assailants had helped themselves."

"To the missing shirts and shoes as well?"

"No, Inspector. They were there, folded on a log."

"And you didn't think that point was important enough to mention in a report?"

The sergeant let forth a sigh that appeared to deflate him and leaned on his desk for support. It was a physical manifestation of desperation, a ritual that Phosy had witnessed and caught himself performing time and again in these frustrating days. The desk creaked in the same key as that of Phosy's own in Vientiane.

"Inspector Phosy," said Teyp, "I've got this one finger that can type, and the typewriter's a monster. Some keys you need to hit with a hammer just to make contact with the paper. Leaving out small details can save me half a day for other duties."

"Is that right? And just how many crimes and misdemeanors has your busy station had to deal with this past month?"

"We have a number of community responsibilities," said Teyp. He looked offended.

"And the vegetable allotment," said Constable Buri.

"That's right," said the sergeant, nodding.

"There are just never enough hours in a day," said Phosy. He went over the report information in his mind. There hadn't been a lot to memorize. "What kind of name is Pan-pan?" he asked. "It doesn't shound very Akha to me."

"His name was Pan," said the sergeant. "But he had a stutter."

"Oh, well, that explains it," said Phosy, scratching his head. "So let's go and visit the scene of the crime."

There was a look of horror on the face of the policemen.

"You want to go there?" asked Teyp, his voice rising to a girly pitch.

"Naturally," said Phosy.

"But . . ."

"I've had just about enough buts for one day."

"It's getting late, and we . . . we haven't cleared it with the villagers."

"Then it'll be a nice surprise for them," said Phosy. "Let's go."

They traveled together on a perfectly good dirt road, Phosy, Sergeant Deyt, Constable Buri, Comrade Xiu Long and Mrs. Loo. Phosy was feeling smug. His decision to collect a token Chinese official as protection had paid dividends. It had nothing to do with protocol. He knew Toothless was anxious to clear the Chinese road gangs of any wrongdoing at any cost. Just why the man would devote himself to this cause so aggressively, Phosy couldn't say. But his instincts told him that here in the remote north, there was a thin line between being a conscientious policeman and being a dead one. If that was the case, Phosy would be in less danger with a Chinese official observing the investigation. He'd considered inviting a clerk or some minor military officer. It was a stroke of luck that such a senior cadre as Xiu Long should be available and willing to travel at short notice. In fact, it was so odd that Phosy wondered what other motives Xiu might have to cross back over the border at the invitation of a police officer. The trade mission and consular offices in Phong Sali and Udomxai had been closed down by the Lao following the new anti-Chinese sentiment in Vientiane. Xiu was currently working out of an office in Mengla on the Chinese side. Why would he be so eager to get back?

But that didn't matter. Xiu was security. Toothless knew about Phosy's family. Alone, Phosy stood no chance. At best, he would have an accident and never be seen again. At worst, Dtui and Malee could be harmed. Phosy had to cover both those risks and give himself an edge in the battle with the scary old guy—a man, he'd learned, who was the senior foreman on the road project.

After fleeing Luang Nam Tha, Phosy had driven to the Chinese border crossing at Ban Boten. It was a village of a few thatched huts, but it was a busy checkpoint. The officers who manned the post seemed to know what they were doing. It was a sensitive political spot, so a senior lieutenant headed the team. Phosy knew him. Within half an hour, they'd cleared the inspector's passage into China and sent a number of messages through the military network. In another hour, he was in Meng La. Given his position within the Lao hierarchy, he could have expected a hostile reception at the new trade office. The Chinese hadn't taken the order to leave Laos in good humor. They'd reclaimed the trucks they'd donated to the northern cities, loaded up every stick of furniture and bulldozed the buildings. A day later they were all across the border with a number of Lao wives and girlfriends in tow.

But trade didn't end. The new office continued to function, and crossing at Ban Boten or Pang Hai was made easy for affluent Lao who had dealings with the People's Republic.

So Phosy was welcomed warmly. The consular staff spoke Lao. Once they'd heard the inspector's mission, they ushered him upstairs to Xiu Long's office, where Mrs. Loo translated for the director. Xiu had stepped out from behind his desk, handed the heavy ledger of forms to his accountant and followed Phosy to his jeep. Loo hadn't been quite so enthusiastic. She'd made enough fuss to be allowed to stop by her residence and pack an overnight bag. The border guards on both sides had been surprised to see Phosy's passenger. The inspector stopped at the Lao post to be sure his messages had reached Vientiane, and with a nod and a smile from the lieutenant—only five hours after having left—he was back in Laos.

It had been an atypical Lao day. In a country where a single activity can take a lifetime, so much had happened: the threats, the border, the reclamation of a police unit and now a visit to the crime scene. He wondered whether perhaps time sped up the closer you were to China.

Yao was not one of Phosy's regional languages, so he had to rely on Constable Buri to translate. The young man looked at his sergeant constantly as if to confirm he wasn't giving anything away. They hadn't been given a chance to collude. The village was the usual mishmash of bamboo and thatch held together by flowering bushes and clotheslines and plastic pipes spidering out of a central water tank. The acting headman didn't seem that surprised to see them. He led them down behind the communal meeting hall along a narrow path to the clearing where they'd found the bodies.

One patch of weeds had been thoroughly soaked in blood, now black, but the scent was unmistakable. Two spears of bamboo sharpened to a point lay to one side. One had been broken in half. Both were sticky with blood. Across the clearing sat the shirts, draped over a log. In front of each were sandals neat in pairs. Then, to Phosy's surprise, two hats—a baseball cap and a straw boater—were perched on top of the shirts. There were no fruit trees around the clearing, no vegetable patches, no signs of recently severed branches.

According to the translator, the two men had been friends. They drank together. But the incident had taken place early in the morning, and there were no empty bottles to be found.

"They probably just came to work in the forest and were set upon by bandits," said Sergeant Teyp.

Phosy smiled and mentally added the sergeant's name to his list of suspects. "That's possible," he said, "but what work would a man do without implements?"

"Could have been stolen," said the sergeant.

"Along with all evidence of being used? Possible. But why would a worker remove his hat and shoes and shirt before commencing work? What's the temperature up here at sunrise? About five degrees?"

"About that," said the constable.

"Bit cool to be removing your shirt, don't you think?"

"Yes, Inspector."

"And what would bandits stand to gain by attacking two unarmed men?"

"Probably a business dispute," said the sergeant.

"Judging from the state of the village we just passed through, I'd say business wasn't a forte of our headmen. No signs of opulence there. And if you want someone dead for business reasons, you kill them. Get it over with. You shoot them or stab them through the heart. You don't make several cursory incisions with a hunk of bamboo and watch them slowly bleed to death. No. This was an example of two men being taught a lesson. They'd pissed somebody off, and this was the result."

"That's an interesting theory," said the sergeant, "but as there are no witnesses, I suppose we'll never know."

"Perhaps. But I'd like to speak to both sets of villagers tomorrow."

"They've all been interviewed."

"There was no record of that in the report," Phosy reminded him. "And no report is complete without transcripts of witness interviews. It looks like you're going to have to train another finger to type, Sergeant."

"They won't—"

Phosy put his finger to his lips. "Shh," he said. "What was that?"

They all listened, but no one could hear sounds other then the insects and the whisper of dry leaves in the breeze.

"I can't—" began the sergeant.

"Listen!" said Phosy.

They stood still and did as they were told.

"Bee Gee," came a voice.

They looked around to see Comrade Xiu Long heading off into the jungle. Nobody had a clue what he'd said. But he was smiling and seemed to have picked up a rhythm. He began to sing. He had no obvious aptitude for melody, but once the music had been identified, the others began to hear it too. Phosy ran after him.

"Inspector Phosy, you really shouldn't . . ." said Sergeant Teyp, but it was too late. Instead, the policemen followed the two visitors through the bush. Mrs. Loo sat on the log and pouted.

Phosy soon caught up with the loping Chinese man who appeared to be having the time of his life. He was singing at the top of his voice. The undergrowth wasn't dense, and they could follow a trajectory almost straight to the source of the music.

They hadn't gone two hundred meters, but the song was already quite clear. *"Ah Ha Ha Ha, Staying Alive, Staying Alive."*

Whatever they meant, Xiu Long had apparently memorized the words. He slowed to a walk. The trees came to an abrupt end up ahead. The music was loud now. Spread out in front of them were hundreds, perhaps thousands, of temporary dwellings. There were tents and grass huts and shelters with corrugated roofs. Beyond them were rows of dirt volleyball and badminton courts all occupied with games in progress and hundreds of men sitting on the sidelines, cheering. And directly in front of Phosy a small group of men sat watching a game of checkers. Beside them was a boom box blaring out its song.

"Ah Ha Ha Ha, Staying Alive, Staying Alive."

Phosy sat on a stump and watched. The pink sun was setting quickly on the shanty camp of Chinese Road Gang Six. Not three hundred meters from the scene of a dual homicide lived an army of itinerant workers from mainland China. It was no wonder both sides were anxious to clear up the murder of the headmen. The list of suspects had stretched into the thousands.

"Bee Gee," said Xiu Long.

4

The Notion of the Potion

The flight to Luang Prabang was overbooked even for cargo. Boxes and sacks and pigs oozing out through the bars of tiny cages were piled to the ceiling. The chances of finding a seat were remote. Siri and Daeng had their note from the Ministry that stated they were priority passengers, but so did all the others waiting at Wattay Airport. They were all hoping to board that one flight. They'd started queuing up at the door forty minutes earlier. From experience, Siri knew that once the glass door was opened, there would be a mad rush for the plane, and the first twenty would get on. It was socialism's way of culling the elderly and unfit.

Siri went to the large window and surveyed the taxiing area. The official responsible for putting people on the plane was guarding the door and palming what they called "the small petals of persuasion": envelopes whose owners hoped would help get them passage ahead of the others. It had worked in the days of the old regime, but this new generation had the audacity to keep the money but continue to give lousy service. Good corruption was something perfected over decades. Siri knew it would be back.

By the time he returned to Daeng, his smile was broad and confident.

"Plan?" she asked.

"Follow me," he said.

They left the departure shack by the front door, which was now unmanned, and walked slowly along the side of the building, Siri taking most of his wife's weight. They went directly to the area where the three remaining embarkation steps were parked. He placed Daeng and their bags on the second step of one of them, released the brake and cast off. It was remarkably easy to push, well-oiled and pneumatically tired.

The pilot of the cargo transporter had his head out the cockpit window, watching the angry frenzy of erstwhile polite people fighting for the right to sit on an onion sack for an hour. The copilot, checking dials against a typed list, looked up in surprise at the knock on the cockpit door. He was even more surprised to see the elderly couple smiling through the window. "Yes?" he shouted above the sound of the propellers.

"Open the door, there's a good boy," shouted Daeng.

The copilot nudged the pilot, who squinted as the rising sun broke free of the horizon. He pulled the sunglasses from his top pocket and put them on. It was then that he recognized the face of his favorite noodle seller.

"Madame Daeng!" He smiled. "What are you doing out there?"

"Trying to get in," she shouted.

"Well, come on, Phot," the pilot said to his copilot. "Don't leave our passengers out there in the cold."

After a little ladder-shuffling, the couple was warmly ensconced on a stack of some unidentified powdery substance just behind the cockpit. Daeng promised the pilot a triple number two noodle special on the house just as soon as her house had a roof and walls.

*   *   *

Phosy awoke with a stiff back and fleabites. He'd been booked into a building on the main street that was scheduled to become a hotel. Currently it was an unsubscribed restaurant with a large empty second floor. Xiu Long and Mrs. Loo had slept at a Chinese business office in the old town, which was one of the many addresses labeled "Chinese Liaison Enterprises." In Vientiane they had started to call them spy nooks.

The manager had brought the former consul and his interpreter to Phosy's hotel at seven. The former was a Lao caricature of a Chinese right down to the horrible accent and the long hairs dangling from a mole on his chin, enough to outnumber those on his head.

Xiu Long spoke to Mrs. Loo, who passed along the offer of this Mr. Woo's help, should the need for it arise. Phosy couldn't imagine a situation when that offer might be accepted. Like Comrade Civilai, Phosy was wary of Chinese influence. From three thousand in the national census of 1931, the Chinese population in Laos had risen to fifty thousand in 1960. He'd worked out that at such a rate, by the turn of the century, whatever Lao were left would have to be fluent in Chinese to get a job in their own country. Every town had its Mr. Woos, and they were breeding like rabbits. Phosy ushered Xiu Long and Mrs. Loo into his jeep and watched in the rearview mirror as Woo waved them off.

Their first stop was to the small hospital where the two bodies had been left. There was a concrete room behind the administration hut which the visitors had been able to smell long before they were told about it. Everyone had been eager to send the two cadavers back to their villages for their respective rights and cremations. But Phosy had insisted they stay put until he could have a look at them. With no electricity to cool them, the bodies were wrapped in various herbal leaves and placed near open windows. The temperature had been low since the killings, but still the rotting flesh announced its decline.

With Mrs. Loo stubbornly anchored in the jeep, Phosy and Xiu Long went into the room and peeled back the leaf shrouds. The wounds were deep and ugly, and already the maggots had come to claim their lunch. Phosy was no Dr. Siri. All he could do was confirm the men were dead, as if there were any doubt. He could see no evidence of anything but an attack with large sharp weapons.

Xiu Long leaned over the corpses and studied them with fascination. "Deceased," he said.

When they pulled up in front of the police station, there was an NJ-130 truck parked out front. Behind the dirty windshield was the man-mountain Phosy recognized from the previous morning even without his AK-47. The man's ears perched squarely on his shoulders. Beside him sat a woman-child with a powdered face and lipstick. She could barely see over the dashboard. Nobody sat in the driver's seat.

Phosy climbed down from his jeep and walked past the open window of the truck. The big man let out a sort of growl. The inspector grinned and proceeded to the open front of the police office.

He was confronted by toothless foreman Goi on his way out. The toothless one put his hand on Phosy's chest. "Where do you think you're going?"

Phosy looked at the hand and took a half step back. "I already warned you about the stick," he said. "I feel even more uncomfortable about greasy hands. If your granddaughter wasn't sitting there in the cab watching, you'd have a broken wrist by now."

Raging red bonfires burned in the foreman's eyes. Had he teeth, he would have bared them. Phosy recognized the signs. This man had killed. The power of life and death, the impunity that came with holding a knife to the jugular of anyone standing in his way, had made him invulnerable. But the difference between this creature and a drunk who took a broken bottle to all comers in a brawl was that this man had a brain and cunning. He planned. He wasn't impetuous. That was what most frightened Phosy.

Foreman Goi looked over Phosy's shoulder as Xiu Long stepped from the jeep, and he nodded at the Chinese man. Goi may have smiled too, but expressions on his face were all a matter of conjecture. He took another step forward and reached out again with his hand. This time he began to brush dust off the detective's shirt with his fingertips.

"Clever Vientiane," he said, not loud enough for anyone else to hear, "you've managed to temporarily plug a few gaps in your leaky life."

"No idea what you mean," said Phosy.

"You know your Chinese backup can't be here forever. And I see your wife and child have left on an unexpected vacation. But you'd be surprised what a small world this is. How easy it is to trace a person. We can—"

Phosy pushed past him, causing the foreman to take a step back. Goi's heel hit a pot of dead flowers, and he toppled backward and thumped into the dust. It was a more dramatic fall than the inspector had planned. He decided to take advantage of the moment.

"Who the hell is this man?" shouted Phosy to the policemen standing in a line on the office step with their mouths open. One of them went to help the foreman but got a slap for his trouble.

Foreman Goi struggled to his feet. "Get off me," he yelled.

"Inspector, you really shouldn't—" Sergeant Teyp began.

"I asked you his name," said Phosy.

"It's Foreman Goi," said Constable Nut.

"And what's Foreman Goi doing here?" Phosy asked.

Sergeant Teyp looked apologetically at the toothless fore-man, then equally apologetically at Phosy. "Foreman Goi has been very helpful with supplies and transportation lately," he said. "He's offered to accompany us to the Yao village."

"He'll do no such thing," said Phosy. "If I see him any-where near that village, or here for that matter, I'll arrest him. You understand that?"

"On what charge?" asked the sergeant.

"We'll start with assault and threatening a police officer, then work our way down to driving without a Lao plate."

The foreman was walking a wide circle around Phosy like a wily bird in a cockfight looking for the vulnerable spots on his opponent. The man-mountain had stepped down from the truck and had his hand under his shirt. Phosy decided he probably wasn't scratching a tick bite.

"Then we'll see if there's anything in the books about him not wearing his false teeth in public," Phosy went on. "If his orangutan pulls that gun out of his belt, we'll have them both for possession of an unlicensed weapon. You name it. We can just make it up as we go along. What's the big guy's name?"

"Silo," said Constable Buri.

"I won't forget that in a hurry," said Phosy.

Foreman Goi had reached the truck after his orbit and was climbing into the driver's seat. He was seething.

"Go on, get out of here," Phosy shouted. He was aware of every nerve in his own body. His fists were clenched to stop his hands from shaking. His legs were wobbling, and his stomach rolled. He'd had no choice but to mark his terri-tory, however briefly. Foreman Goi was right. Soon Xiu Long would be gone, and the allegiances of the Luang Nam Tha police force would return to the status quo. Phosy would be mincemeat. But at least there was this one small stand that might be remembered in dispatches to Vientiane when his body was returned to the capital. Something for Malee to boast about to her friends at school.

Foreman Goi turned the key, pulled the ignition knob and revved the engine. Before taking off, he reached for the woman-child in the seat beside him and kissed her full on the mouth. She didn't pull away, just hung there like a cloth doll all of thirteen years of age. The foreman grabbed the steering wheel and drove forward in a trajectory that would sideswipe the inspector. Phosy's step was not backward to avoid it, but forward, forcing the driver to either hit him or swerve and skid on the loose dirt road. Goi obviously wasn't ready to kill him just yet. After a second of slithering across the red dust, the truck righted itself and sped off in a cloud of red dust.

Phosy exhaled. He'd been holding his breath all this time. With that first gulp of air came a feeling of stupidity. Like the opium addict who'd climbed into the bear cage at Hanoi Zoo, Phosy knew he was just begging to be ripped apart.

The youngest of the police officers whistled. There were smiles on everyone's face—apart from that of Sergeant Teyp. But even he seemed to have adopted a reluctant expression of admiration. Xiu Long looked delighted. He turned to Mrs. Loo and asked something, but she was too stunned to reply. Phosy was a temporary star, if not of the show, then of one short scene. He stood in the middle of the road, watching the dust settle, but he wasn't waiting for an ovation. His legs wouldn't move at all.

By the time they landed in Luang Nam Tha, Siri and Daeng were both feeling poorly. At first they put it down to the rocking and bucking of the flight initially to Luang Prabang, then the connecting prehistoric Li-2 to Luang Nam Tha. It didn't help that the temperature was dipping deep in the low-Arctic twenties. The porters who gathered around the plane were dressed like Sherpas in balaclavas and socks with flip-flops rather than climbing boots. Their friendly banter had lasted only until they realized the old couple really didn't have anything for them to carry. But in the spirit of opportunism, they offered to piggyback Daeng to the guesthouse. Siri told them that the only man who'd have contact with his wife would be him, although he didn't offer to piggyback her himself. Instead he took her arm, and they walked slowly across the field beside the runway where goats grazed and little black pigs ran around their ankles like puppies.

The walk took longer than Madame Chanta's hand-drawn map had suggested. Siri coughed most of the way. On three occasions, Daeng took a rest in front of strangers' huts. On each occasion, she was treated by the householder to local sweet sticky rice and tea. So they reached the Nam Tha River in good spirits. Although there was no sign to announce it, the small wooden guesthouse perched on the riverbank looked exactly as Madame Chanta had described it. The owner was a Thai Lu from a village eleven kilometers upstream. His wife had been a weaver there before they got a taste for innkeeping. Her name was Nang Uma, and she was a close friend of Chanta. She apologized that her husband was away and not able to see them, then welcomed the guests and read Madame Chanta's letter of introduction with joy.

"What fun," she said in heavily accented Lao, even before they were shown to their room. "Show me you piece."

Siri pulled the half-*sin* from his pack and removed it from the plastic. Nang Uma took it from him and opened it up. She looked a little confused at first but then smiled. "Is one of Auntie Kwa's," she said.

"How can you tell?" Daeng asked.

"Well, it clearly Lu," she said, "and weaver here in Luang Nam Tha have own pattern. Is not so—how you say?—not

detail like other tribe but easy recognize. We so close to
China, the weaver here like to sew in ribbon from China
make stripe. Ribbon make on machine. We no have. Sometime overlap ribbon make brocade look pretty. Auntie Kwa
go to border often barter for silk. She love the pink too much.
See that?"

"And where can we find Auntie Kwa?" Siri asked.

"She up in Muang Sing. Everybody know her up there.
And you lucky. Have three bus every week go to Muang Sing.
Today have bus. It stop here outside twelve o'clock. Give you
time eat lunch before you go."

"So soon?" said Daeng. "In fact, we were hoping to catch
up with a friend of ours. A policeman. He's working on a case
here in Luang Nam Tha."

"You know where?" asked Nang Uma.

"Not the name of the village," said Siri. "But I imagine he'll
be lodging in town somewhere."

"Okay," said Nang Uma. "We do like this. You not get the
bus today, you have to wait Saturday for next one. Muang Sing
fifty kilometers. Use to take almost one day. Now have new
road, take couple hour. I say you catch bus today, visit Auntie
Kwa. Do what you have to do. If you finish, come back on
Saturday bus. You can write letter to you police friend, and I
take bicycle to new town and give to policeman at police station. He have a car?"

"A jeep," said Siri.

"Okay. Good. He can drive Muang Sing meet you there."

"He won't know where we're staying," said Daeng.

"Muang Sing, not Peking, Madame. He find you."

During their early lunch, Siri and Daeng composed a note
to Phosy. They mentioned that Dtui had stopped by to see
them before they left Vientiane. She'd received Phosy's wire
from the Chinese border and had gone somewhere "perfectly
safe" with little Malee. They were at a place he knew well.

Siri offered to help with Phosy's case even though the doctor was aware the request for forensic assistance might have been invented by Judge Haeng. Either way, Siri would be delighted to tag along as a Dr. Watson to the great Sherlock Phosy. Phosy had spent many hours listening to Siri's renditions of Holmes's clever detections. In the note they explained why they were going to Muang Sing and hoped he could find time to visit them there. If not, they'd probably be back at the guesthouse on Saturday.

The twelve o'clock bus arrived at two, which Nang Uma told them was normal. She waved them off and took the note in its sealed envelope back into the guesthouse. Her husband was sitting at the communal table. "They've gone," she said.

She sat opposite him and used a table knife to open the envelope, then handed him the note. He read it once, screwed it into a ball and threw it off the balcony into the gently flowing Nam Tha River.

Phosy's visit to the second village was entirely different from the first. He appeared to be getting more respect and cooperation from the local police. Constable Nut even offered to carry the inspector's briefcase. Ban Bouree was an Akha village, and Phosy could speak passable Akha. He'd neglected to mention this fact when they set off that morning. But by the time he'd met the village elders, introduced himself and told them the Akha produced the best rice liquor in the country, he owned the village. The fact that nobody in his entourage had any idea what he was saying was a tremendous advantage. He'd allowed them to sit in on the meeting but provided only scant and selective translated feedback.

"How's your relationship with the Chinese at the road camp?" he asked the middle-aged man, Ahpah, who had taken on the mantle of spokesman. He was a weedy specimen whose hair had never seen a comb.

"Very good, sir," Ahpah said without enthusiasm.

"Have you had any dealings with them?"

"They came to buy eggs or pigs in the beginning. But we don't have much. After a couple of days, they knew we couldn't provide their groceries."

Mrs. Yoo interrupted, "I'm afraid I have to insist on a translation."

"Preliminaries," said Phosy. "Just breaking the ice a little bit."

"Preliminaries," said Xiu Long. His smile had never been brighter. Phosy wondered how a man who understood so little could be so content. The Chinese man winked at the inspector, who wasn't sure what to make of the gesture. He opted to ignore it and return to the elders.

"Any problems at all?" he asked. "With the Chinese, that is."

"What do you mean—problems?" asked the spokesman.

"Come on. There are a thousand-plus men camped over your back fence. No drunkenness? Threats? No attempts to flirt with your young ladies? No burglary?"

"No," said the spokesman.

"No to which part?"

"To all of it. They've been most polite."

"What about your deceased headman's dealings with them?"

"Just the initial negotiation."

"About what?"

"Renting the land. The fields back there belong to our two villages."

"Do you have land documents to prove that?"

"No. The provincial governor knows what land belongs to which tribes. That is our shared land. We all agree."

"And the road builders were okay with that?"

"Of course. Both the headmen attended the meeting."

"And who negotiated on behalf of the road people?"

"Their foreman, Goi."

Phosy felt a prodding in his ribs and a fluttering in his stomach.

"Inspector Phosy," said Mrs. Yoo. "Really . . ."

"A lot of ice here," said Phosy. "A veritable glacier. But it won't be long." He noticed Sergeant Teyp whisper something to Constable Nut, who stood to leave. "Stay!" said Phosy.

Nut sat like a trained terrier.

"So the two villages got a fifty-fifty split of the rental," Phosy concluded.

"Down the middle," said the spokesman.

"And what amount are we talking here?"

"A quarter of a million."

"I assume you aren't referring to US dollars."

"Lao *kip*."

Phosy hummed. For a quarter of a million *kip* in 1979 you could get a very nice wall calendar. So money was hardly a motivating factor in the killings.

"All right then," said the policeman. "Can you tell me why your headman and the Yao headman were meeting on neutral ground at sunrise?"

Until that moment, every response to Phosy's questions had been succinct and apparently honest. But this question produced a good deal of eye contact amongst the Akha. It was brief, almost imperceptible, but to a policeman with a keen eye it was as loud as a Tannoy conversation.

"No," said the spokesman. His first lie.

"No, you can't tell me?"

"No—we . . . I don't really . . ."

In Phosy's dealings with the Akha, one characteristic had always floated to the surface. Telling an outright lie was a truly uncomfortable experience. They could be annoyingly direct and blunt to the point of cruelty, but untruths seemed to curdle their blood. Phosy rephrased his question. "Why did the two men meet?"

"A matter."

"What kind of matter?"

One of the elders, a ginseng root of a man who had thus far remained silent, stood and stretched and cracked several bones in his fingers. "I think it's time to get to the fields," he said.

And with that, the meeting broke up. The elders left the hut, being sure to shake the hands of the visitors before leaving. Phosy smiled and said to his baffled observers, "Well, I think that went very well. Don't you?"

The seven-hour bus ride to Muang Sing had been delayed by Mother Nature and haunted by the ghosts that lurked in machines. The single Look Up tree that lay across the road at kilometer eighteen shouldn't have presented the problems it did; it was no more than sixty centimeters in diameter, but that was high enough to serve as an impassable buffer to the old bus. There were no axes or machetes on board, and the nearest village was half an hour's walk. The driver said the situation was hopeless and started to perform a sixteen-point turn on the skinny road.

It was Siri who solved the problem. On the roof of the bus was a basket of cooking pots to be collected by its owner in Muang Sing. The passengers took the pots and filled them with rocks and earth from the roadside embankment. With these they constructed a ramp on and off the log. Naturally, Dr. Siri, a hands-on educator, was wheezing pathetically by the time the bus landed on the far side.

The bus continued its journey. There were several stops for maintenance, which the driver seemed to have mastered from experience, but the cracked piston was another matter. Ten kilometers from Muang Sing, the engine suddenly had no moving parts and the bus became a landmark. So it was that Siri and Daeng arrived in Muang Sing on a cart pulled by a small pony. The animal and the passengers were coughing loudly. The twelve-year-old driver was not. Dr. Siri examined himself and his wife and announced that they had undoubtedly caught Dtui's cold. He wasn't carrying any cold remedies. There was one pharmacy in Muang Sing, but it was dark and shuttered as the pony clopped past. 8 P.M. was well past the town's bedtime. The travelers couldn't even find a guesthouse.

At the recommendation of the cart driver, they went to the house of the local cadre in charge of visitors. He checked their *laissez-passer*s. His own residence was already full of Chinese dignitaries, he said, but he led them to a two-story wooden building at the intersection of Muang Sing's main streets. It had no rooms and, of course, no electricity. The cadre, keen to get back to his more important guests, left them a beeswax lamp, a bucket of drinking water, bedding and four kapok mattresses that smelled of mothballs. The bathroom was way out back, and there was a good deal of wildlife between them and it.

But vermin or no vermin, if old folk have to go, they have to go. Each wrapped against the cold in an embroidered counterpane, Siri and Daeng coughed and spluttered to the outhouse, did their business by lamplight and almost stepped on a rat on the way back.

The couple had made themselves a sort of spring-roll casing from the soggy mattresses and quilts and were squashed together as the filling—purely for the preservation of body heat, of course.

"Still miss the adventure?" Siri asked.

"Every day with you is a lifetime of adventure, Dr. Siri." Daeng smiled.

*   *   *

The residents of Siri's halfway house for vagrants and strays in Vientiane were thinking about retiring for the night. The children were already in their bedrolls, and the women were waiting for their turns to shower. They'd wash their hair in the afternoon when the sunshine helped to dry it, so they spent as little time as possible on their evening ablutions. It was Mrs. Fah's turn at the water trough. As there was no lock on the door, she was singing—badly.

Some of the men were playing their last hand of rummy. Noo the forest monk had accrued a veritable log cabin of toothpicks in winnings, which he promised to donate to a worthy cause. None of the others would accuse him of cheating, although it was quite obvious he had been.

The transistor played Thai pop from across the river interspersed with monotonous advertisements for luxury items the Lao had long since stopped dreaming of owning. What good was a blender/mixer when there were no fruits and vegetables to blend or mix? They'd paused the game briefly and were listening to how they might change the pigment of their unsightly dark skin through daily applications of Snowflake cream—now available in half-liter jars.

That's when they heard the scream. Gongjai, the ex-karaoke lounge hostess, came running into the kitchen wearing her baby-doll nightdress. She was closely followed by two men wielding machetes. "These bastards manhandled me," said Gongjai.

"Shut up," said Machete One.

"Which one of you's Nurse Dtui?" said Machete Two. For effect he clunked his machete into the Queen of Hearts on the kitchen table, perhaps envisioning splitting the table in two and everyone saying, "OOH." Instead, the fat knife embedded itself in the old teak table, and he blushed as he attempted to pull it out.

A third man, unarmed but naturally frightening with the left side of his face like melted cheese, burst into the kitchen. "Where is she?" he shouted.

Alerted by the singing from the bathroom, he strode across to the wooden door and kicked it down. Though Mrs. Fah narrowly avoided being hit by the falling door, she did not avoid being seen in all her splendor by everyone in the kitchen. "How rude," she said, but didn't hurry to cover herself.

"The garden!" shouted Half-Face. The man who wasn't standing on the kitchen table astride his machete like Arthur attempting to free Excalibur ran into the backyard.

Crazy Rajhid and the lost woman were sitting silently at the garden table staring at each other. Ugly the dog had been tied to a post with heavy-duty electrical cable for fear he might have attempted to follow Siri's airplane. He obviously hadn't given up that hope, because he'd patiently spent his days chewing through the copper wire. When he saw an assailant burst through the back door carrying a weapon, he charged. The cable snapped. Ugly soared through the air like a country rocket and buried his fangs in the man's face. The man screamed, fell backward, lost his machete and landed with a thump on the path. Crazy Rajhid was at the man's chest like an attack of angina.

Taking advantage of the distracting sounds from outside, Inthanet the puppet master reached into the shoulder bag that hung from his chair and produced a Browning pistol. He fired twice into the ceiling, then leveled the weapon at Half-Face. Splinters of plywood rained down. The house invader on the table was dragged down to the nicely tiled floor, where he found himself in an armlock and staring into the face of a bald man with no eyebrows.

"I forgive you," said Noo.

Half-Face looked back from whence he'd come, hoping for reinforcements, but the man he'd placed as lookout at the front gate appeared with a teenaged girl clamped onto his back. The fingers of her left hand gouged into his eyes. In her right hand, she held a shaving blade to his throat. Behind him were assorted women and children with bamboo broom handles prodding and poking him into the kitchen.

"What the . . . ?" Half-Face began. "What's wrong with you guys? These are old men and kids and damned women. Pull yourselves tog—"

He was interrupted by the excruciating pain of a screwdriver being buried into his shoulder. He turned to see the lost woman at his back, eyes burning like flares, teeth snarling. She yanked out the shaft with little effort and was primed to strike again, this time at his throat. He cringed and sank to his knees, but she had hold of his hair. She looked—to all who witnessed the scene—rapturous. It was Rajhid who caught her wrist before she could plunge it into the invader's jugular. She had found a reservoir of incredible strength, but the Indian was its equal. Whatever demons were inside of her would have to wait for their exorcism. She settled for slapping the gang leader around the head with her free hand, two, three times. Then, as quickly as it had arrived, her energy was gone, and she was frail and vulnerable again.

"Help!" came a distant call from out back, accompanied by Ugly on the growls.

Inthanet walked up to the cowed gang leader. "I'm afraid Nurse Dtui isn't in right now," he said. "But if you'd care to leave a message . . ."

Daeng and Siri rose with what should have been the sunrise having slept hardly at all. One would fall asleep only to be awoken by the coughing of the other. Eventually they fell into an exhausted trancelike state where they didn't have the energy to cough or the wherewithal to sleep. Although the temperature hadn't risen a single degree, they came to sit on the wraparound balcony of the old building to watch for the frenzied comings and goings of Muang Sing's main intersection. After ten minutes, a cheroot-smoking man on a bicycle squeaked past. It was another fifteen minutes before a woman with a bouncing shoulder cradle full of fruit headed in the same direction.

That was, apparently, as exciting as things would get. The old couple were left with the feeling they were the last survivors. The mountains that surrounded the town on the maps were not apparent in the flesh. Instead, the mist gradually deleted the buildings only a block from Siri's viewpoint and left him in the hollow of a cloud. He had no sense of the vibrancy he'd read about in the old tomes of the French explorers. Of the days when Muang Sing market was the Ginza of the Golden Triangle drug trade.

"Fancy a coffee and croissants?" he asked.

"I think I'd prefer a bowl of hot stew," said Daeng. She nodded toward the bank of mist to the east. "Looks like the masses are heading in that direction. I bet the market's in that fog somewhere. And where there's croissants and stew, there's bound to be drugs."

"We don't need drugs," said Siri. "Water and vitamin C, that's what's called for. It's a nasty cold. It'll be gone in twenty-four hours. Trust me. I'm a doctor."

And with that he fell into another coughing fit.

Compared to Muang Sing's downtown, the market was throbbing in a slow, early morning, sleepy kind of way. The morning trade leaned toward fruits, vegetables and opium. Despite all the international suggestions for drug eradication, nobody had come up with a crop that could bring in higher profits. There were no oranges, but Siri bought a large bag of pomegranates, and they gorged and dribbled as they ambled along the aisles. It was still fun to admire the hill tribe women in their traditional costumes—the Akha jangling in their piaster hats and the Hmong in their embroidered finery. They were accompanied by a soundtrack of languages they didn't recognize and the whinnies of ponies tethered to posts. The clothing and electrical goods stalls didn't bother to open until after eight, when the villagers had made enough from their cane or bananas or edible wildlife to buy a T-shirt or a battery for the community radio.

But against the odds, there was one stall selling *pha sin*. A woman sat cross-legged on top of her cloths in a long Tottenham Hotspur football scarf and earmuffs.

"Sister," asked Siri, "where might we find Auntie Kwa? She's a weaver."

"She's a common seller," said the woman with a morose expression. "She's a mother to ingrates, a wife to a drunk killed in a useless war. She's the sister to a drug addict. She's a pauper because nobody has money to buy her beautiful wares. But somewhere deep in all that tragedy, yes, she's a weaver."

The reply was somewhat more complicated than the question deserved, but Madame Daeng got it. "You're Auntie Kwa," she said.

"To some," said the woman. "To others I'm dirt."

Siri unwrapped the half *pha sin* from its plastic bag and held it up. "Did you weave this?" he asked.

Auntie Kwa looked at it curiously, then up at the customers. "Oh, it's you."

She climbed down from her perch. "Did I weave that? Yes and no," she said as she rummaged around in a large pack, finally producing another plastic bag, this one stapled shut. "I'm to give you this," she said, and handed it to Siri. "Glad to be rid of it. It's brought me nothing but bad luck."

Siri doubted whatever was in the bag could curse her life to a greater extent than she herself. He ripped open the staples, reached into the bag and pulled out another *pha sin*.

"Don't open that here," said Auntie Kwa.

"It's just a rectangle of fabric," said Siri.

"It's never that."

Siri unfolded it anyway, took hold of the corners and let it drape to the ground. To his untrained and disappointed eye, it looked rather similar to the one they'd received in Vientiane. There were one or two minute differences that he would have called insignificant. He started to run his fingers around the hem.

"Do you know where this is from?" asked Daeng.

"No," said Auntie Kwa, and looked away.

"It's Lu, isn't it?" said Daeng.

"I don't know."

"Yes, you do," said Siri. "Could I borrow some scissors?"

"What for?"

"Look here," he said, and handed her the *sin*. "Feel this?"

She reached out and squeezed the hem. "What is that?" she asked.

"I'm guessing it's a finger," he told her.

"A what?" said Auntie Kwa, stepping back in horror.

"A severed finger like the one you sent to me in Vientiane."

"Are you mad? I never did any such thing."

"Sister," he said, "I work for the Ministry of Justice. We found a finger in the hem of the *pha sin* you've admitted you wove. That makes you a murder suspect."

"Don't be ridiculous."

"If this second one also contains a finger, that's what we

at Justice call a . . . a double-digit dilemma. You're in a lot of trouble. Now . . . the scissors, if you'd be so kind."

Auntie Kwa handed him a pair of shears as big as his chest. Daeng laughed. "Could you just pick the hem for us?" she asked the woman.

Reluctantly, Auntie Kwa took hold of the cloth and began to pick with a thin blade. As in most markets, this small but significant break from early morning tradition had attracted a silent gathering of curious onlookers come to see what the outsiders were doing. Shoppers in blankets tied at the waist with string or in ex-army trenchcoats crowded in on the old couple.

"I didn't do this. I didn't do this," Auntie Kwa mumbled. She didn't dare look inside even when the opening was wide enough. She handed the skirt to Siri, who probed into the hem with a pair of tweezers from his morgue kit. He withdrew the object slowly, but it wasn't a finger he found in there. It was a bullet of a type he didn't recognize.

"That's not a finger," said Auntie Kwa.

"It's no less incriminating," said Siri. "It could be the bullet that killed the owner of the finger, for all we know. I think you'd better tell us everything."

"I had nothing to do with this," she said. "There's nothing to tell. I sold one of my *sin*s to some woman. She gave me twice what I asked for it. Then she handed me this plastic bag and told me an old man would bring back my *sin* one day, and I was to give him the bag—this one. I never even opened it."

"When was this?" Daeng asked.

"About six weeks ago."

"What did she look like?" asked Siri.

"Normal. Nothing special. Not tall, not short. About my age."

The gathered onlookers had begun a mumbled translation for their fellow tribesmen.

"Lao?" asked Siri.

"Far as I could tell. I didn't check her ID."

"How was she traveling?" asked Daeng.

"Just turned up on foot here, like you two."

"Do you know anyone who's missing a finger?" Siri asked.

"No, I do not," Auntie Kwa replied.

"All right," said Daeng. "Then that brings us to the original question. Where was this second *sin* made?"

"Really, I don't know."

"Look carefully," said Siri.

"It's a cheap rip-off," she said. "Poor quality. A Lu design, but nothing personal about it. We Lu take a pride in our weaving. It's a family-based tradition in the villages. This was probably made over the border in a sweatshop. That's why nobody buys my high-class *sin*s anymore. They go for the cheap ones."

"Over the border?" said Daeng. "You mean, in China?"

"Yes. No, perhaps not China. You see this fabric? The green hem beneath the brocade? That's Burmese. Here in Muang Sing we only produce black, indigo and blue."

"And is there a trade in green fabric between Muang Sing and Burma?"

"No, too far. Not enough interest. If we needed it, we could get it cheaper from the Chinese."

"So if I wanted to buy Burmese cloth . . . ?"

"You'd go to Chiang Kok, on the Mekhong."

"Do you know any Lu weavers over there?" Siri asked.

"There's only the one. Her name's Peu Jin. She lives by the river."

"No, wait," said Daeng. "That doesn't make sense. You say they don't produce green cloth here. But the *sin* that was sent to us—the *sin* you wove—has a green hem. So doesn't that make it Burmese?"

"No, sister. That's why I said yes and no when you asked me if it was mine. I did weave that cloth, but I used good old-fashioned Muang Sing spun cotton. Someone's dyed the hem green, and a shoddy job they made of it too."

"Why would they do that?" Siri asked.

"Your guess is as good as mine, old man."

Inspector Phosy had spent the night in his jeep on a remote hill. He'd found paranoia had saved his life on several occasions. In this case, it was more like a shivery touch of the inevitable that kept him away from his boardinghouse. He'd broken the face of probably the most influential villain in the province. Following his initial interviews at the Yao village, Phosy had driven his Chinese guests back to the border crossing at Pang Hai. From there they'd found their own transportation to the trade commission in Meng La.

Lieutenant Tang on the Lao side had been interested to hear of the inspector's run-in with Foreman Goi. The lieutenant had collected a good deal of information about the toothless one. His interest had been piqued following a visit the foreman had paid him a year earlier. Goi had quite openly suggested mutual rewards in turning a blind eye to certain imports and exports. Ninety times out of a hundred, such a deal would have been accepted, and a Lao military man on five dollars a month could have himself a very cozy life. But Lieutenant Tang was no ordinary soldier. He was one of those rare devout communists who detested capitalist doctrines and the selfish pursuit of money. He could most certainly not be bought. He slept in a rattan hut, drank in moderation and wrote daily to his wife and children. Phosy liked him.

Over coffee, Phosy heard that toothless Goi was actually called Guan Jin. He was Thai Lu but born on the Chinese side of the border. Like the Lao, the Lu race had been cut in half by a random demarcation. Goi had studied engineering in Peking and risen to the rank of sergeant in the

People's Liberation Army. He had been accused of some unlisted infringements that were never proven, but he had been kicked out of the military. Soon he was managing engineering crews as a civil engineer in the southern provinces. There his language skills made him invaluable to the monolingual Chinese. His personal record was clouded with accusations of violence, cruelty and profiteering, but his professional accomplishments were many. His teams were always the most efficient and effective. His projects were concluded under budget and to the satisfaction of the regional cadres. Once the Chinese road program was launched in Laos, Goi was given instructions to get the job done without draining the limited resources of the People's Republic of China. It appeared nobody looked too deeply into how he achieved that.

Rumors were a national pastime in Laos, and nowhere were they more extravagant than along the border. But even if rumors about Foreman Goi were greatly exaggerated, they all pointed in one direction. The man was criminally insane. There were stories of executions, of beatings and torture. Goi had become a dark legend in the north, and his name spread fear in the hearts of those who worked for and with him. Phosy had felt that manic energy, and there was no doubt in his mind that Foreman Goi was a dangerous man. To make matters worse, his influence extended beyond Luang Nam Tha all the way to the capital. He had to have contacts in Vientiane to have been able to gather information about Phosy's wife and child. Those same contacts proved a constant threat to their lives. Phosy could have called for backup from Vientiane, but he felt he'd need a small army to compete with Goi and his road builders. And waging war against a warlord had never proven wise or successful.

Phosy and Tang might have been able to glean more information from Vientiane about Goi's record, but communication had been down for twenty-four hours. The border post was completely cut off from the outside world. Even their shortwave signals had been blocked. And, for some reason, traffic into Laos from China had halted completely.

"They do it every now and then," said Tang. "The Chinese. They get a new directive from Peking and shut border crossings. Then they show off with their technical skills. It'll all be back to normal in a day or so."

With no observers and no police escort, Phosy returned to the Akha village at Ban Bouree. He parked well off the main road behind a patch of untidy banana trees. From there he walked along the track leading to the village. At one point, he passed a small gaggle of women dressed in threadbare costumes that didn't seem to represent any clan he'd ever seen. The women were carrying baskets of firewood on their backs. The basket straps formed a band across their foreheads. Phosy nodded. The older women ignored him. The younger ones giggled and probably made some ribald comments in their language, because everyone laughed.

It was a young girl at the back of the group who caught his attention like the tongue of a cartoon frog lassoing a fly. She was stunningly beautiful, but not in a modest girlish way. She was about fifteen, sweet and ripe as an orange mango, and she walked as if she'd learned the arts of grace and poise at a finishing school. He stopped to watch her pass. She looked back, smiled, rolled her hips and licked her lips. Phosy's heart bunched like a fist.

It had been a brief encounter, the details of which he would most certainly not be sharing with his wife when he returned to Vientiane. He was disturbed by how the girl had made him feel. Phosy was not a flirtatious man, and very rarely was he excited at the sight of a teenaged girl, no matter how pretty.

But this young vixen had made a papaya salad of his hor-
mones and thrown in a handful of chillies. Any other man
would have been flattered and stimulated by such a show.
But the inspector was embarrassed. He thought he was past
such adolescent weaknesses. He was still unsettled when he
arrived at the village.

Most of the adults were out cutting sugarcane. The girls
of ten or eleven had been entrusted with the care of the
younger children. They were playing with toddlers or rocking
babies on hips not yet fully formed. One of the girls remembered him from his visit the day before. She waved. She'd
tied a tin can on a string to the tail of a young pig and set her
three small charges the challenge of being the first to strike
the can with a stick. The pig, quite naturally, kept its distance
from the stick, and the game seemed unending. The girl had
probably played the same game when she was three or four.
With the exception of the pig, it seemed to thrill everyone.

"Hello, Uncle," the girl said.

"Hello, little mother," said Phosy.

She laughed. Her teeth already showed signs of a sugarcane diet. Phosy sat on a tree stump and watched the game.
"You're a policeman," she said.

"Yes. Do you have anything to confess?"

"Not yet."

"Not yet?"

"You see that one?" she said, pointing her chin at a chubby
child who was throwing clods of earth at the pig. "He makes
me angry. I might kill him."

Phosy laughed. Had there been schools up here in the
wilds, this girl would get the education she deserved and
become the Minister of Culture. There was no doubt about it.
As it was, she would dutifully await marriage at far too young
an age and fade out of the landscape of potential. "Do you
suppose someone got angry at Headman Panpan?"

"No."

"Really? It looked like someone didn't like him."

"Only Headman Mao."

"Headman Mao didn't like Headman Panpan?"

"They used to be best friends. Then one day they broke up. They started arguing a lot."

"What did they argue about?"

"Don't know. They only ever argued in Lao. I don't speak Lao."

"Can you think what might cause two men who were close friends to suddenly stop liking each other?"

"Mama said it was the potion. When a man drinks the potion, he doesn't know what's right."

"What kind of potion was it?"

"Don't know. Mama said I'm too young to drink it. I'm guessing it's like Coca-Cola. I drank a bottle once, and it made me throw up."

"Did your headman ever fall over and say silly things when he was drinking this potion?"

"No, you're thinking of rice whiskey. That just makes people drunk. The potion makes people stupid."

Phosy didn't get any further with the potion theory. He thanked the girl and told the chubby kid to be good. The chubby kid threw a clod of earth at him.

"Go ahead," Phosy told the girl.

The inspector walked down the winding path that led to the clearing. He passed along tight jungle tracks where the leaves reached out to caress him on either side. Where anything could have been lurking around the next bend. Where the sounds of birds and insects took on human form. Reaching the crime scene came as something of a relief.

He sat again on the log. The clothes had been removed now. The sharpened bamboo poles were gone. He'd told Sergeant Teyp and his men to take everything to the police office. They'd looked at him as if he were mad when he handed them the plastic gloves and insisted they touch none of the evidence without wearing the gloves. Many of Dr. Siri's methods stuck. So now Phosy had only the crime scene and his skill at visualization. It had been early morning when the men died. No signs of alcohol. A meeting in a place where there was no work to be done. It's cold in the morning, yet they removed their shirts and hats. What could . . . ?

"The potion," he said aloud. All of a sudden the parts fit neatly together. He was embarrassed that it had taken him so long. Dr. Siri would probably have worked it all out in his sleep.

It was a tragedy, but the important point was that the scenario he'd arrived at had nothing to do with the Chinese road builders. He could sign the statement now with a clear conscience. China was innocent.

Phosy walked through the forest toward the work camp, not with the intention of announcing this fact, more to burn up the adrenaline that pumped through him when a case was solved. It still remained to be seen why toothless Goi had been so keen to clear China's name. Given the man's record of illicit dealings, Phosy doubted the motivation was purely, or even partly, political. But that was a larger issue and one he wasn't about to tackle.

When he arrived at the camp, it was deserted. The shanties stretched out before him, but there were no people. He assumed he'd come before the end of the work detail, that the men were still at the road site. But as he walked from hut to shack, he saw no personal effects. No bags. No bed mats. The volleyball nets had been taken down. There were no pots in the mess tent. In the twenty-seven hours since he'd last seen them, 1,117 Chinese road workers had disappeared.

5

Chasing Skirt

There were three motorized vehicles in Muang Sing—all jeeps. One belonged to the police. One to the military. And one to a nebulous aid group by the name of Physicians Eschewing Agendas. The group had supported the Pathet Lao enthusiastically in the international press during the struggles. Like the Quakers and the Mennonites, PEA had been invited to stay on in the country and do . . . whatever it was they'd been doing before the takeover. Nobody was too clear exactly what that was. But brotherhood had to be rewarded.

All this Siri had learned from a hot berry drink seller at the market. He and Daeng had spent an hour there thawing out and pumping in vitamin C. It wasn't working. They were still in need of transportation to the Mekhong, sixty kilometers west.

The consensus at the market was that there was nothing faster than an ox cart heading in that direction. They could see no earthly chance of wresting jeeps from the police or the army, so they followed directions to a quaint old wooden building on stilts behind Xieng Yeun Temple. They arrived in the middle of a rendition of "Jingle Bells" sung by twenty small children seated beneath the house. The choirmaster was an elderly balding version of what Santa Claus might have looked like after a crash diet. His hair was long, and his beard bore two plaited strands that looked from a distance like dribble. When the song was over, he introduced himself in Lao as Bobby from California and sang the word "Lola."

Lola, his wife, came down the staircase with a tray of pancakes cut into small triangles. Siri had never met Henry Kissinger, but he'd seen photographs. Lola bore such a resemblance, she could have been his mother. She wore a frock with a hibiscus print that made her look like a garden trellis.

Within minutes, Siri and Daeng had been hugged and shaken and squeezed until they were intimates. Lola and Bobby, Siri learned, had been holed up in this house for six months because the government hadn't yet decided what they were allowed to do. They were both qualified and experienced doctors, but they were kept away from the understaffed hospital, couldn't see patients at the house and were not allowed to "teach, train, fraternize or proselytize." This was spelled out in their letter of welcome from the government that now hung framed on their kitchen wall. The same letter concluded, "We respect PEA for its ongoing support of the Pathet Lao revolution and thank you for your continued assistance to the poor in remote areas."

In short, PEA could stay in their Muang Sing home, chat to health care workers and conduct singalongs with the kids, the lyrics of which were "picked up" rather than taught. And, of course, they could make pancakes. The kids treated the snack with great deference and refused to eat it in one sitting. They left reluctantly for home, jingling all the way.

Despite the couple's overindulgences in the area of bonhomie, Siri and Daeng rather liked them. Bobby gave Siri some of their stock of herbal cold medicine as a gift and, having heard of the visitors' need for transportation, he led them out back. In the rear corner of the open yard was a large object wrapped in burlap sacks and rope. As Bobby peeled off the sacks, he explained, "This beauty belonged to Dr. Tom Dooley back in the sixties. When they moved on, the Lao staff at the clinic didn't know what to do with her. None of them could drive. So she sat there. Medico—the sponsors—said we could use her. I rescued her just in time. Her name's Agnes."

He yanked at the last rope, and the sacking fell away to reveal a Willys Jeep in remarkable condition.

"They don't make 'em like this any more," Bobby continued. "I'm a car guy. We've been sitting around here twiddling our thumbs, so I put all my energy into this baby. It works just fine. But the local cadres won't let us go anywhere in it. I drive it around the grounds when nobody's looking. The carburetor hums like a hive o' hornets. You'll have to find gas for it, but you're welcome to use it."

"I feel like I belong to some tribe of cave dwellers," Siri told Daeng later. Bobby was polishing his Willys. Lola was cooking them lunch. The cold remedies had swaddled Siri and Daeng in a cocoon of cotton.

"Well, technically, you do," she reminded him. "The revolution was conducted from the caves of the north."

"But not in one million BC, Daeng. We've got a hospital up here that's still practicing bloodletting and chicken sacrifices, and we have two experienced, Lao-speaking doctors waiting to help, and they're all tied up in PDR red tape. It makes me sick."

"I know it does, dear."

"I want to—"

"I know you do, dear." And she watched as Siri's outrage dissipated into one more coughing fit.

Even though they'd only known the new arrivals for three hours, the Americans provided an emotional goodbye. Lola sobbed into her handkerchief as she and Bobby stood on the front step waving them off. "Our hearts go with you," shouted Lola.

Sitting proudly at the wheel, Siri watched them shrink in the rearview mirror.

"Do you suppose they're that enthusiastic with everyone?" Daeng asked.

"It's the grapes," said Siri. "California. Wine. It makes people love each other. Look at France. *L'amour* every damned where."

"The French aren't nearly so gushing," said Daeng.

"They've been doing it a lot longer. They went through their gushing period. History irons gushing out. Now they only have romance. The Americans will get there."

Daeng leaned over and kissed his ear.

"What?" he said.

"I love it when you talk rubbish."

"I'm not . . ."

"What do we do for petrol, my husband?"

"That will take care of itself. I have a good feeling about all of this."

At Muang Sing's only petrol pump at the old China road intersection, the proprietor announced boldly that they weren't accepting *kip* that day. Siri stared at him. He was tall and nicely postured like a matinee actor in hard times.

"Have they moved the border since we got here?" Siri asked.

"A lot of Chinese vehicles heading home today," the proprietor replied. "They're in a hurry. They can't be bothered to count out all those small bills in *kip*, so they hand over wads of *yuan*. It usually works out better for me to have foreign currency. Our people are forever devaluing."

"That's the spirit," said Siri. "What happens to the poor Lao who don't have *yuan*?"

"That's not my problem. I've been told to get the Chinese out as quickly as possible."

Daeng leaned across her husband. A full logging truck cast a shadow over them and blasted its horn. "Surely there's some way to get petrol here without using foreign currency," she said.

"No," the proprietor barked. "Now do you want to pull over so this guy can get filled up?"

"I'm not moving," said Siri.

"Suit yourself, Granddad," said the man. "Those trucks have bull bars the size of Alaska." He waved the truck driver forward.

"Don't you have parents?" Daeng asked. "Can't you help an old couple get to Chiang Kok to visit their dying grandson? He only has half a lung."

The proprietor held up his hand to the truck driver. "You're going to Chiang Kok?" he asked.

"We're trying to," said Siri.

"Well then there might be a way, after all," said the man. "If you'd be prepared to take a passenger."

"We could be persuaded," said Siri.

The truck driver blasted his horn again.

"I've got this important politburo man out back," said the proprietor. "He's been here all day. He's asked me to keep an eye open for anything headed west. He's on some top-secret mission, or so he keeps telling me. I imagine he'd have a petrol budget if he's as important as he says. He's had no trouble paying for the end of my stock of Tsingtao beer."

"Show us the way," said Daeng.

The truck started forward, and Siri pulled aside. The fumes weren't helping his condition. The proprietor put some petrol in the tank and was counting out his *yuan* as he led Siri and Daeng to the rear of the pump building.

"What's happening in China?" Daeng asked him.

"What?"

"You said everyone's in a hurry to get back."

"You're joking, right, lady?"

"If I was I wouldn't have found myself particularly funny," she said. "Just answer the question, young man."

The proprietor stopped and looked back at the old lady. "You really haven't heard?"

"Heard what?"

"China's invaded Vietnam," he said. "The Vietnamese are putting pressure on Laos to kick out all the Chinese. The Chinks are getting out all their heavy equipment so it won't be confiscated as war booty. Some of the work teams have left already."

"China invaded Vietnam?" said Siri. "I don't believe it."

"Don't you listen to the radio?"

"All I can hear is Chinese."

"They have a program in the Lao language. They reopened the channel and announced it officially a couple of hours ago. Their army's already captured two provincial capitals in Vietnam. The locals are dropping like fireflies."

"And what's Laos doing about it?" Daeng asked.

"The Chinese reckon all the hill tribes are siding with them, and units of Lao militia have already defected. But I imagine that's Chinese propaganda. You can't believe a word those bastards say. I suppose you'd have to ask the politburo guy for the real story. He just arrived from Vientiane. He'll probably know."

They followed the proprietor around the back of a small cottage and heard him say, "Hello, Uncle. I think I might have found you a ride out west."

When Siri and Daeng arrived at the veranda, they saw an old man sitting on a porch swing with a bottle on his lap. He looked up at the arrivals and smiled.

"Civilai?" said Daeng.

"Hello," said Civilai.

"What are you doing here?" Siri asked.

"You know him?" asked the proprietor.

"I'm the honorary war attaché for Luang Nam Tha," said Civilai. Siri sat beside him and started to swing the seat. "Steady. You'll spill my beer," said Civilai.

"What happened to the Chinese Relations Committee?" Siri asked. Daeng sat opposite on a good solid bench.

"It folded," said Civilai. "It's really hard for one to have relations with people who are waging war with one. Or at least with one's ally. There's more than the usual chaos in Vientiane. Nobody knows how to react. Do we send greetings cards to both sides wishing them the best of luck? Or do we take up arms and defend our borders? We didn't know about it until the Chinese were twenty kilometers into Vietnam and it was a bit too late to lodge strong objections to the buildup of troops."

"Is that why you're up here, Civilai?" Daeng asked. "Defending our borders with a beer bottle?"

"They call it a nonaggressive diplomatic mission," he said. "I'm just here to observe and report back. I'm having a few drinks because it's a very stressful job."

"Did you have a choice?" Siri asked.

"They did offer me the ambassadorship in Phnom Phen again."

"Again?"

"For the third time. Nobody wants it. You might even qualify by now, Siri."

"But you refused," said Daeng.

"I most certainly did, Madame."

"Then why couldn't you refuse this posting?"

"I knew you two were up here. I thought we might meet up and have an adventure like in the old days. You both look absolutely awful, by the way. I hope it's nothing contagious."

"Flu," said Siri, blowing the word into his friend's face.

"I doubt a little cold will prevent Civilai from single-handedly beating back a Chinese invasion of Laos," said Daeng.

"They assured me in Vientiane I wouldn't need a weapon," Civilai replied. "Once the official order for the Chinese to leave is announced, I'm here to supervise the orderly withdrawal of the rest of the road crews."

"We're kicking them all out?" Siri asked.

"I imagine it will be a temporary measure. Just a wee show to keep Hanoi happy. Once the Chinese pull out of Vietnam, we'll have them all back in a heartbeat."

"All this responsibility and they don't give you transportation?" said Daeng.

"I have a chit for unlimited petrol," Civilai told her. "But I was supposed to be using the military jeep. I went to look at it when I arrived. Army wages haven't made it up here for the past two months, so they took off the wheels and sold them to buy rations."

"I like to see initiative in the armed forces," said Siri. "Let's hope they don't have to retreat in a hurry."

"And what wheels do you have, brother?"

"A Willys. Prime condition. Name of Agnes. Only lacking petrol."

"Perfect," said Civilai. "Then there's nothing stopping us."

These were the days of what Civilai liked to call "bedroom farce" politics. Countries were frantically jumping in and out of bed with other countries who had once been mortal enemies. In the USA, *TIME* magazine had named Deng Xiao Ping their man of the year. The Chinese Premier traveled to Washington, where amnesia had apparently set in over the insults they'd lavished upon him just a year before.

The Soviet Union, sensing a Chinaless void to flood with its style-less domestic appliances, had hurriedly thrown together a peace delegation to visit the region. They had agreed to several educational and cultural projects in the spirit of socialist harmony. The Soviets were currently airlifting Vietnamese troops out of Cambodia to shore up Vietnam's northern borders. On the southern front, capitalist Thailand had put together its own love team led by a Prime Minister who had suggested just a year earlier that Laos was a backwater run by idiots. The Mekhong had been reclassified from a volatile border to a waterway of opportunity. The Morning Market was stocking up on Thai-made junk. Thai bottled soft drinks were already on sale in the south. One advertising campaign from a company never shy to overplay its potential featured the motto COCA COLA IS LOVE. Inspector Phosy had brought a crate for his journey north. That's why the little girl's Coca-Cola reference had clicked for him.

Phosy had called a meeting of elders from both villages. For effect it was to be held in the clearing where the deaths had occurred. Sergeant Teyp and Officer Buri were there, and an invitation had been extended to toothless Foreman Goi, whom Phosy was certain wouldn't show. All the talk in Luang Nam Tha was about the Chinese invasion and the expulsion of anyone with links to that country. Goi would surely be too busy to take time out to attend a dénouement.

Phosy waited until the forum was full before appearing from the village track. Despite an impending war, there was a good turnout. The two concerned villages had sent their elders, who apparently had arranged interpreters of their own. Both the military and the town hall were represented as well as someone from education and the Woman's Union. Other tribespeople had put in an appearance, including some of the women he'd seen on the track the previous day—minus the young temptress. But, then he saw him: Foreman Goi. He was seated on a folding chair beside his junior concubine and the neckless henchman. The latter had selected a saber as a belt accessory for the event.

Phosy clenched his right fist behind his back. What were they doing there? Didn't they know there was a war on? But all being well, the results of the inspector's investigation would please the Lu foreman, and everything would be jasmine and hollyhocks between them.

Phosy had once taken his family to see the Russian Circus—or a stunted Lao version of it—in Vientiane. Here he felt like the ringmaster as he stepped into the circle. Except the ringmaster with his fine top hat had exuded confidence, and Phosy had stage fright. None of the lines he'd rehearsed on the way down the path now seemed to make any sense. He nodded to the audience. There was a respectful silence rather than a round of applause, and Phosy cleared his throat.

"Comrades, brothers and sisters," he began. "We are gathered here today to determine the cause of death of Headman Mao and Headman Panpan, although I believe many of you present already know what happened." He looked into the eyes of the village elders, but not one was able to hold his gaze. "I offer that the cause of death was good, old-fashioned love."

He'd been hoping for an audible intake of breath at that moment, but the silence continued.

"Or," he continued, "perhaps I should say 'desire'? Both men, you see, had fallen for the charms of a beautiful young woman from a nearby village. The girl had inflamed such desire in the hearts of the two men that they began to hate each other, and a terrible feud had arisen. The only way for the two men to decide who would marry the girl was to fight a duel to the death. Winner take all. And so they met that morning. The weapon of choice was the sharpened bamboo spears we found here at the site. The fight began, each man scoring points as the spikes pierced the skin of the combatants. But the two were evenly matched, and blood was shed and the men grew weak. At last, neither had the strength to strike at the other. Blood leaked from the open wounds, and first one, then the other, died. Bled to death."

Phosy had been proud of his explanation, but still there was no applause. The lack of response left him with no idea what to say next. He supposed that many in his audience had already heard the story. "I'm now open for comments and opinions from the floor," he said in desperation.

To his surprise, the elders of both camps huddled and engaged in intense discussions amongst themselves. The Akha group was first to respond. Their interpreter put up his hand. Phosy nodded. "Is there anything illegal about what happened?" the man asked.

The question of legality was always a contentious one, as the old royalist constitution and its rules had been thrown out along with the French texts. Until a new law book was drafted, the term "legal" would remain a matter of conjecture.

"As it stands, no," said Phosy. "If one of the headmen had lived, he would be arrested for murder. But as they died together . . ."

Up went another hand.

"Right," said the Yao representative. "That's what we need to know."

"What?" Phosy asked.

"Which one died first."

"We didn't send anyone to observe," said the Akha. "That wouldn't have been respectful. The arrangement was that they'd be left to fight it out. The winner would be the one who came out of it alive. When neither of them showed up, we walked down here and found the two bodies."

"That didn't work for any of us," said the Yao.

"Why not?" asked Phosy.

"There was a sort of contract. The prize would be the property of the village whose headman won the duel."

"That's why we needed the police here," said the Akha. "To decide who'd died first. We didn't know it was going to cause so much trouble with the road workers and Foreman Goi and Vientiane."

A throaty laugh rose from a toothless mouth.

"Once we found out they'd be sending an inspector from the capital, we decided it was best to say nothing," said the Yao.

There was a long silence. "So?" said the Akha finally.

"Who died first?" asked the Yao.

Phosy realized the question was directed at him. "I don't know," he said.

There was a disappointed groan from the audience.

"What?" said Phosy. "How can I know?"

"You're a police inspector," said the Yao. "You're supposed to deduce these things. Science has come a long way."

"Not in Laos, it hasn't."

There was another groan.

"I'm not a coroner," said Phosy. "We have professionals to do that job."

"Shame you didn't bring them," said the Akha.

Phosy agreed. He also realized the situation had lost its true focus. He'd slipped from brilliantly intuitive to professionally incompetent. He wasn't able to answer the question that everyone had come to hear. Only a small group of women off to his left showed any positive reaction at all. They slapped palms like successful basketballers and bled betel juice smiles at one another. It seemed so out of place Phosy assumed this was a private joke that had nothing to do with him.

"I suppose I could take another look at the bodies," he said, eager now to get away from the meeting.

"Well, hurry up," said the Yao.

*   *   *

Late that afternoon, Phosy returned to the smelly room behind the hospital with little hope of learning anything new from the bodies, short of cutting them open. And there was a frog's chance in a French restaurant of that happening. But he had failed to impress the country folk in Luang Nam Tha, and his pride was at stake. Surely he could turn his logical mind to the time of death. He had learned one or two things from the doctor. First, he knew that rigor mortis set in three hours after death and took twelve hours to affect the whole body. These bodies were soft as crème caramel, so that was no help at all. He knew that body temperature dropped one degree per hour if you happened to be anywhere but the tropics. On this steamy afternoon, he knew a thermometer would tell him nothing.

With a thick towel spread with Tiger Balm wrapped around his face, he leaned over the bodies. There were no marked differences between the lividity or the hypostasis of the two men, not that he really understood all that technical stuff. He wasn't about to examine the rate of digestion of their last meals. He rolled them both onto their stomachs and stood back. "Tell me, Siri," he said. "What am I looking for?"

The room remained silent but for the buzzing of flies. With no great objective in mind, Phosy counted the number of wounds to see who had received more. He wondered whether that might have some bearing on the speed of death. There were around twenty on each man. No help. He rolled them back and counted the wounds on their fronts. On their . . . fronts. Their fronts bore the same number of wounds. About twenty each. And of course, there was the answer.

He turned with a satified smile on his face just as the crank handle crashed into the side of his head, dropping him to the ground like a ripe coconut. He remained conscious for long enough to see toothless Goi lean over him. And even though the inspector was unable to respond, Goi continued to strike him with the metal.

The jeep crossed the last bridge and rounded the last turn at Chiang Kok, where the mighty Mekhong spread before them all the way to the blue-grey mountains of Burma. Siri and Daeng had seen it in all its guises—churning and violent at Khong Falls, slow and shallow as a puddle in Vientiane, deep as a great lake in Xayaburi—but they never failed to show the mother of rivers the respect she deserved. Siri came to a halt just down from the lonely customs shed high on the bank, and the couple afforded the river a courteous *nop*, hands in prayer.

"Closet royalists," said Civilai, climbing down from the rear box seat.

"Closet heathen," Siri responded.

Civilai trudged up the hill and knocked on the door of the hut. He heard the rustles and grunts of someone waking and hurriedly dressing. The door was opened by a dormouse of a policeman in a wrongly buttoned tunic. "Yes?" said the man.

Some people look intelligent but are not. Others look stupid but are not. Every now and then you come across a stupid person who looks the part. Civilai held up his government *laisser-passer*, but he doubted this fellow could read it.

"I'm government," said Civilai. "All you have to do is answer one or two quick questions. Understand?"

"Umm, yes."

"Have you seen any signs of a Chinese invasion?"

"What?"

"Signs. Invasion. Chinese. Gunboats sailing down the river on their way to blow up the capital. That sort of thing."

"I . . . err . . ."

"No? Very good. Dismissed."

"Wait, hold fast," said Daeng, hobbling up the hill. "Perhaps you'd have an idea where we could find Madame Peu Jin."

"Madame Peu Jin?" said the man.

"Yes. She lives here near the river. She's a weaver."

"Oh, you mean Peu Jin," said the man.

"Perhaps I do," agreed Daeng.

"Oh, wait. It's you," he said, and disappeared back into the hut.

"I fear we've overtaxed him," said Civilai.

But the river guard returned almost immediately with a plastic bag stapled at the top. "You're the old man," he said. "She told me to give you this."

"I most certainly am not the old man," said Civilai. "That's him down there."

He pointed at Siri leaning against the jeep, admiring the river. The guard stepped out of his hut and into his sandals, even though the floor inside was dirt. He felt obliged to wave at the doctor, who waved politely back.

"But I'm the old man's wife," said Daeng, and she took the bag from him. She removed the staples with her strong fingers and removed the latest *pha sin*. She held it up and whistled to Siri, who summoned all his strength to jog up the hill. He was a quarter dead by the time he reached the others, spluttering and wheezing.

"Steady there, old fellow," said Civilai.

"I'm fine," said Siri.

The doctor took the skirt from his wife and held it up. It was similar to the previous two but had a single band of tapestry woven between the plain colors. As with the first *sins*, the hem was green. There was some type of figure represented in the band.

"We need someone to tell us about this," said Siri. "Where's Madame Whatever-Her-Name-Is?"

"Peu Jin? She took a boat up river yesterday," said the river guard. "She's lived here for years, but she's Thai Lu. All her papers are Chinese. A few others have left too. There are rumors being spread on Chinese radio about what the PL will do to ethnic Chinese who refuse to go back."

"Any other weavers in town?" Daeng asked.

"No, Granny. She was the only one."

"Then we're stuck," said Daeng. "No expert to direct us to the next weaver. Dead end."

Siri was feeling along the hem of the skirt. "There's something in here," he said, and started to pick at the threading with his penknife.

"What about the motif?" asked Civilai. He held it up to the sunlight and ran a finger over the raised embroidery. "Perhaps that's a clue. What is it, a cat?"

"No, Grandpa," said the guard, and laughed. "It's an elephant."

"A what?" said Civilai. "I've seen many an elephant, young fellow. Never in sobriety have they looked like this."

"It's two-headed."

"Oh, well, that explains it. How would you know that?"

"It used to be the symbol of Muang Long, Grandpa," said the man. "That's where I'm from."

Siri had produced the next clue from the hem of the skirt.

"What is that?" Daeng asked.

"It's a pipe stem," said Civilai. "The bowl's been unscrewed. My father used to smoke one just like it."

"And what do you take it to mean?" Daeng asked. "A finger, a bullet and a pipe stem?"

"I don't have the foggiest idea," Civilai confessed. "You, Siri?"

"No idea. But my brain is being dulled by the cough medicine. I'm sure it'll come to me."

"Then it looks like next stop is Muang Long," said Daeng. "Driver!"

*   *   *

Muang Long was one more dusty village along the straight dusty road back to Muang Sing. It was the district capital, but not one a district might take a pride in. The ramshackle township sat in a picturesque valley amid gently rising hills on each side. A new road had been recently cut beyond the bridge to give access to villages that had been lost in time since their establishment.

The director of Muang Long's education department was from the northeast and had no interest in local history or culture. But the woman who made Siri's tea recognized the tapestry right away. She sent the visitors up the new road to the village of Bak Haeng. Finding the house with its old loom beneath was not a problem. At the loom sat a neat, compact woman who was totally engrossed in her weaving to the point that she hadn't even heard the noisy jeep pull up at the bottom of the hill or the annoying hacking of Dr. Siri. She could see nothing but the complex inlaying of multiple colors. The visitors were fascinated by the length of time and the amount of skill that had been invested into the beautiful work in front of her. At the end of her row of weft, she looked up to see three strangers sitting on the fence and watching her.

"Hello." She smiled.

"Hello," said the visitors.

"How can I help you?" asked the woman.

"Just come to admire your work," said Daeng. "It's very beautiful."

Daeng noticed bruises on the weaver's arms and neck. Some were fresh. Siri saw them too, but something more peculiar happened at that moment. Auntie Bpoo, his resident transvestite, stepped in front of him as if she'd been projected onto a screen before his eyes. She was clearly attempting to get his attention, but there was no sound. She was not a particularly skillful mime, so all her gesturing and prancing meant nothing to him. With a shake of his head, she was gone and the message was left undelivered.

"That's very kind of you," said the woman who had been oblivious to this manifestation.

Siri made a rapid recovery of his senses. "And we were hoping you'd have something for us," he said.

A look of fear replaced the gentle smile on her face. The weaving shuttle fell from her hand, which had began to shake. "Oh, my word. Yes, of course I do," she said. "I'm sorry. Really, I am. I don't know where my head is these days. Dotty as a ladybird. Excuse me."

She scurried off into the backyard. There were sounds of hoeing from behind the latrine and the distraught voice of the weaver apparently berating herself in her own language. The visitors exchanged glances and raised eyebrows. There was the sound of a rusty hinge, a grunt, and the little woman came scurrying back, wiping dirt off a canvas bag the size of a folded parachute.

She handed it to Siri. "You'd better be off before someone sees you," she said, and took a step back.

Siri began to unfasten the leather buckles.

"What do you think you're doing?" the woman asked, horrified.

"I'm opening the—"

"Not here," she said. "Not in full view of everyone."

"But there may be questions," said Siri.

"I don't care. Take it away."

Back in the jeep, as Siri drove them to Muang Sing, Daeng unfastened the pack. It was full of fist-sized plastic bags, each packed tightly with a fine white powder. Civilai leaned over the seat. Siri almost drove off the road. For once, none of them had a funny comment.

"If I didn't know better . . ." said Daeng. She made a slit in the top bag and poked in a finger. She licked it.

"I bet that isn't table salt," said Civilai.

"Heroin," said Daeng. "Pure."

"Why would they—whoever they are—why would they give us a stash of heroin?" Siri asked. "And what's it all got to do with the *sin* hunt?"

"Technically, I suppose we should hand this over to the authorities," said Civilai.

"Do you think we've been set up?" Daeng asked. "We go round the next bend, and there's an army checkpoint."

"I happen to know they're a bit short of vehicles up here," said Civilai. "Perhaps this is the reward for successfully following the clues. It's the treasure."

"Somebody's gone to a lot of trouble to set this all up," Siri said. "We're supposed to be learning from it. Paying attention. This isn't just an adult game. Are there any other clues in the pack?"

Daeng had all the plastic bags out spread over her lap and across the floor.

"No, nothing," she said. "It's just—"

They rounded the bend, and a ten-wheel truck came hurtling along the center of the road toward them. The driver was invisible behind a muddy windshield and obviously hadn't seen the jeep. There was nowhere to pull off the road. Siri slammed on the brakes, and the jeep slithered across the dust. At the last second, the truck swerved to its right and slapped Agnes's wing mirror, which folded inward but didn't snap off. The truck didn't stop. By the time the dust had settled, Siri was coughing up chunks of laterite, and everything in the jeep, including the passengers and the heroin, had a dirty brown crust.

"Some people need a course in road manners," said Civilai.

The jeep bumped on along the old French road. Siri

and Daeng were deep in thought. Civilai had wiped off the dust and neatly replaced the plastic bags in the pack. They were twenty-five minutes out of Muang Long when Siri pulled over.

"It's not ours," he said.

"What?" said Daeng.

"The heroin. It was a mistake. We asked her if she had something for us, and she assumed we meant the stash. It has nothing to do with the treasure hunt."

"How can you be so sure?" Civilai asked.

"Intuition," said Siri. "Common sense. And even if I'm wrong, we shouldn't be driving around with twenty kilos of pure heroin in bandit country. This is the Golden Triangle. Hard characters rule up here. Hoods with tattoos and gold needles under their skin to ward off bullets. If anyone knows what we've got, invasion or no invasion, they'll come looking for us."

Civilai had taken to nursing the pack in the backseat. "I don't see—" he began.

"He's right," said Daeng. "He's right."

The return journey to Muang Long was slower but more comfortable because Siri had learned when to stop for pot-holes. They passed the kamikaze truck parked beside the road just outside Muang Long. That and an ancient tractor dragging a trailer of bananas were the only vehicles they saw. They returned to Bak Haeng village and parked at the point where the lane became too narrow to drive. Siri and Civilai left Daeng in the jeep while they returned the stash.

It later transpired that Siri and Civilai had come to the same wrong conclusion when first they saw the weaver spread-eagled on top of her loom. That it had been a long day, and she was tired and that this was how weavers relaxed—illogical though it may have seemed. When they got closer, they saw a face that advertised a fresh beating.

"How could . . . ?" Siri began. He leaned over the loom to check for signs of life.

"We've hardly been gone forty minutes," said Civilai. "Will she be all right?"

"In her next life perhaps," said Siri, and closed her eyelids.

"No! Who . . . ?"

"Forty minutes was obviously long enough," said Siri. "My guess is that the real couriers turned up just after we left. She spun some yarn about a jeep full of oldies who came by to collect the stash. And she was left splayed on her own loom as a message to the neighbors that you don't mess with Big . . . insert name of Drug Baron of the Month."

"We killed her," said Civilai.

"Most certainly. If we hadn't taken the parcel . . ."

The old boys did the rounds of the surrounding huts. Naturally, nobody had seen or heard anything. Most were hostile in a subdued country fashion. Few seemed to give a damn that these were high-ranking lowland Lao officials. They showed no respect. The tribes in the north had been screwed by just about everybody. They had no allegiances. They looked after their own.

Siri and Civilai returned to the hut. Their brief search produced further evidence that the weaver had been guilty of mistaken identity. They found a plastic bag, stapled shut. It contained one more skirt. But the game had lost its fun. The return journey to Muang Sing was conducted in silence.

6

The British Medical Journal of June 1877

The four men being held at the central Police Headquarters in Vientiane weren't giving anything away. Nurse Dtui had been asked to come and see if she recognized any of them. She didn't. And even when she walked past the cell in which the men sat, none of them appeared to recognize her. Sergeant Sihot, who was handling matters in Inspector Phosy's absence, suggested the men were thugs for hire. The fact that they'd been overpowered by a household of women, children, old men and a monk suggested they were in the wrong profession. But they were loyal. Either that, or they didn't know who'd hired them to kidnap the inspector's wife and child.

Of course, Dtui had not been staying at Siri's house. That would have been far too obvious. Word had been spread that she was there, but in fact, she and Malee were hiding out at the abandoned embassy compound of France, another victim of Laos's fickle bed partner politics. She'd been growing more anxious with every passing day. It had been a week since Phosy's message ordering her to go into hiding. She'd tried everything to get word to her husband that she was safe but to no avail. Nobody had anticipated the blatant thug invasion of Siri's house. That battle was won, but new security measures had to be put in place.

"Any news from Phosy?" she asked the sergeant.

"Communication's really—"

"—bad up there, yes, I know, Sergeant. But it's not impossible. He was able to get through a week ago."

"That was before the conflict started," said Sihot. "And he got in touch from the base on the Chinese border. He'd be wise to stay away now. Nobody knows what's going on up there. You don't need to worry, Dtui. He can look after himself."

"He's on his own in a province he doesn't know well. Someone up there has made threats and sent out assassins. And there's a war on. If I choose to worry, I'll worry, and so should you."

"Fair enough."

"What happens to the four thugs?"

"No papers. Two of them don't appear to speak Lao. We'll keep working on them. We have modern interrogation techniques."

"Yes, I noticed the bruises."

Dtui was just leaving Police Headquarters to begin her circuitous return to the French compound when a *samlor* bicycle taxi pulled up alongside her. Fearing the worst, she stepped to one side and braced herself for the shot.

"Dtui!" came a husky voice.

On the seat was Teacher Ou in a pathetic state. Dtui's cold had cleared, but it appeared Ou hadn't been so lucky. She looked like she'd been passed through a mangle. Her face was white, her hair greasy, and sweat stained her pink blouse.

"Ou," said Dtui. She stepped up to the bicycle. "You look terrible. What . . . ?"

The teacher tried to get out of her seat but fell against the rider's back and dropped sideways. She tumbled like a string puppet onto the broken paving stones. Dtui knelt and took hold of Ou's head. The teacher tried to speak.

"What? What is it?" Dtui asked.

"Siri . . ." said Ou. "Must warn . . . Siri."

"Warn him? Warn him about what?"

"Paris."

With that, her eyelids folded shut, and a slight dribble of blood crept from between her lips.

"Ou! Ou!" shouted Dtui. She felt for a pulse. Slapped at her friend's face, once, then once more. It was then that she felt the spirit leave the body. To Dtui's shock and amazement, Teacher Ou was dead.

Siri, Daeng and Civilai had slept roughly, parked five kilometers before Muang Sing, hidden from the road by a field of tall grass. Siri had been banished to a distant farmer's gazebo where he could cough all he wanted without keeping the others awake. But it was turning into more than a cough. The donated medicine was finished, but the doctor could tell it had subdued his symptoms rather than cured them. He had something more than mere flu. He felt like hell.

They'd decided against returning to the wooden house downtown where the jeep would spend the night parked out front. If the weaver had given away any information before she was killed, the rightful owner of the heroin would be looking for three old folks in a jeep. They wouldn't have been hard to find.

When the sun came up, none of them could claim to have slept well. They were hungry and cold and in need of a good wash to get the red dust out of their wrinkles. They sat around the warm embers of last night's fire and watched as

Daeng unpicked the hem of the latest *sin*. Rolled inside was a Chinese ten-*yuan* banknote.

"I'm getting sick of this," said Siri.

"Come on," said Daeng. "It's a challenge. You're just grumpy because you're sick. Get a shower and a hot meal inside you, and you'll be raring to go. We came all this way. We can't stop now. Let's go to the market. We'll be safe with people around. We can eat and ask about this."

She held up the *sin*. It was beautifully crafted and heavy from the quality of the cloth. But there were still the familiar Thai Lu bands they'd come to recognize. Yet it was a single gold thread that drew their attention. "I'm sure somebody will recognize this," Daeng said.

They decided not to go to the central market but instead returned to a small local marketplace of seven or eight stalls they'd passed the previous evening. There were only food-stuffs on sale at most of the stalls, but one did have a heap of cheap T-shirts and the knockoff *pha sin*s they'd seen before. They approached the seller. She was in her seventies and sur-prisingly jolly for such a poor woman.

"Auntie," Daeng said, "we were hoping to ask someone about a *pha sin*."

"What type of question would you be asking then?" the seller asked.

"We'd like to know who wove this cloth." Daeng held it up.

"Hmm, it's good quality," said the woman. "My sister might be able to help. She used to be a weaver."

She called to a young boy who was sitting in the dust with a block of wood that might, with the right imagination, have been a truck that day. She told him to fetch Granny, and he seemed delighted to have been given a task. The sister arrived within a few minutes. She was a clone of the first woman. Daeng lay the *sin* across the stall.

"Ah, she's still using it," said the ex-weaver.

"Who?" Siri asked.

"Mae. She used to work with the Americans at the clinic before. They had this gold thread sent over especially for her. She uses it sparingly now, but nobody else has anything like it."

Daeng shook her head. "How do you all know these things?" she asked. "You have no TV. No telephones. How does a remote village learn about the weaving habits of another village?"

"Ah, little sister," the ex-weaver said, "the *sin* is our telephone. When we travel—when we were still allowed to—we'd wear our best *sin*. At a distant market the aunties would come up to us and ask about our skirts. Back in the days before the cheap copies, you could tell anything about a stranger just by admiring her *sin*. There's no question at all that this is one of Mae's."

"Any idea where we might find her?" Civilai asked, still cuddling the large parcel to his chest.

"She used to live in Muang Sing," said the woman. "No idea if she's still there. Just ask around. 'American Mae,' they call her."

There are moments that remind a coroner that his or her job is more than merely the slicing and cataloguing of meat. Looking down at the slab into the lifeless eyes of a friend is perhaps the most poignant. As a nurse, Dtui had been trained to help the sick. Her interest in pathology had grown from admiration for Dr. Siri. In fact, from outdated text books and trial and error, they had learned the craft together. Were it not for an unplanned pregnancy, Dtui would have traveled to the Eastern Bloc to learn the skill from experts. And in a country where handling the dead was considered taboo on many levels, she would have become the first coroner of Laos who actually wanted the job. All she had now was a nursing certificate and a hunger to learn more.

Even so, Judge Haeng, back in his role of Head of Public Prosecution, had ordered her to find the cause of death of a teacher at Vientiane's most prestigious school. Dtui had called back Mr. Geung from the house of his fiancée. She knew she'd never be able to perform the autopsy alone. That morning, Geung was already on the steps sweeping when she arrived at the morgue. The old welcome mat was back in its place. They hugged and cried for a very long time over the loss of their friend Ou. Geung had set about cleaning the building and had said nothing to Dtui, who sat on a stool beside the slab, holding her friend's hand.

At last she told him, "Geung, I can't do it."

"I . . . I can show you," he said.

"No, honey. I know how, I just can't bring myself to do it."

"Her d-d-dad said it's all right," he reminded her.

"I know. He wants to know what happened. We all do. But . . . I don't know. There must be another way. Geung, let's put Teacher Ou back in the freezer and go for a walk."

"Okay."

For a large woman and an uncoordinated man, the *lycée* was a brisk thirty-minute walk from Mahosot, but the weather was pleasant, and there was enough cloud cover to shade them from the midday sun.

The principal was still depressed at the loss of his most experienced science teacher. "But she studied in Australia," he said, as if that were enough to exempt her from death.

"I know," Dtui replied.

The principal showed Dtui and Geung to Ou's small office behind the science lab. There was barely enough space for two, so the principal left them to it. Unvarnished wood shelves crammed with bottles reached high up two walls. The labels were in Russian and German. None was in Lao or English.

There were photographs of Ou's son, Nali, on the only vacant patch of wall. He would never get to know his mother. Dtui found herself squeezing Geung's hand.

"Hurts," said Geung.

"Sorry, pal. So where do we start?"

"At the start," said Geung.

"All right."

She felt a sniffle as if her cold might be returning. "Any signs of medication?" she asked. "I suppose she might have taken some wrongly labeled cold medicine. But if she did, how would we know? After this, we can go to her parents' house and take a look in the bathroom."

Geung burst out laughing.

"What is it?" she asked.

"Look in the ba—the bathroom."

It wasn't easy to tell what might tickle Mr. Geung or why, but he never failed to make Dtui laugh, even on a dour day like this. "Geung, you're a nutcase."

"I'm a nut nut."

Dtui turned a slow circle and took in the details of the alcove. "All right. So she would have been sitting at her desk. She was a scientist. What was she working on?"

Dtui sat on Ou's chair and looked around. There was a clunky black Soviet microscope to one side of the work bench. Beside it was a box of slides. Each one was hand labeled with a date. The latest slide contained a single strand of material. The label was marked COLOR TEST N34. Dtui knew that color tests were conducted to check for volatile substances. The combinations and the colors they produced were outlined in a book Siri had obtained from Chiang Mai University in Thailand. They had used the tests successfully on stomach contents and identifying pills and powders. Teacher Ou kept methodical notes in a ledger open on the desk. Slide N34 had featured in eleven tests. The teacher's handwriting had deteriorated rapidly over the last five pages, and the final page was almost illegible. But Dtui could make out the word *negative* beside each entry.

She opened the color test book. Teacher Ou had worked on the toxins in the same order they appeared in the book. The next toxin due to be tested for was arsenic, but there was no entry for it in the ledger. She sat at Ou's desk and had pulled up the chair when her left foot kicked something on the floor. It was a book, a thick textbook. She picked it up and read the English title: *Toxicology*.

"What's it doing on the floor, Geung?" she asked.

"Teacher Ou . . . d-d-dropped it?"

"I bet she did. So this was what she was last reading."

Dtui went through the pages. There were no bookmarks or dog-ears. There was nothing highlighted. "But what was she reading? What was it that made her leave in a hurry and drop the book?"

Then she remembered the last word her friend had spoken.

"Paris," she said. "Something to do with Paris."

She turned to the index. There were two entries under Paris; *Paris: 1968 Toxicological conference*, and *Paris Green*.

She turned to the latter and read aloud in English for Geung to hear but not to understand.

> *"Paris Green: According to the British Medical Journal of June 1877, it was reported that cases had been brought before the notice of the medical profession in which severe symptoms were experienced by patients who were being slowly poisoned with arsenic. This slow poisoning was going on at the time very extensively due to an arsenical coloring matter contained in the green calico lining of some bed curtains and the green muslin,*

which was much used for ladies' dresses' coloring. For months and months, this source of poison was not discovered, and the symptoms were treated as those of natural disease. This lining containing a green coloring pigment known as Paris Green was, doubtless, producing severe suffering. Dr. Debus, the Professor of Chemistry in Guy's Hospital, made the examination of the bed curtain lining above alluded to; and thinking that other green colored goods might also contain arsenic, he purchased some muslin of a very beautiful pale green tint for analysis. It proved to contain upwards of sixty grains of an arsenical compound (Scheele's or Paris green) in every square yard, and this was so slightly incorporated that it could be dusted out with great facility.

"'Imagine, sir,' the doctor exclaimed, 'what the atmosphere of a ballroom must be where these muslin fabrics are worn, and where the agitation of skirts consequent on dancing must be constantly discharging arsenical poison. The pallor and languor so commonly observed in those who pass through the labors of a London season are not to be altogether attributed to ill-ventilated crowded rooms and bad champagne, but are probably in great part owing to the inhalation of arsenical dust shaken from the clothing of a number of poisoners."

Dtui looked at the green strand in the slide. She understood enough of the article to know what had happened to Teacher Ou. "Oh, Geung. That was it. We didn't have colds. We were both suffering from arsenic poisoning. But why is it that I got over it, but she didn't?"

Geung was holding up the slide to the light from the high louver window.

"It . . . it's the same color," he said.

"As what?"

"As the chair cover."

Dtui scrambled to her feet and looked back at the chair. Geung was right. On the seat back was the half skirt that Siri had left behind for Ou to examine. She was using it as an attractive chair cover. She'd sat at this desk every day between lessons, exposing herself more and more to the poison. It wasn't flu that had killed Teacher Ou. It was Paris Green. In ten days it had destroyed the system of a healthy young woman. What chance, at their age, would Siri and Daeng have?

It had been a long morning, and Siri and Daeng were feeling the worse for it. Daeng had been right. A good meal and a bath had improved her husband's mood but not his health. Still they followed the treasure trail of *pha sin*s with no idea where or into what it might lead them. They had spent the morning in search of American Mae, who incorporated gold thread into her skirts. She had worked for the eccentric American doctor, Dooley, in the sixties and still lived nearby, they were told. They found her, as was usual in Laos, by being passed from hut to hut, from person to person, until they were rewarded by an, "Oh, yes. She lives near the old fort. I'll show you."

Civilai insisted on staying in the jeep with his highly addictive new friend on his lap while Siri and Daeng walked to the house. They found American Mae sitting on the floor with her family, about to start their midday meal. She was thin, as were her relatives, and she had a curiously wide parting that was starting to look like the pate of a Japanese samurai.

Ignoring apologies and protests of, "Really. We've just eaten," the family insisted the visitors join them for a bite to eat. And a bite was all they seemed to have. Siri and Daeng nibbled sparingly and apologized for their diarrhetic uncle in the jeep who never ate.

After lunch, with the sun still hidden behind a thick mist, Mae led them into her pretty garden where the frangipani and mimosa blooms looked like snow on the bushes. She took them through a gap in the broken fence and along a path that ended at a small cottage. After hearing a highly abridged version of their venture to the north, not including the murder of the weaver or the presence of twenty kilos of heroin in the jeep, Mae had told them about the old guesthouse and insisted they stay there while they continued their quest. She too had a plastic bag for them that had been left by the same plain woman.

"This is where Dr. Tom stayed," she told them while they settled in. She pointed through the window at a long gray building in need of a coat of paint. "The clinic is just over there. There's nobody staying here. I keep it clean out of habit, mainly."

The Lao knew all about the Muang Sing medical team. The old clinic had once been occupied by Dr. Tom Dooley, the American upper-class dandy who had dedicated much of his life to work with the poor—although he never suffered his hardships in silence. He was a master of self-promotion. The building was situated opposite the old French military compound on the road to Ban Khuang. Some had seen Dooley as a saint. Others called him a glory-seeker and a CIA plant. But whatever his motives, a lot of people in the north who would otherwise have died from the absence of medical care had survived. The Chinese had hated him and his team and made daily radio broadcasts to say that they were practicing witchcraft and murdering babies. To have upset the Chinese so seriously, Civilai considered the Americans to have been doing something right.

The guesthouse had three actual beds with spring bases, a refrigerator and a piano. Civilai hid the stash under his bed and joined the others in the living room. Daeng, coughing heavily now, was laying out the *sin*s on the floor.

Siri opened Mae's plastic bag and took out the latest. "They're all Thai Lu," he said, recognizing the pattern.

"It's from Muang Xai," said Mae.

"There it is again." Daeng laughed. "The weavers' grapevine. Tell us, Mae. How can you tell where it's from so precisely?"

"Auntie Duang in Muang Xai has been having trouble with her loom for a couple of years. It's an ancient monster, impossible to get spare parts for. It's like a typewriter that has one broken key. A weaver can recognize the effects of a broken loom. Weaving a *pha sin* is like raising a child. You have mishaps. You have moments you're proud of and others when you know you could have done better if you'd concentrated. By the time you've completed a skirt, you can make out all the characteristics and the flaws and the happy moments you've been through together. It's like recognizing your own daughter. You see this loose gathering here?"

"Barely," said Daeng.

"That's a result of the comb not beating evenly. The wood of the frame is warped."

"So we're looking for Auntie Duang in Muang Xai?" Civilai asked.

"It's hers for sure," said Mae. "But if you're going to see her, I'd better warn you about her."

"What?"

"She's a little bit . . . eccentric. Some of the locals call her Auntie Voodoo."

"I'll be sure to make a note of that," said Civilai, no longer shocked by such a warning.

"I don't think there's anything in . . ." Siri began. He had felt around the hem of the new *sin* but found nothing. So he began to cut away the stitching. "No, wait. There is something."

He reached in with two fingers and pulled. It was brown tape, the type used in cassette recorders. It was about three feet long. "I don't suppose your Dr. Tom left a cassette recorder behind, by any chance?" Siri asked.

"You think something's recorded on it?" Civilai asked.

"Fat lot of use if there isn't," said Siri.

Mae explained that some of her neighbors had radios to pick up the Chinese music station, but cassette recorders were far beyond their budgets. So the tape would have to wait. She left them to relax, but none of them could sleep. Instead they sat in the living room, staring at the odd gallery of *sin*s spread out on the floor.

"Five *sin*s, five clues," said Daeng.

"Technically, four and a half," Siri reminded her.

"Nice collection though," said Civilai, who was clearly coming down with the flu too. "Do you suppose they spell out some message if we arrange them right? Some semiotic signal? How's your naval training, Siri?"

"Once across the Mekhong on a log was as close as I got to the navy," said Siri. "You know, I think the *sin*s are just the *laissez-passer*s. They get us from one place to the next. I think the locations are important. What we have to do is collect all the clues and work it out from there."

"To be honest," said Daeng, "we have no idea how many there might be."

"Too true," Civilai agreed. "This prankster could keep us snapping at the tidbits she tosses for us indefinitely."

"We should give it a couple more days," said Siri. "We'll head off to Muang Xai early tomorrow when we're rested up. Enjoy the scenery."

"Well, this adventurer has no intention of going anywhere tomorrow," said Daeng.

The men looked at her in surprise.

"What? I'm no good to anyone with this cold," she said. "My plan is to wrap myself up in blankets and sweat the blighter out of my system."

"Perhaps we should all do that," said Siri.

"Oh, husband. You could no sooner sit still all day than I could dance the tango in stilettos."

"Good," said Civilai. "Girls always were a burden on road trips. Just you and me, Siri. Off to the wilds of Muang Xai."

"Didn't you have a Chinese invasion to uncover?" said Siri.

"Exactly," said Civilai. "We'll be passing right through the heart of Udomxai, the most logical province from which to launch an attack on Vietnam. Why else would the Chinese have built all those roads to Dien Bien Phu if not to invade the place?"

The next morning with the scenery a blur and the sun nowhere to be seen, Siri and Civilai set off on the trip to Un Mai. There had been one contentious moment when Civilai headed for the door with the stash over his shoulder.

"What do you think you're doing, brother?" Siri had asked.

"We can't possibly leave a defenseless woman alone with twenty kilos of heroin."

"And you would sooner take it through half a dozen military road checkpoints?"

"I have a letter which states that I represent the government."

"You do know most of those boys won't be able to read your travel documents? But they do have a nose for drugs."

Reluctantly, Civilai had secreted the stash beneath the lid of the old piano. He sulked as they drove away. Daeng, wrapped in a blanket, had waved them off from the front steps.

When they were out of sight, which didn't take long, she turned back, hobbled into the house and locked the door. Shedding her itchy blanket, she walked to the piano and lifted the lid. She took one plastic bag to the sofa, then retrieved her service penknife from her pocket. This was something she badly needed to do. Her husband would never have approved, but some forces were stronger than love.

She dug the knife into the pack, releasing a gentle cloud of white powder. She breathed it in and could already taste its influence. This was the real thing.

"We appear to be on the wrong road," said Civilai.

"We aren't on the road yet," said Siri. "We're visiting some old friends."

"Since when did you have friends?"

Siri ignored him and pulled up in front of the two-story wooden building, then turned off the engine. The mist crawled around the yard like on a B-grade horror movie set. Siri beeped his horn, and Bobby poked his head through the window.

"Breakfast?" he shouted.

"Do you have a cassette recorder?" Siri called to him.

"Of course."

"Then yes to breakfast."

They ate waffles slathered in syrup and drank sweet black coffee. The Americans had brought a huge food hamper with them, but supplies were running low. PEA continued to send them hardship packages, though not much in the way of edibles from overseas made it through the Lao postal service. Bobby sat at the table splicing the section of tape onto an unwanted cassette. It took him no time at all. He pressed

PLAY on the old cassette player, and they heard a few seconds of a tune that was familiar.

"Simon and Garfunkel," said Lola.

"That's the name of the song?" Siri asked.

"The singers," said Bobby. "The song's called 'Bridge Over Troubled Waters.'" He translated the segment from the tape. "Like a bridge over troubled water, I will lay me down."

"I think we have the full lyrics upstairs," said Lola.

"No need," said Siri. "I think that was the only part we were supposed to hear."

Bobby was ecstatic to have an ex-politburo man in his house. He took several photographs to send home and even asked for Civilai's autograph.

"Is the song relevant to something?" Lola asked.

"No," said Siri. "We're just practicing our English."

"So," said Civilai. "We have one finger, one bullet, a clay pipe stem, a Chinese banknote, a stash of heroin and a song about a bridge."

The old pair was driving through the mountains of Na Maw on a road that had obviously been built with one jeep and two hand-pulled carts in mind. In the two hours they'd been traveling, they hadn't seen another vehicle. The unkempt vegetation reached out to them on both sides, caressing Agnes's flanks. Every now and then they'd be stopped by boulders broken loose from the overhanging rocks. The pair had briefly considered climbing down and rolling the rocks out of the way but ultimately used the jeep's thick metal bumper to clear a space.

"I don't think you can count the stash," said Siri.

"Even so, it's pretty obvious."

"You've worked it out?"

"Simon and Carbunkle are singing about a bridge when a

goat herder comes by and says, 'Would you mind shutting up, because my goats can't get to sleep, and I want to sit back and smoke some weed in peace.' Simon and Carbunkle don't take any notice of him and keep singing. He offers them twenty *yuan*, two months' salary, to stop their racket, but no luck. So he goes home, gets his rifle and shoots Carbunkle's finger off. End of story."

"How much of Bobby's cold medicine did you take, exactly?"

"Siri?"

"Yes?"

"Do you really think it was wise to leave Madame Daeng back there alone with all that dope?"

Siri slammed on the brakes, and they slid to a stop. "What exactly do you mean?" he asked.

"I mean . . . considering her little opium problem."

"Opium isn't a problem. Arthritis is a problem. Opium is the solution."

"And there I was thinking you were a doctor."

"Your point?"

"Is that you know better than I do that opium isn't a solution to any ailment. It just makes you forget you've got it for a little while until it wears off and you need some more. And as the pain gets worse the more you need. Heroin is a step up into the big league. That's an awful lot of temptation we've left with her."

"Daeng isn't stupid, Civilai."

"No. But she's suffering."

7

Warped

Inspector Phosy slowly came to in pitch darkness and all he could feel was pain. The stink of excrement was all around him. His wrists and ankles were bound. When he turned his head and moved his mouth, one side of his face cracked like partridge eggshells underfoot. He could smell his own dried blood. He didn't know where he was or what was expected of him. As a soldier he had spent time behind bars, had been tortured and beaten. But he'd known and understood his enemies back then. Knowledge was a powerful tool. But here, Phosy was shrouded in ignorance.

He rocked from side to side and shimmied back and forth and decided he was in a pit the size of a grave. His hands were tied behind his back, and he didn't want to think about the slime upon which he lay. He had no idea how long he had been in his pit, but his stomach rumbled and his throat was parched. The Buddhists had a neat assortment of hells, but most provided fellow sinners to keep a man company. Isolation and deprivation of the senses were far worse than purgatory as far as Phosy was concerned.

*   *   *

American Mae was awoken from her afternoon nap by the sound of banging. She retied her light cloth skirt and walked to the front of the house. The sun had finally found a niche, and its light blurred the body that stood in the open doorway. In one hand the visitor held a pestle which she was using to beat against the wooden doorframe.

"Sister Daeng?" said Mae. "Is that you? You frightened me."

As she neared the door, it was clear to Mae that Madame Daeng was not in perfect array. She had hitched up the *pha sin* she wore to a point just above her knees. Her blouse was open at the top to reveal her bra.

"Let's go," said Daeng, swaying slightly despite hanging on to the doorframe.

"Where would you like to go, sister?" asked Mae. She was face-to-face with Daeng now and could see the woman's pupils were mere pinpricks.

"A miracle happened," said Daeng.

"What is it?"

"My legs. They're cured."

"Sister Daeng, why don't we go back to the cottage and have ourselves a cup of—"

"Don't you . . . don't you dare deprive me of this moment of pain-free bliss. We're going dancing. We're going to the market."

"For what?"

"For men. Young men to dance with. Here I go." She turned and skipped down the path.

"Wait!" said Mae. "Wait, I'll . . ." She turned back into the house, found her bag and put on her hat. But by the time she returned to the door, Daeng was nowhere to be found. Mae shook her head and started off to the market. She'd seen this too many times in her years as a nurse. The old lady was high—and she'd taken a lot.

*   *   *

Agnes the jeep pulled up in front of the post office in Muang Xai. The town was a short main street with old trees that offered shade to the few businesses there. Nothing new had been built for a very long time, which gave the town some grubby historical charm but also made it look in need of a good wash. Like in several other provincial capitals, there was one long-distance phone line and a vast number of locals waiting to use it. Civilai wasn't one to stand in line, not that the principle of queuing had made it this far north. He called for the manager. The middle-aged paunchy man at the desk hesitated before saying, "That's me, comrade."

Civilai took out his letter of recommendation and held it out for the man to see.

"I'm from the government," said Civilai. "I need a line to Vientiane now. It's a priority."

The manager pulled his reading glasses down from the top of his head and read the government document . . . very slowly.

"That means 'immediately,'" said Civilai.

"You have to fill out a form," said the manager. He opened a drawer and began to fumble through papers.

"I'll fill it out later," said Civilai.

The manager opened a second drawer, which stuck a little, before pulling out a handmade pistol with a hollow handle and placing it on the counter in front of him.

"Forms were designed for people like you," said the man.

Civilai had never been threatened at gunpoint in a post office before, but then again, he hadn't spent much time in the wild north. He took the form the man handed him. "I'd ask to borrow a pen, but I'm afraid you'd toss a hand grenade at me."

The manager produced a pen from the top pocket of his navy blue shirt. Civilai squinted as he tried to read the fading print. "I don't suppose . . . ?"

The manager took off his glasses and handed them to the old man without complaint. For an armed gunman, he was most accommodating.

Meanwhile, across town, Siri had located the market and was making enquiries about the latest *sin* in the treasure trail. As usual, the market was all but deserted by afternoon, but there were one or two small stalls that sold cheap Chinese clothes as well as a few local *pha sins*.

"I'm looking for the woman who made this," he said, holding up the skirt to a small gaggle of sellers.

"She's not the type of doctor you'd be looking for," said one stall holder.

"What makes you think I'm looking for a doctor?" Siri asked.

"Look at the state of you," said the woman at the next stall. "You're on your last legs. You need a hospital."

There's nothing more effective for making a man feel ill than to be told he looks like death. Siri became aware of just how bad his condition looked to others. The cough medicine top-up from Bobby was having no effect at all. "Then what kind of doctor is the weaver?" he asked.

"She's a voodoo woman," said the first stall holder. "Crazy as a loon. You don't want to go over there. Buy one of mine instead. Much better quality."

"What kind of crazy?" Siri asked.

"She thinks she's a witch, a shape-shifter, a medium . . . you name it."

"But she's not," said the other. "She's just nuts. You'd best stay away in your condition. The excitement might kill you."

"And if I chose not to stay away," said Siri. "Where might I find her?"

*   *   *

Siri was back in front of the post office hacking his guts up when Civilai emerged. The old politician climbed into the passenger seat and slapped the dashboard two or three times. He hurt himself far more than he hurt the jeep. He was fuming.

"You took your time," said Siri, wiping his mouth.

"I was mugged," Civilai told him. "Not only did I have to stand in a disorganized scrum with the riffraff, I had to pay for the call."

"It's a post office. Isn't that normal?"

"I'm a special envoy of the politburo."

"This is a socialist state. You aren't supposed to have privileges."

"That's just in the pamphlets. It's theoretical. It doesn't apply to the real world."

"Someone obviously convinced you otherwise."

"He pulled a gun on me."

Siri laughed hoarsely and stamped on the gas pedal a few times before engaging a gear. The roar caused the few pedestrians on the main street to turn their heads. A hundred meters later, the jeep was already on the outskirts of town.

"I reckon that's the only way we're going to spread Communism around the globe. At gunpoint. Did you get through?"

"To a clerk. She said she'd pass on my message as soon as the minister gets back from his herbal spa."

"I see they're all on edge worrying about the Chinese invasion. You do realize you'd get more respect and better service if you did all your research through military bases?"

"I don't want a unit of soldiers following me around. I'm incognito. The invisible spy. Civilai the ghost agent who sees enemy occupations."

"I still get the feeling you aren't taking any of this seriously."

"Basically, who cares? If they don't invade us militarily now, they'll invade us commercially at a later date. We're too ripe for plunder to be ignored, and none of the hill tribes up here have any great love for the Lao or the distant administration in Vientiane that does nothing for them. They'd switch allegiances tomorrow if they thought they'd be better off."

"I can't think why they didn't keep you on the politburo with such a positive outlook."

"Where are we going?"

"To see a crazy woman."

"That's all of them, isn't it?"

"Would you like me to run over the next elderly cripple with a puppy that I see?"

"With your driving skills, you'd miss."

"You do remember I'm your only friend, don't you?"

"Friendship is highly overrated."

Siri abandoned all hope of drawing love and caring from the old diplomat and set his sights on locating the green-and-pink house of Madame Voodoo. In fact, it found them before they found it. They'd just crossed a small bridge and were on a downward slope traveling at some fifty kilometers per hour when a woman darted across the road in front of them. Siri braked and swerved, narrowly avoiding a catastrophe. As it was, his left headlight thumped the woman's ample rear end. She stopped, looked back, cursed and ran on.

The house she disappeared into was green and pink. It was apparently the only painted house in the province.

The old talisman that hung at Siri's neck began to vibrate. That was always a bad sign. It invariably announced that he had arrived at a sight with dense paranormal activity. He decided not to announce this fact to Civilai.

Still a little shaken from the near miss, the old boys parked in front of the house and walked up the ladder that led to the large front deck. A very pretty girl of about eight was rocking there on a rattan chair. "Hello, uncles," she said.

"Hello, young miss," said Siri. He kicked off his sandals at the top of the ladder and creaked across the bamboo floor. "Was that your mother we almost hit?"

"My aunt," said the girl. "She does that all the time."

"Why?" asked Civilai, joining them on the deck.

"The shadow spirit," said the girl, quite matter-of-factly. "He follows her whenever she's out of the house. It's really annoying."

"So she runs in front of cars?" said Siri.

"Yes."

"Why?"

"Because she's hoping that the shadow spirit will be hit by the car, of course. It'll break his leg, and he won't be able to keep up when she goes shopping."

"That makes sense," said Siri.

Civilai glared at him.

"But wouldn't your aunt be hoping that the shadow spirit is killed by the car?" Siri continued.

The girl laughed. "Don't be silly," she said. "It's a spirit."

"Right," said Siri, smiling. "Can we see your aunt, do you think?"

"She's at the loom."

"I didn't notice it under the house."

"It's in the bedroom. We're afraid they'll steal it."

"The spirits?"

"No, the Chinese. They steal everything. This way."

The girl left the chair, which continued to rock even without her in it. She took a key from her pocket and unlocked a huge padlock that held shut the door to the only room in the house. She walked inside before them. Siri and Civilai paused and looked at each other, perhaps wondering how the aunt had managed to enter the house and lock herself in from the outside.

"We've been waiting for you," said the girl. The creepy moments just piled up one on top of the other. The loom sat auntless in the center of the room. There were some mattresses rolled on one side and a cardboard case, but no other signs of habitation.

"She's not here," said Civilai. "Perhaps we should . . ."

"She'll be back," said the girl.

Siri looked around. There were no other rooms. No doors. His cough had let up for the first time in a week.

"Back from where?" he asked.

"Phi bung bot," said the girl. "The door to other dimensions. She steps in and out often."

Siri was fascinated. Civilai rolled his eyes. "Can we expect her back in this lifetime?" he asked.

"Never can tell," said the girl. "Sometimes she vanishes for weeks."

"Marvelous," said Siri. "Does she tell you about the places she visits?"

"Look, we have to get back before dark," said Civilai. "You said you were expecting us. Do you perhaps have something for us? A *pha sin*, maybe?"

"Yes, of course," said the girl. "It's over there in the corner."

Civilai located the latest plastic bag and started to remove the staples.

"I should do that," said Siri.

The girl watched, fascinated, as Siri removed the latest *sin* from its bag. He held it by two corners. It was not remarkably different from its predecessors. The hem was black, and there were two pale green bands in the brocade. It did feel considerably older than the others, however. There was something musty about its smell. It was perhaps antique but in remarkably good condition.

Siri was distracted by some slight movement at the loom. The treadle began to pump. The harness lifted. And like some cinematographic sleight of hand, a woman appeared on the bench, weaving. She was round like a watermelon and belted her skirt almost beneath her armpits. Her cheeks were pink, and she wheezed as if she'd been in a hundred-meter dash.

Siri clapped his hands. "Bravo," he shouted. "Good show."

Civilai put his head in his palms. "It's the monosodium glutamate," he said. "They told me to lay off."

But it was as if Madame Voodoo had always been in the room, always been weaving at the loom. Siri turned to show the girl how delighted he was, but she'd vanished. Odd, as she'd been nowhere near the open door. But marvelous. Madame Voodoo made one last toss of the shuttle and sighed as she beat her last weft threads. It was not until she'd placed her shuttle on top of the fabric that she noticed her guests for the first time.

"Good day," she cooed. "What brings two such handsome men here to my modest home?" She smiled at Siri and looked at the *pha sin* he clutched to his chest.

"Now that's a pretty piece," she said, climbing down from the bench and walking toward him. Suddenly she stopped as if hitting an invisible wall. "Oh," she said. "Oh, dear."

"What?" Siri asked.

"You are terribly congested," she said.

"I think it was the sticky rice and pork we had on the road," Siri joked, knowing full well what she was actually talking about. His talisman was biting into his chest. He became instantly aware that this was a junction. Spirits traveled, of course they did, and Madame Voodoo's house was the Paris St. Germain of mystic travel. He could feel it. "Any suggestions as to how I might clear the blockage?" he asked.

"Hah," she laughed. "No."

"I don't believe you."

Civilai sat with his fingers in his ears, whistling the Lao national anthem. He'd always been averse to the psychic art, preferring to shut it out than to believe in it.

"I make potions," said Madame Voodoo. "The ingredients come to me in dreams. Some say they help with minor spiritual problems. But you? You need a complete paranormal enema."

"That sounds rather erotic. Would it help?"

"It might, but these things find a way to cancel each other out."

"How do you mean?"

"Well, you might be cured of dipsomania, but you'd grow a tail. Do you know what I mean? You could be rid of a demon but lose the ability to speak your native language. That sort of thing."

If Siri hadn't seen her materialize out of thin air, he would have put her down as a freak just as the women at the market had done. But rematerialization was a tough act. He had no choice but to follow through. "Do you have any remedies for arthritis?" he asked.

"Easy," she said.

"How bad could the side effects be?"

"Siri!" said Civilai. "Stop it."

"I'm only asking," said Siri.

"I never can tell until the course is complete," said the woman. "But it wouldn't be worse . . . physically."

"How much do you charge for these remedies of yours?"

"Siri, enough!" said Civilai.

"I can't charge," said Madame Voodoo. "They wouldn't let me back in my own dreams if I did."

"I'll take a jar."

"Don't, Siri."

"Civilai, do you believe in any of this?"

"Of course I don't."

"Then what's the harm?"

"It's just . . . it's that you're bartering in an area that you don't understand. You don't know what poisons this witch puts in her brews."

"I have something you can take for unpleasantness too," said the woman, looking at Civilai.

"I'll take it to Teacher Ou at the *lycée* and have her analyze the contents," said Siri. And all at once, an image of the teacher walked across his mind, paused there and smiled before fading away. For that to have happened, of course, Teacher Ou had to be dead. But it was such an unlikely event and so unexpected that Siri put it down as one more technical fault in his already faulty extra sense.

"I'd like some," he told Madame Voodoo. "Please."

She swayed her enormous backside toward the door. "I have some in the backyard," she said. "Won't be long."

Once she'd left, Siri inspected the hem of the latest *sin*, and Civilai went into detail about his bad instincts around this whole affair. One part of the hem was thicker than the rest. The thread was brittle and easy to pick open. What he found was a document rolled into a sausage shape and flattened.

Civilai came to watch as Siri unrolled it and ironed it with his palm. "It's Chinese," said Civilai.

"Brilliant," said Siri. "It's some sort of list. Handwritten. The page is ripped as if it was torn from a pad or a notebook. Where can we get it translated?"

"The way things are going, we just sit here and wait for the first wave of Chinese troops to wash over us. I'm sure we'll find a literate one—if they don't shoot us first."

They were interrupted by the return of Madame Voodoo.

"Sorry to have kept you waiting," she said. She carried a vial in each hand. She went to Siri and held up the first vial.

"This," she said, "is for Madame Daeng. One milliliter each morning until it's all gone." Siri hadn't mentioned his wife's name. "This . . ." she held up the second vial, "is for you."

"I don't need—"

"It's for your blockage. It will help you deal with your other visitors."

"I'm not sure . . ."

"I know. You're worried that once you let one in, you'll be swamped. That might well happen. But you know you have to find out before you're on the pyre yourself."

She'd touched several nerves. The most frustrating element in his life was that he carried around so many souls, but despite the odd outburst or dream, he couldn't talk to them. He had at least two spirit mediums, and neither had been able to break through. But he didn't totally blame himself. With so many competent shamans around, how dense would a ghost have to be to settle in him?

"Thank you, sister," he said, not totally convinced she wasn't insane. "I'm afraid we have to go now. But perhaps you'd be able to tell us where we might find the weaver of this fine *sin*?"

Again he held it up against his chest for her to see.

"If times were different," she began, "if art and culture had a value, this would be kept in a museum. It's a piece of Thai Lu history."

"Where might we find the weaver?" asked Civilai.

"Grandmother Amphone? In the afterlife. I could ask around."

"She's dead?"

"At least a hundred years already."

"Splendid. So the hunt ends in a cul-de-sac in the hereafter."

"When she was still alive, where do you suppose she might have lived?" Siri asked.

"I believe there's a small shrine in her honor in Un Mai," she said. "That would be the logical place to look. She probably has relatives there."

They paraded out of the room and onto the bamboo deck. Siri noticed there was no longer a padlock on the door . . . or a hasp. The little girl must have just left because the chair was still rocking. "Your niece seems to have abandoned us," said Siri.

"Niece?" said Madame Voodoo. "I don't have a niece."

Time spent in isolation, in misery, becomes a personal infinity. The self and beyond it blend to a point where you abandon your role at the center of your universe and admit you're nothing.

Inspector Phosy was nothing.

He no longer felt the biting insects nor the wounds nor the repulsion. He'd decided already to wait for death with dignity. There was nothing to see, but he looked toward a point where the horizon between black and black might be. The sunrise would come, he believed, from that direction. A pencil-thin crack opening to a beautiful, delicate dawn.

So when the sky opened above him and the light flooded his space, he was overwhelmed with disappointment. Dizzy from hunger, nauseated from fatigue, he could make no sense of it at all. He clamped his eyes shut but still the light burned into him. Through his lids he could make out the shapes that eclipsed his sky. Movement. An enormous hand reached down and grabbed his collar, wrenching him upward and out of his tub of filth. He was a string of beads, limp and unresponsive. When he was tossed onto the cold floor, he felt nothing. He could see the jet of water that hosed him down but had no strength to fight it as it pummeled him head to foot.

The water was turned off, and someone kicked him onto his back. His eyes were wide open now, and he could see where he was. It was some sort of rustic warehouse. The underground grave he'd been in for hell-knew-how-long had a thick zinc lid on hinges and a lock. There were three similar tombs running parallel to it. It was night. The windows were full of black, and the high-roofed room was lit by fluorescent lights. His hearing slowly returned: the growl of a generator, shouts in Chinese and some other language, mosquitoes at his ears.

Lastly came the sense of touch, although he wished it hadn't. He had it all, discomfort and pain, a head that felt split in two and hanging loose, the soul of every bruise and gash and fracture awoken by the freezing water.

"You really should take more time on your personal hygiene," came a voice. Phosy recognized the graveled words of Goi and found his outline carved against a ceiling light.

"Look at you," continued the voice. "And you were so handsome when you arrived. Lucky your wife's dead, or she'd never let you back in the house."

Phosy felt a torrent of rage and horror well up inside him. As a soldier he had learned not to tame but to contain his considerable temper, especially when venting it would serve no purpose. His mantra over the years had always been, *Never let the enemy know how you feel.*

"Perhaps you didn't hear me," said Toothless Goi.

He was crouching now beside Phosy's body. He wore a military topcoat and a fur hat. It made Phosy even more aware of the cold. His teeth had begun to chatter, so he forced his tongue between them.

"I said—"

"I heard you," said Phosy. His own voice was the crushing of chalk blocks in a grinder. One of his teeth was loose.

"Surely you're just a little sad."

"I wasn't that fond of her."

"Then what about that sweet child? Malee, isn't it? We kept her alive—just. Always helps to have one bargaining chip. She got a bit damaged in the kidnapping, but she might pull through."

Phosy was tugging so hard on his wrist binding that he could feel it slice into his skin, feel the warmth of the blood. But his face betrayed nothing. "I'll get over it," he said.

Goi spat on him. Phosy considered that a victory.

"It's been nice, this little family reunion chat, but here's the truth of it," said Goi. "You're going to die. You can either die very soon and get it out of the way, or we can go through this routine two or three more times. I say three because nobody's ever survived more than three trips to the pit. You think you're a tough guy, but bigger men than you have given up long before that."

"A quick death sounds good," said Phosy. "What do I have to do?"

"You just tell me the results of your investigation—what information you sent to Vientiane."

"You were there," said the inspector. "You heard the results. The headman—"

Phosy was interrupted by a boot to his jaw. He spat out blood. Perhaps another tooth.

"You ignorant commie bastard," said Goi. "Insult my intelligence again, and you go into the pit facedown. Think about that prospect before you speak again. You're the head of special investigations at Police Headquarters. They aren't going to send you up here to investigate a scuffle between two piddling little villages. You were sent here to look into my activities. You were cooperating with the Chinese. It's a joint investigation. Now your stupid politburo is kicking us all out and spoiling a very nice party. Before I go, if I go, I need to know exactly what you think you learned and how much of it you shared with the Chinks."

Phosy tried to speak, but his words came out in a dry cough. Goi nodded, and his henchman turned the water back on, drilling it into the policeman's face. Phosy took as much in as he could without drowning. He needed the water and the time to think. Would the government have sent Phosy north to sort out a problem between two ethnic groups? Given the paranoia in the capital that the hill tribes were being recruited by the Chinese, you bet your life they would. A central subcommittee had been set up, fueled by exactly that fear. But this? This was something else.

Goi's paranoia made the politburo seem rational. Admittedly he wielded a great deal of power in Luang Nam Tha, but he had reached a far greater status in his own mind. Everything centered around the toothless one. It was a weakness, and Phosy needed a weakness in his opponent to survive this torture. The policeman would have to admit he was at something of a disadvantage.

Some might call it a hopeless situation. But Phosy carried with him a fertile optimism. He was optimistic that his wife and child had been protected by the Vientiane network. He was optimistic that at some point he would meet Toothless face-to-face on equal terms and beat him to a mash. But in the short term he was optimistic that one more session in the pit would not be the death of him. In fact, right now, the warmth of the earth was appealing. Foreman Goi probably considered this brief encounter a victory. The bully stamps his authority. The victim understands his hopelessness. But in fact, it had given Phosy a weapon. Hope.

"Perhaps we could discuss this over a meal," he said.

Toothless raised his boot.

"All right," said Phosy. "That wasn't such a good idea. Why don't we do it like this? You list the things you've done wrong, and I tell you whether the Chinese know about them."

*   *   *

The zinc cover slammed shut on Phosy in his damp grave. But now he had ammunition. He had knowledge. He had motivation. At his next exhumation, he would have a plan.

Or be dead.

"She's off her head," said a woman.

"It's sad," said her friend. "And at her age."

"But look at her fancy clothes. She's from the city. They can afford to be out of their minds most of the day."

Madame Daeng was on her third tour of the Muang Sing market and was currently scratching at some imaginary gnat bites. She'd spent her time helping herself to fruit and embarrassing the stallholders. It has to be said that Muang Sing stall holders can take a lot before they're embarrassed.

"Look at these legs," shouted Daeng. She hitched her skirt even higher. "See how pretty they are? They could have been dancer's legs. I could have been a race horse even. Then the evil spirit of arthritis took root in them and turned them into radishes. See? See this?"

Her heavy eyelids dropped shut then sprang open again. She picked up two thick radishes from the nearest stall and walked them in front of her like puppets from stall to stall. "But I'm free now," she said.

The local policemen had gathered at one end of the market and were discussing what should be done with the unruly woman. Madame Daeng began to dance, overbalanced and fell onto a pile of carrots. She rolled around in them and laughed.

"I've found the magic," she said, scratching at her skin as if she were coated in red ants. "Now look at these carrots.

Riddled with lice they are. Riddled. How can you sell such infested carrots?"

She ripped off her blouse and scratched at her chest. This was the point at which the young policemen moved in. She protested but seemed to have little fight in her. They took an arm each and marched her out of the market. American Mae had watched the whole thing. She could have stepped in and claimed Madame Daeng as a friend, but experience had taught her that addicts rarely appreciated acts of kindness. It was best to stand back and leave them to self-destruct. But she felt sorry for the husband. The old doctor was kind and polite. He didn't deserve a wife like this.

Nurse Dtui and Mr. Geung arrived at the central post office on Lan Xang early in the afternoon when the employees were still stodgy with lunch and lethargic from the heat. They'd be mellow and more likely to answer questions. Dtui knew the assistant manager from the days when the nurse was in gynecology and the manager was carrying her third child. She was happy to take them to the room out back that housed their mail-vetting department.

Some twenty employees, most hired and trained by the Ministry of Foreign Affairs, sat at large tables and talked amicably amongst themselves while they opened private correspondence and parcels from overseas and distant provinces. Almost every item was noted in a ledger with the time of meddling and the listed contents. Every now and then, one might notice employees chomping on chocolate Tim Tams from Townsville or tooth-cracking pistachios from Pasadena, but none of those items made appearances in the ledgers.

Fortunately, Dr. Siri's *pha sin* wasn't edible, and the assistant manager found its delivery date in the registry. She called over the employee who had handled the item. She was a frail, slow-moving woman who made up for her lack of bulk by teasing and curling her hair into a masterpiece of ornamental cosmetology. She glared at Dtui through a cascade of tight curls. "Yes, I remember it," said the woman.

"Why?" Dtui asked. "I'm sure you get a lot of articles like this. *Pha sin*s from the countryside to relatives working in Vientiane."

"Ah, but they would give a return address. Our workers in the country post offices would insist on it. It's for situations when we can't deliver the parcel, and it has to be returned, not that we have staff to perform such a service. On top of that, the frank stamp was blurred. All in all, a suspicious package."

"So you opened it," said Dtui.

"Yes."

"And found?"

"A *pha sin*."

"No note? No letter?"

"No. Just a *pha sin*."

"And what happened to it then?"

"I attached a note to the package informing the postman that a charge had to be levied because of inappropriate notification."

"Wh-wh-what color was it?" asked Mr. Geung.

Dtui looked at him in surprise, but the hair woman didn't miss a beat. "It was from the north," she said. "Lu, I think. Bands of green and pink and blue."

"Thank you," said Dtui, and turned to leave.

". . . and a black hem," added the woman.

8

A Little War with China

The old boys had spent the night in Muang Xai. They had both been feeling poorly after their day of post-office muggings and shape-shifting weavers, so they stayed in a room over a nightclub. It was the only place available. They'd made the effort to drink alcohol and dance to taped music with powder-faced plump girls, but their night was all over by nine. The flu or whatever it was that had accompanied them to the north kept them awake all night.

"When we were young," said Civilai from the depths of his blankets, "a cold would last half a day. You could stand out in the rain in your underpants all afternoon and think nothing of it. Remember that?"

"Now I'll never get to sleep with the image of you in the rain in your underpants," said Siri. "But for the flu, we can blame the influx of foreigners."

He hadn't intended to sound racist. That was Civilai's territory.

"They bring in their personal strains of flu," he continued, "and leave us with a casserole of germs that our antibodies aren't trained to cope with. By the year 2030, flu will be wiping out more victims than the Black Death. There's no such thing as a slight cold anymore."

"That makes me feel so much better," said Civilai.

"I do my best," said Siri.

They lay awake, inhaling the scent of cheap dancers on the counterpane and listening to the distant croaking of frogs in search of melody.

"I haven't yet told you of Muang Nam," said Civilai.

"Have we been there?"

"You have such a poor memory for places, I'm surprised you make it to the outhouse every morning."

"Some days I don't bother. Civilai, there are so many *muang*s and *ban*s up here. How am I supposed to remember all of them? Where is Muang Nam?"

"Nowhere."

"Good. Well, that's the end of one more worthless conversation."

"But according to Hanoi and Russian observers, it's been occupied by Chinese troops."

"How does a town that is nowhere become occupied, exactly?"

"According to a letter that was issued by the ambassadors of both Vietnam and the Soviet Union, an area at the Chinese border has been overrun by two units of Chinese military. They agree that unless the CRA withdraw immediately, this will become an international incident. The area in question is called Muang Nam."

"Which does not exist. Aha. I see. So our good allies have invented an invasion to discredit the Chinese. Didn't they think we'd know we didn't have a Muang Nam?"

"In fact, it took awhile to be sure. A lot of documentation was lost or destroyed during the fighting. We couldn't be absolutely sure there wasn't a Muang Nam. We had to do a search in all the border province archives to be certain."

"This all gets more peculiar every day."

Siri sucked on the fumes from the last of his jar of Tiger Balm, wondering how many inhalations it might take to empty the little glass container. Could one actually suck a balm bottle dry? Was there . . . ? And then a thought occurred to him.

"Civilai?"

"I'm asleep."

"Then allow your subconscious to ponder this. I have a theory."

"Good for you."

"My theory is that you weren't sent here as the goodwill ambassador to negotiate a peace settlement with the warring Chinese or observe enemy troop movements. Hardly a one-man job, I'd say, especially for one so frail. Especially for an ex-politburo man who argued with and upset almost everyone on the Central Committee. My theory is that you were sent up here to check the map archives of Muang Sing. That they sent half a dozen old farts like yourself to pore over curling land documents and village records of all the border provinces for a few days. Nice, safe, little job to keep you out of the way. How's that for a theory?"

The reply was in the form of unconvincing snores from an ex-somebody, caught out.

By 5:30 they were in Agnes and on the road. They calculated that, without mishap, they'd be back in Muang Sing by lunchtime. They just needed to stop briefly in Un Mai and pick up the next clue from old Grandmother Amphone's family. The road was named Highway One, which signified that it was the first, rather than the best, of the northern roads, but it had weathered well and allowed a good deal of uninterrupted speeding. It passed directly through Na Maw.

There was nothing spectacular about the scenery. A few hills. One or two valleys. Forgettable villages with no signs. The previous day they'd made the entire journey in three hours. Civilai had conceded that, although the Chinese couldn't cook to save their lives, they did put together a damned decent road. Indeed, with only three stops to empty old bladders and throw up that morning's breakfast— a greasy plate of eggs—they arrived in a little village they didn't bother to ask the name of. It would have been perfect timing for an early lunch, but neither was feeling well enough to eat. They stocked up on fresh fruit and clean drinking water and hoped that an appetite might catch up with them on the road.

Twenty kilometers before Un Mai, on a blacktop that had been as deserted as Mars the previous day, they ran into a roadblock. It was piled high with freshly cut logs. Though unmanned, it was impossible to go around without leaving the road and crossing open terrain that sloped downward at an acute angle.

"That's odd," said Siri. "I didn't notice this yesterday."

"Me neither. In the past twenty-four hours someone has erected a barricade worthy of *Les Misérables*. It is obviously here to tell us that the only road to Muang Sing is now inaccessible."

"It's symbolic," said Siri.

"Why so?"

"There are better places to build a roadblock. Spots where you wouldn't be able to pass even with four-wheel drive. The barrier builders can still use the road. It's a warning to others."

"So what are our options?"

"We ignore the warning and continue on, or we turn around and hide out in the room above the nightclub until the road is cleared and spend the rest of our lives wondering what would have happened if we'd had the balls to keep going."

"The rest of our lives being . . . ?"

"In my case, it could be days."

"So let's do it. I mean the former."

Agnes headed down toward the valley. There was one point so steep that the old boys instinctively leaned to their right as two wheels left the ground. The jeep hovered for a second before bumping back to earth. They scrambled up onto the roadway and heard the thump of mud against the undercarriage as the wheels cleaned themselves. The scenery hadn't changed, but the atmosphere was thicker on this side of the barrier. Siri's foot wasn't so heavy on the accelerator. Civilai didn't sing off-key French communist campfire songs. The deserted road was fraught with tension as if some evil spirit lay around every corner. And it didn't take long to learn the reason for their apprehension.

They rounded one of many sharp bends and came to a second barrier. This was merely a single line of rocks. Siri braked, and even before the jeep had shuddered to a stop, they were surrounded by dozens of armed soldiers. They swarmed down on the jeep from every direction in their almost-matching green uniforms and dented helmets. They were yelling and screaming in Chinese and punching the muzzles of their weapons toward the old men.

"Don't put up your hands," said Civilai.

"Are you mad?" Siri asked.

"Just trust me. Keep your hands down."

The swarm had reached the jeep, and despite the fact that neither Siri nor Civilai could understand Chinese, it was evident the gentlemen would have been most grateful if the Lao should put up their hands and, perhaps, get out of the jeep. One soldier went so far as to fire a bullet above their heads to emphasize the seriousness of the situation. Instead, Civilai slowly raised his letter of introduction and held it in front of his face. He smiled as if it were an invitation from the Chinese Premier himself.

An officer barked an order, and some of the men stood back to let him approach the jeep. He said something in Chinese, and Civilai replied in Lao, "I do not speak Chinese."

The officer tried again in English. Civilai's only competence in those two languages was to recognize them. He replied in French, "I do not speak English." As the officer had apparently run out of languages, Civilai said in Lao, "Sir, the least you can do is have the decency to learn the language of the country you're invading."

The officer snatched the paper from Civilai and looked at its unfathomable lettering. He was obviously unsure as to how to proceed. The lack of fear on the faces of the old men, their refusal to adopt a pose of subjugation, and their ages called for the intervention of a higher authority. He barked another order.

One soldier handed his gun to a colleague and climbed all over the two old men, apparently in search of weapons. He found none. The officer called his unit to regroup, all but a dozen who took up positions around the jeep. The others scrambled up the rise and were swallowed by the thick vegetation. The only sounds that remained were the chirping of birds and the clicks of the cooling jeep.

"Well," said Siri, looking around at the silent circle of armed men, "if I was feeling a bit better, I could take them on."

"If you were feeling better—and if you were Bruce Lee," said Civilai.

"You'll recall that the twelve men Bruce engages are invariably armed with little balsa-wood sticks or bath sponges. I haven't yet seen him take on submachine gunners."

"All right, boys?" Civilai shouted. "Anyone here speak Lao?"

If they did, nobody owned up.

"Where do we stand, brother?" Siri asked.

"I suppose that depends on whether we've run into a small advance party or the entire Chinese Third Army. My intuition tells me the latter."

"What? Why?"

"Because they left us here rather than take us to their camp, where we'd see just how large a force they have. Once we knew that, they'd probably have no choice but to shoot us. I imagine their commander will want to know why we're here and how much we—and by *we*, I mean the Lao government—know of their plan. As the roadblock wasn't up yesterday, and we're about twenty kilometers from the border, I suspect they've only just arrived. They would have hoped to make it to the Vietnamese border without any resistance. I suspect that this is the second front, hoping to sneak across Laos unnoticed."

Siri had a huge grin on his face.

"What are you smiling about?" Civilai asked.

"You."

"What about me?"

"For all the years I've known you, I thought you were quite useless."

"Thank you."

"I mean, pleasant company, but not exactly practical. I thought your diplomacy was all tea and compliments and taking foreign leaders to 'wink, wink' traditional masseurs. I've never been with you in your element before. I'm impressed. What's our next move?"

"I have no idea."

"Don't spoil it for me. Surely you had all this planned out back in Vientiane?"

"I didn't expect for one second we'd actually find an invading army up here."

"Oh."

"Don't panic. I'll think of something."

Nothing happened for forty minutes. The guards got hot once the sun had broken through the mist, and they retreated to the shade of the trees. The old boys' adrenaline drained rapidly, leaving only the symptoms of flu, diarrhea and nausea that had been Siri's travel companions for much of the journey. They were dozing in their non-reclining seats when they were roused by the sound of a snapping to attention. They opened their eyes to see the first officer and a high-ranking commander marching toward them accompanied by a man both Siri and Civilai recognized immediately. Colonel Bouaphan had been the Lao Vice Minister of Economic Affairs until a year before. One day he'd emptied the contents of his office safe and left a note to say he'd be defecting to Communist China. Nobody, including his wife, cared very much, and nobody had heard from him since.

The first officer barked something, and the defector stepped forward. He wore a Chinese uniform that was too small for him. "Hello, comrades," said Bouaphan. He was pigeon-toed and pigeon-chested which made him look a lot like . . . a pigeon.

"How's treachery treating you?" asked Civilai.

"Ooh, can't complain. The food's good, and I have a sweet new wife. How's poverty and mismanagement?"

"At least it's our poverty and mismanagement," said Siri.

The officer barked again. His oral skills all seemed to be canine.

"Right," said Bouaphan. "So I'm in a bit of a spot here."

"I really hope we'll be able to help you out of it," said Civilai.

"You see," said Bouaphan, "I had certain influence in the decision to pass innocently through Lao territory on our way to Dien Viang Phu. My appraisal was that—given the Lao inability to tie its own bootlaces—you'd not realize we were here until long after we entered Vietnam. So what I'd like to know is how you found us."

Civilai smiled and said, "I seem to recall underestimation was your forte back at the finance ministry. That's why nobody particularly missed you when you left."

Bouaphan didn't find the comment funny.

Siri coughed. It started as a *don't push your luck* cough but soon became bronchial.

"You be nice now, Comrade Civilai," said Bouaphan. "I'm the only one who can get you out of here in one piece."

"Don't flatter yourself," said Civilai. "You know who I am. Do you really think I'd just happen to be here on vacation? We've been monitoring your troop buildup for a week."

"Don't be ridiculous. I know for a fact you don't have the resources."

"We don't, no. But our new Big Brother does. The Soviets have been very interested in your movements. You'd be surprised what technical strides they've made since the tsars moved on. My mission here is to politely ask you to turn around and cross back over the border to avert, amongst other things, a third world war. If you refuse, and if my brother here and I do not arrive in Un Mai in an hour, not only will your advance meet heavy resistance long before you reach the Vietnamese border, but your retreat will have been cut off completely, and you'll be stranded here."

The commander had said nothing thus far, but Siri noticed that he had his head bowed slightly. He was listening to a short man who stood directly behind him. This, Siri realized, must have been an official translator. It appeared that the Chinese did not completely trust their defector.

"Utter nonsense," said Bouaphan. "There have been no Lao troops anywhere near this border."

"You seem to have also underestimated the hill tribe

militia," said Civilai. "With Soviet comradeship comes Soviet funding. It's amazing how unified a country can become with a few rubles jingling in its pockets."

"I don't believe you," said Bouaphan.

"I don't care," said Civilai.

There was a moment of silence during which a great deal of brain matter was stirred. It was Siri who broke the deadlock. "Young man," he called.

The interpreter leaned out from behind the officer and pointed to himself, eyebrows raised.

"Yes, you," Siri continued. "Tell your boss that this is Laos. We've been an ally to China since our ancestors taught you how to make gunpowder and the paper to write about it. We're two old men in a jeep. We're here in the spirit of friendship. We don't want Chinese corpses on our soil. Tell him to go home and kiss his wife and think of another plan."

The interpreter did his job, ignoring the interruptions of Bouaphan's stilted Chinese. The commander stared at the old men in the jeep, who shrugged and did their utmost to seem indifferent. There followed a heated discussion, a bark, and the men fell in. They followed their commander back up the rise. Before disappearing behind the tree line, the officer stopped and handed something to one of his men. The soldier ran down to the jeep and gave Siri back his key. Bouaphan was left in the no-man's-land he'd created for himself.

"You'd better run and say farewell to your sweet concubine," shouted Civilai. "I think you've underestimated yourself into a political toilet."

The defector was lost for words. He jogged up the hill every inch a pigeon, even down to the egg he'd laid for himself.

Siri and Civilai enjoyed five minutes of silent isolation until they sighed in unison, then laughed.

"Do you suppose anyone in Vientiane will believe this?" Siri asked.

"That we averted a Chinese invasion?"

"Yes."

"Not on your life."

"Too bad. I'm long overdue a medal."

"Nice touch, that wife-kissing line."

"Civilai, you are the maestro of diplomacy. I'm going to put you in my will."

"You have nothing I want."

After another frustrating hour of attempting to get word to Phosy and Siri, Nurse Dtui, with Mr. Geung in tow, found the postman who had delivered the poisoned *pha sin* to Dr. Siri. He was sitting under a tree munching instant noodles directly from the packet. He washed it down with red sugar water. He was a man in need of nutritional advice amongst other things.

"Hello, Uncle," she said.

He looked up at her, then across to Geung. "Taking the moron for a walk, are you?"

If it was a joke, it was bettered by Geung saying, "If you don't have s-s-s-something nnnice to say, don't say any—anything."

"You remember this?" Dtui asked the postman, holding up a photo of the half-*sin* Siri had left behind.

"No," said the postman, barely looking at the photo.

Growing up, Dtui had always seen mail delivery as a social occupation. Its perpetrators were friends to all, caring and happy. So it didn't take her long to realize that this postman was in the wrong profession. "It's a *pha sin*," she said.

"I can see that."

"You de—delivered it," said Geung. "When?"

"Look, lady, call the monkey off, will you?"

"You'll answer his questions," said Dtui. "And show some manners if you don't want to lose your job."

"Who do you think you—?"

"The post office put the *pha sin* in your delivery pouch on the sixteenth," said Dtui. "It wasn't received until the eighteenth. What did you do with it for two days?"

"I don't know nothing about it."

"Perhaps I can . . . I c-c-can jog your memory," said Geung. "It had no reeeeturn address and a faint f-f-frank stamp. You were supposed to coll—"

"Collect a fine," said the postman. "I don't have enough years left to wait for you to finish a sentence, boy. Yeah, I remember. I handed it over the day I got it. And I collected the fine. You can check the ledger."

"We did," said Dtui. "And we found the signed document. But that wasn't the owner's signature."

"That's none of my business."

"In fact it is. You're supposed to get a positive identification of the owner before you hand over mail. That's the rule of the post office."

"She walked out of the front yard. I told her about the fine. She handed it over without question. Who but the owner's going to do a thing like that?"

"So you didn't ask to see her national citizen card?"

"She said she was his wife," said the postman.

"An-an-and I'm the king of Thailand," said Geung.

Dtui suppressed a laugh. "What did she look like?" she asked the flustered postman.

"I don't know," he said.

"Try," said Geung.

"Skinny. Old. Long grey hair in a chinois. Neat. Polite."

"Thank you," said Mr. Geung and kissed him on the forehead.

Agnes arrived in Un Mai long before the fictitious deadline that would signal hostilities between Laos and China. The old boys still had no great hunger despite their encounter with the Chinese third army. The only pharmacy in town was boarded over. The neighbors said the owner was Chinese. He'd fled with his family. They also gave directions to the house of Kew, the granddaughter of the famous but sadly departed Grandmother Amphone. Compared to border transgressions, the treasure hunt was becoming something of a triviality.

"Do you suppose that might have been the purpose of this wild goose chase?" Civilai asked as they crossed the small bridge before the village.

"What?"

"To have us arrive here in time to meet the invaders. To avert disaster."

"I doubt it," said Siri. "These clues were laid two or three months ago. I shouldn't think the Chinese had a date in mind back then. And I doubt even more that anyone could have predicted when we'd be here."

"That's too bad. I'd rather like to go home now. Adventure isn't nearly so thrilling when you have a cold."

"It's flu. It'll pass."

"So you keep telling me. But I can never forget that you're a coroner rather than an MD. All I can hear is, 'It was flu. He passed away.'"

"More people worldwide die of being sucked into pneumatic airplane toilets every year than influenza."

The house they were looking for stood alone beside a disused rice field.

"You made that up."

"Prove me wrong."

Kew, Grandmother Amphone's granddaughter, was about fifty and had a skeletal system that seemed too large for her.

Bones jutted out at the pelvis and shoulders and connected poorly at the elbows. She walked to meet the jeep like a knight in armor but she was soft-spoken and easy to like.

"You are the gentleman come to collect the *pha sin*," she said, not a question.

"You're expecting us?" said Siri.

"She said you'd come."

She had the two old men sit under a breadfruit tree, where a plastic jug of water was waiting for them.

"And who is 'she,' exactly?" asked Civilai.

"She never did give me her name," said the woman, joining them on a wooden bench. "But she spent an entire day here looking at my grandmother's *sin*s. She was very knowledgeable."

"What did she look like?" asked Siri.

"You don't know her? I assumed you'd met."

"Why?"

"She talked about you so affectionately. That's why I agreed to let her take one of the collection with her. She said you'd be bringing it back. You do have it, I hope?"

Siri opened his pack and pulled out the latest *sin*. "I'm afraid the seam is a little unraveled," he said.

"Nothing that can't be repaired," Kew said, inspecting the returned skirt.

"So . . . the woman?" said Civilai.

"Oh, sorry, yes. She was pleasant enough. Elderly. Long hair. Rather thin."

"She didn't mention what she intended to do with the *sin*?" Civilai asked.

"I rather got the idea it was something like a game," she said. "I'm supposed to give you the next clue. Wait, I'll get it for you. Help yourselves to the water."

She disappeared into the house, and the old boys drank heartily from the jug. "Some game," said Civilai.

Kew returned with a familiar plastic bag and watched as Siri unfastened the staples and pulled out the next *pha sin*. It was markedly different from all the others. The colors were brighter, and there were more bands with pink and blue and green elephants parading along a high track and brown-and-orange deer heading in the opposite direction below.

"What number is this?" Civilai asked.

"Seven," said Siri. "Six and a half in hand."

"My, so many," said the woman. "What fun."

"What fun, indeed," said Siri. "I don't suppose you recognize this weave, my dear?"

"Of course I do," she said. "It's what you might call a *nouveau* Lu. There's a village south of Luang Nam Tha on the river. They're producing some really exotic *sins*. Far more modern than anyone else."

This sounded familiar to Siri. "About eleven kilometers south?" he asked.

"About that, yes."

"You know the place?" Civilai asked.

"It appears we've come full circle," said Siri. "When Daeng and I first arrived in Luang Nam Tha, the owner of the guesthouse where we took lunch was from a Lu village eleven kilometers down the river. It has to be the same place."

"Well, thank goodness for that," said Civilai. "At last we can stop somewhere long enough to get well and start drinking again."

Siri was picking at the hem of the newest *sin*. "What are you doing?" asked the woman.

"A clue has been sewn into the hem of each of the *sins*," said Siri.

"How delightful," said the woman. "Here."

She handed him a small knife from amongst the instruments in her shirt pocket. From the hem, Siri produced one more flattened roll of paper. It appeared to be another page ripped from a ledger. Again, it was written in Chinese in five columns. But unlike the previous page, this was lined and written in a much neater hand.

"Are there any Chinese living here?" Siri asked.

"Mr. Lee, our pharmacist, was the last," she said. "They've all been told to go. But if it's a translation you want, I'd be pleased to do that for you."

"You read Chinese?"

"I spent twelve years at school in Shanghai. Our family made a lot of money in China from our granny's *sins*. She was quite a celebrity across the border. She sent all her grandchildren there to study. The opportunities were much better up north. Look, it's too late for you to travel. Why don't I make you a good hot meal, and we'll look through your clues together. I'll send my husband to the market to get some natural remedies for your condition. You both look like you could use some rest."

"Well, nice to see you at last," came a voice, bass, sarcastic.

"Bpoo?"

The concoction Kew's husband had returned with from the market was vaguely alcoholic and most certainly opium based. For a while, Siri's dreams sped by in color like billboards outside a train. And then he was on the Normandy Express, and Aunti Bpoo the transvestite fortune teller was seated opposite. Her demise had gone no length toward bringing down her weight. She leaned forward and put a hand on his knee.

"So this is a dream, right?" he asked.

"As opposed to . . . ?"

"To reality. Actual conversation."

"Call it what you like."

"Why can't we talk when I'm conscious?"

"Because you don't believe."

Auntie Bpoo stood on the seat and started a very slow striptease.

"Believe in what?" Siri asked.

"In us."

"Of course I believe in you. How can I not? I see you all the time. Do you really have to do that?"

"Your scientific side continues to reject us. Your doctor logic."

She peeled off a long green opera glove. The other passengers on the train, some of whom Siri recognized from obituary photographs, began to clap—egging her on. She found the rhythm and let her micro-skirt slide to the seat. Fortunately she was wearing thick tights with designs of cakes on them.

"But the doctor is part of me," said Siri. "How can I ignore him without leaving myself . . . incomplete?"

"Take the potion," she said.

"What potion?"

"You know what potion. The brew the witch gave you in Muang Xai."

Bpoo pulled her tank top up over her pot belly, over her empty bra.

"She said there might be . . . side effects," said Siri.

"So what?" said Bpoo.

The tank top across her face caught on her earring and disoriented her. She spun around, lost her footing on the seat and fell to the floor with a thump. Siri felt the same thump and awoke on the floorboards in the backroom of Kew's house. Civilai snored beside him.

9

The Black–Clad, Evil–Eyed Men at Dr. Dooley's Place

The door to Dr. Dooley's clinic guesthouse burst open, and two black-clad evil-eyed men ran inside. Each held a flashlight.

"In here," said one of them.

The other came to join him, and they found the old woman facedown on the bed. The room smelled of vomit and booze. On a bedside table was a teaspoon. Evil-Eye Number One dabbed a finger into it but he knew what it would contain even before he tasted it. He nodded.

His partner slapped the old woman across the face five, six, seven times. There was no reaction. "Is she alive?" Evil-Eye Number One asked.

His partner shone the light on the woman's face and pried open her eyelids. The pupils were full stops. She was out of it.

They tore the place apart: the furniture, the out-of-tune piano, inside the ceiling tiles. They threw the old woman out of the bed and sliced open the mattress. There was no sign of the stash. In desperation they dragged her to the shower, turned the water on cold and left her lying there. Still she didn't come to. They walked around the building looking for signs of recent digging. They broke into the old operating theater. It was a shell.

They decided the only choice they had was to wait until she came out of her drug-induced stupor and beat it out of her. They knew from experience, given her state, that she wouldn't be conscious for another three, four hours. So they left her soaked in the shower stall, and each made a nest from the shredded mattress kapok and curled up to sleep.

It couldn't have been more than twenty minutes later that Evil-Eye Number One was awoken by a flicker of light. A single candle burned across the room. In its staccato flame he could just make out the sleeping form of his sidekick. The candle painted a hideous shadow on the man's face. His tongue hung loose like a dog's, and there was . . . was that blood seeping from a wound on his neck, or just a trick of the light? Evil-Eye pushed himself up on one elbow to get a clearer look, but a boot to his neck forced him back down with a crunch. Out of the corner of his eye, he could see the old woman standing over him with a penknife in her hand. It was dripping blood. She was smiling.

"That's not possible," he wheezed, the boot constricting his larynx.

"Slap an old lady, would you?" she said. "Nasty bastard."

After talking to the postman, Dtui had yet again been told at the long-distance phone booth that communication with Luang Nam Tha was impossible. Not even Party members were getting through these days. Altogether preoccupied, she taught her lone afternoon class at the nursing college. In the summary session, she appreciated for once the dearth of questions from the would-be—heaven help them—nurses. Her mind had wandered elsewhere. She was positing the ridiculous.

She considered the postman's description of the woman he'd met in front of Siri's house. Who was she? She had brazenly stolen a *pha sin* that had been sent to Dr. Siri. She perhaps thought it was a gift unbeknownst that there was a severed finger sewn into the hem. Or had she put it there? She had, overnight, bleached one segment of the skirt. She had applied a coat of Paris Green, a toxic pigment rich in arsenic. Two days later, she or a colleague had delivered the altered *sin* to Dr. Siri's house knowing full well that prolonged exposure to the material would sicken and eventually kill anyone in close proximity to it.

What type of woman would go to so much trouble? What type of woman would have access to deadly poison? Who would hate Dr. Siri and Madame Daeng so? Nurse Dtui could think of only one person, and she was dead: executed for crimes against the state based largely on evidence from Siri and Daeng. The spy they called The Lizard had already made elaborate attempts on the lives of the couple. It had been one of the first cases they'd all worked on together. Dtui had kept Lizard's wanted poster. It had once hung on various walls around the town, but now it was in a drawer at the morgue. After her class, she'd taken the poster to the post office and caught the obnoxious postman coming off his shift.

"Your b-b-b-b-boyfriend not with you, honey?" he asked.

She held up the poster. "Is this the woman?" she asked. "The woman you gave the parcel to?"

"What do I get if I tell you?"

"You get me not going home to tell my policeman husband how unpleasant you are. Is this the woman?"

"Yeah."

"You sure?"

"Yeah."

*   *   *

Nurse Dtui had never felt so alone. She'd been used to group support in troubled times. Late nights around a table at Madame Daeng's noodle shop, Daeng and Siri and Civilai. And her husband Phosy. Where the hell was Phosy? She needed confirmation that she'd interpreted everything correctly. She had a clue now, and a suspect, but no idea what to do about either. She went to see the only ally she had. Mr. Geung could neither read nor tie his shoelaces, but he had a memory that would shame an elephant. She found him rocking in a non-rocking chair in front of the hospital dorm.

"Geung," she said, "do you remember the night at the Russian Club when we celebrated the death of The Lizard?"

Of course he did.

"I had a beer," he said. It had been a rare indulgence.

"Yes, but—"

"I . . . I vomited in the Mekhong."

"Good job. But do you recall anything that was said that night? Anything that might have suggested the execution of The Lizard could have been canceled?"

He didn't have to think. "No."

"Right. I didn't think so. So there was nothing suspicious? Nothing that made you wonder?"

"Yes."

"Oh, well. It was worth asking. Thanks, pal."

"Yes m-m-m-means yes," he said.

"I know. Wait. You mean there was something?"

"The ring," he said.

"What ring? Oh, shit. Right. The ring."

In a final moment of remorse, on the eve of her execution, The Lizard had apologized to Siri and Daeng. She had taken a very expensive ring off her finger and told them the bastard soldiers would only steal it once she was shot by the firing squad. She told them if they took it to the Russian Club, the owner would take it in lieu of payment for a night of food and drink for them and all their friends. She explained that only the manageress of that establishment would know the worth of the ring.

And she'd been right. They'd eaten and drunk to excess that night and all had appropriate hangovers the following day. And nobody had given a second thought to the ring. Could it have contained a message?

The Russian Club had changed management shortly after, and none of them had followed up with the military. There was a slim chance that the ring had alerted allies of The Lizard's location and led to a rescue.

That faint hope was enough for Dtui. The military would never announce or admit to such a debacle, and there was no way a simple nurse would be given such information.

So there she was in police headquarters, sitting opposite Sergeant Sihot. He'd been a good soldier, but he would never be a general. He filled in the forms and listened politely, but he didn't put on his bulletproof armor and charge into battle. That's what Phosy would have done. That's why she needed her husband.

Sergeant Sihot listened to the entire story of the *pha sin* and the poison. Dtui told him about the deceased woman who might have come back to life in order to kill Siri and Daeng. In fairness, he listened with a straight face.

When the story was told, he put down the pen and leaned back in his creaky chair. "Must say, it all sounds a bit espionage-like to me," he said.

"Espionage-like?" said Dtui. "Of course it was espionage-like. She was a spy. That's what they do. All you'd have to do is get in touch with the military and get a confirmation she was executed."

He pursed his lips. "Oooh," he said. "That wouldn't be easy at all."

"Why not?"

"Military and police. We don't get along that well."

"How could you not? You were a colonel in the military. Phosy was a general. The police force is just an offshoot of the army. There must be people over there you can ask."

"I suppose so," Sihot said without enthusiasm.

"You suppose . . . ? All right. Then bear this in mind while you consider it. Our friends Dr. Siri and Daeng went up-country to follow up on where the mystery finger came from. They'd already been exposed to arsenic. They took half the *sin* with them. They were already ill when they left. But what if The Lizard's up there too? What if she's exposed them to more of the stuff? What if she wants to watch them have a slow and painful death? Could you live with that?"

"That's an awful lot of conjecture, young Dtui."

"You're right. But we live in a time where it's advisable to expect the worst. Could you at least promise me you'll contact the military and ask about The Lizard? A man of your resources must have old friends in the armed forces."

Sihot smiled. He was missing a good number of teeth. "I'll try," he said.

She stood to leave. "And it would be a good opportunity to have the military get in touch with Phosy and get him on the case."

"He'll be in touch," said Sihot. "Don't worry."

10

Geckos Don't Wear Trousers

Buddhism probably prepared a man to lay in a puddle of effluent for long periods in total darkness. But Phosy wasn't Buddhist, and his eclectic animist upbringing hadn't helped at all. He needed to keep his mind active through some activity other than meditation. The endless hours of arse-numbing political seminars had trained him to look fascinated while plotting long-term projects; his thirst for revenge on toothless Goi would have kept him alive for weeks. He had formulated a plan. It wasn't perfect, but he was hardly in a state to expect perfection.

He had also kept his mind alive by retracing the events of the morning the two headmen had purportedly killed each other. Once he'd studied the bodies and applied logic to the findings, it had become obvious what had actually transpired. He would never be able to prove it, and he decided it would be more than his life was worth to run his suspicions by the perpetrators.

But he was confident he had reached the actual scenario. The wounds on the bodies were most certainly those from sharpened bamboo poles—there was no doubt about that. The curious part was how both men had as many wounds on their backs as they did on their fronts. These might have occurred on one corpse as the impending victor gave chase to his opponent and administered the final blows. But there were no circumstances that he could imagine whereby the two men were both attacking and retreating. In a stand-up fight, the rivals would be facing each other.

So how did the wounds arrive on the backs of the fighters? There was only one possibility. They were attacked by somebody else, or rather, by a group armed with the same type of sharpened bamboo poles as those of the headmen. But who could have been responsible for such a thing? The Chinese road gang had no vested interest in the duel. If one of the headman's own villages had been involved, that headman would surely have only attacked the opposing headman. So what group would stand to gain from the death of both of them?

At Phosy's embarrassing dénouement in the clearing, only one section of the crowd had shown any pleasure at his announcement that he was unable to declare a winner from the two villages. The mysterious tribeswomen whose youngster had caused the lust-fest in the first place had clapped and grinned when they heard the girl would not become the possession of either camp. Of course, who would want to see such a prize condemned to poverty in a dirty village in the middle of nowhere? No. They had better things planned for their nubile virgin princess. A rich city type. A dowry. Aid. By killing the two headmen, the girl was back on the market.

When the zinc roof to his tomb opened this time, he was prepared for it. When he heard the padlock being unfastened, he closed his eyes tight against the glare, took a deep breath and twisted around to be facedown. There he lay perfectly still. As still as death. The same hand grabbed his collar, but the material ripped. There was yelling. Someone had climbed down into the grave and was manhandling him

out. He took a long slow breath through his nose and was
dumped on the dirt.

Someone felt for a pulse. Phosy was a man who took a pride
in keeping his pulse to himself. Dtui, an experienced nurse,
had only been able to find it on rare occasions, all of those
after sex. She'd pronounced him dead many an early morning. His veins were deep and embedded in a thick endoplasm.

He doubted his captors would give him mouth-to-mouth.
A finger lifted his eyelid, but he was already staring at the
inside of his brain, another trick he'd learned at Siri's slab.
There were punches and kicks. He'd expected those. There
was angry shouting in a strange language. The voices were
probably saying what a coward this Vientiane policeman was,
taking his own life.

But then he was ignored. One eye closed. One turned in
on itself. No sounds. Patience. He was dead. He'd lie there all
day if necessary, fighting back the goosebumps. He wondered
how they'd dispose of his body. It was a matter he'd given a
lot of thought to while down under.

But he didn't have long to wait. Another hand, this one
smaller, took ahold of his ankle and dragged him slowly
across the dirt. His body bumped over a step. His back and
his wrists with their open sores sent slithers of lightning
pain through his body. His physical self could take no more
abuse, but his confidence grew. Somehow he would harness
that confidence to find the strength to escape. To have his
revenge.

Still not prepared to look around him for fear of being
discovered, he kept still, but he could hear the labored
breathing of the man dragging him. A wheeze, spitting, a
cough, and then his leg was allowed to drop to the ground.
They had reached their destination. Phosy had envisioned a
pit rather than an individual grave. A pit where other corpses
lay and no hurry to fill it in. He was ready for that. There were

other possibilities. Benzene and a Bic lighter, weighted down and thrown into a pond. As long as his hands were tied, he couldn't foresee a way out of either. He wasn't Houdini.

He lay on his side. He decided to take a chance and bring down his lazy eye. He saw nobody. He was on a flat surface. The warehouse was some thirty meters away. It was a lone building surrounded by vegetation. He heard another cough, and then a pair of skinny feet in flip-flops stood directly in front of his face. One foot stepped on his chest. He anticipated another kick, but instead the foot rolled him gently onto his back.

And there was nothing beneath him. He dropped like a shot partridge. He watched the sky, then the cliff, race past him. He was in free fall and knew he had time for no more than a kiss from the heart for his wife and child. And were it not for some blessed rock that jutted from the cliff and knocked him unconscious, he knew that he would have fallen forever. And all the spirits that lie in wait for falling men would have taken over his body and carried its soul to their hell long before the body hit the ground.

Siri and Civilai arrived in Muang Sing at exactly lunchtime as planned. Only they were a day late. On the road they'd been sharing their opiate dreams of the previous night. Although they'd both rationed the natural remedies from Kew, they'd topped up after breakfast and enjoyed a hilarious drive back. And their colds were all but forgotten, though the symptoms remained. It was Civilai who recommended they become addicts.

"I'm sure you wouldn't want conflicting addictions," said Siri.

"Opium and . . . ?"

"Food," said Siri. "You haven't stopped eating since you

left the politburo. Look at you. You look like a gecko with a basketball down his trousers."

They'd laughed for a kilometer.

"Geckos don't wear trousers," said Civilai at last.

More laughter.

"Opium is so much more plentiful up here than food," Civilai added. "Did I ever tell you how the CIA were producing heroin here and sending it to their own troops in Vietnam?"

"On a number of occasions."

"Ironic, isn't it? The British get the Chinese addicted to opium. The Chinese get the hill tribes to produce it, then kick them out when they refuse to pay tax on it. The hill tribes flee south, and the French buy up all the stocks to subsidize their occupation of Indochina. Then the Americans fund a war with it. And here they all are, blaming us for the flood of drugs on the streets of Paris and London and New York."

"Not to mention the Germans," said Siri.

"Damn, did they invade us too?"

"In a way. We can thank the Germans for taking those important scientific steps of mass-producing morphine and heroin and distributing them around the globe."

"See?" said Civilai. "The Western world got rich on the backs of our weak wills. We should do it too."

"Do what?"

"Cash in on the backs of the weak-willed. Let's sell our stash and live the life we've always imagined. Mercedes-Benz. Air-conditioned house. Pool."

"That's our dream?"

"Too true."

"I thought our dream was that everyone has an equal share of the wealth of the world."

"Absolutely. I'll have a maid and a gardener, and they can

share my wealth in monthly installments. Perhaps a pool boy and a hair stylist."

"If you weren't stoned, I'd submit a report about you to the Ministry of Interior."

"Come on, you stick-in-the-mud. Let's go back to the house and get into that pure heroin. I bet Madame Daeng's already off her face."

They pulled up in front of the clinic guesthouse, and Madame Daeng hobbled down the steps to meet them. She was wearing an apron that gave the impression she might have been cooking. Siri hopped out of the jeep and gave her one more culturally inappropriate hug. Civilai turned away in embarrassment. There was no telling how she knew the men would be back at that time on that day, but she'd put together a fine spread of pickled fish and vegetables and sticky rice. She'd also set up a table on the balcony so they could watch the imperceptible flow of traffic on the main road. There was even rice wine with various local fruit juice options as mixers. Whereas the men's health had become progressively worse over the three days, Madame Daeng had apparently made a full recovery.

They ate, drank and were merry over a long period that afternoon while Siri and Civilai regaled Daeng with all the tales of their odyssey. Of their dealings with the voodoo woman, their night of opium hallucinations and their single-handed repulsion of the Chinese invasion. She knew from experience to take their fairy tales with a large handful of salt.

"History will prove us heroes," slurred Civilai.

"So, my wife," said Siri, "apart from cooking and cleaning, what have you been up to?"

Daeng looked at Siri, then at Civilai. "I killed one man and have another tied to a post," she said.

"Ha!" cried Civilai. *"Vive la femme."*

But Siri could tell immediately that it was not a joke. Daeng shrugged and stood and walked down the steps and across to the clinic. Siri followed her with Civilai, still chuckling, tagging along behind. Daeng opened the door to the clinic, and there, in the center of the room, tied to a central pillar, was a short-haired man with bruises that stood out defiantly against his dark complexion. He looked up and spat in their direction.

Civilai fell against the doorframe. "You did this, madame?" he said.

Daeng nodded.

"And the dead one?" Siri asked.

"Buried behind the latrine," she said. "Or to be more accurate, I buried him in the old latrine and relocated the latrine. The ground was softer there."

"Oh, my goodness," said Civilai.

"What did they do to you?" Siri asked.

"We'll need a coffee for that story," Daeng replied.

They were back on the balcony, but the mood had altered somewhat. The coffee was sweet and hot, and the late, low mists were starting to crawl in.

"It was the stash day," Daeng began. "The poor woman—the weaver—was so confused when all these outsiders landed on her. It was obvious the heroin wasn't meant for us. She had the *pha sin* in its plastic bag. We should have asked for it specifically. She just got confused. As we said, she was a simple woman someone had forced to mind a large stash of drugs. In fact, we were responsible for her death. It was obvious that the traffickers had killed her, and I wanted to meet them. So I advertised the fact that I had their precious stash."

Siri dropped his head. Civilai threw his arms aloft in

frustration. "How does one advertise such a thing, madam?" Civilai asked. "A small ad in the local newspaper?"

"She acted stoned," said Siri. "You had it all worked out the day we set off without you, didn't you?"

"Not all of it."

"And what were you hoping to achieve?" Civilai asked.

"Probably nothing in the overall big picture of drug trafficking in the Golden Triangle," Daeng said. "But . . ."

"But she got bored," said Siri. "She wanted a taste of some of those old thrills. Right, my precious?"

"Old habits die hard," she agreed. "And these were unsavory characters. You saw the bruises on the weaver. She'd been beaten before. I don't like bullies. I let the word spread that I was intoxicated. I went to the market. I exposed myself a little bit. Got arrested. Then I came back here. I made sure everyone knew where I was staying."

"You are completely mad," said Civilai.

"Not completely." She smiled. "I have a little way to go."

"But aren't there certain physical manifestations of drug taking?" Civilai went on. "I thought there were physical signs you couldn't fake."

"A lot you can act your way through," she said. "The most difficult sign is the constricted pupils. But you can mimic the affect by using carbachol eyedrops. They gave me some when I was having my glaucoma treated. It's always at the bottom of my bag, just in case."

"So the thugs came to claim their lost loot," said Civilai, who was now clear-headed and sober but developing a headache. Siri merely reached across and squeezed his wife's hand.

"And I was ready for them," said Daeng.

Civilai rolled his eyes. "And what now?" he shouted.

"Now we interrogate the prisoner and find out—"

"Prisoner?" Civilai yelled. "Are you a policewoman, Madame Daeng? No. You will interview your bully over there and discover that he works for a super-thug who in turn works for a super-thug who is in the employ of some third-world tyrant, and you and I and what we do are unrecognizable on a microscope slide compared to them."

"They killed a woman because she made a mistake," said Daeng. "And then they tried to kill me. They're cowards."

Civilai reached heavenward in desperation. "Tell her, Siri," he said. "Tell her."

"I'm very fond of you," Siri said to her.

Civilai waved angrily, as if he were conducting a large but invisible orchestra of tone-deaf musicians.

"That's . . . that's not what I want you to tell . . . I want you to let her know she's not working underground for the Pathet Lao any more. It's not hand-to-hand fighting. Tell her she's standing in front of a speeding freight train. Heaven help me. What a match you two are. A pair of perfect idiots."

"Nobody's perfect," Siri reminded him.

"Pray tell me what you intend to do with your 'prisoner' once he's spilled whatever beans you expect to get out of him," Civilai continued. "Or heaven help him if he refuses to talk because you know he knows that you killed his partner. Are you going to make him swear an oath not to tell anyone, and he can go on his way? Or should we just stroll over there and beat him to death right now?"

"Brother, you need a lie-down," said Daeng.

"I need . . . ? I . . . ? Yes, you're quite right. I shall go for a little sleep. When I wake up, this will have all been just a nightmare."

Civilai headed for the door of his sleeping quarters, stopped, turned around and came back. He almost said something but instead picked up the last bottle of rice whiskey and took it to bed with him. It was barely 6 P.M. Siri and Daeng watched him go.

"He's right," said the doctor.

"He's always right," said Daeng. "That's why he's so annoying."

"Exactly what plans do you have for your captive over there?"

"I didn't even need to torture him to get a confession. I mentioned the weaver in Muang Long, and he came straight out with it. He told me yes, they'd beaten her to death, and he'd be doing the same to me as soon as he got free."

"I can imagine he was a little put out by being overwhelmed by an arthritic woman in her sixties."

"You know what else he said? He said, 'We own the police. We own the army. All the village headmen and the mayors and the governor. We own the lot of them. What do you think you're going to do to me?'"

"Is that when you hammered him?"

"My hands aren't up to it anymore. I had to use a book."

"Oh? Which one?"

"Don't know the name. It was on the shelf. There was a bear on the cover and a little boy in boots."

"Ah. Good choice."

They sipped at the last of their drinks. Siri suppressed a cough.

"I'm worried about you," said Daeng. "It's not a cold, is it?"

"Probably something tropical. My body will sort it out."

"You look awful."

"You got over it. I just need a little rest."

"You mean, the type I got?"

"Oh, right. You were busy. What should we do with your hostage? We can't hand him over to the police. You can't kill him in cold blood."

"This is a different planet, Siri. We can't use southern morals up here."

"Even so . . ."

"I don't mean kill him. Just find a way to use him to win

the next little battle. To make a statement that not everyone kowtows to the drug barons."

"It's a big fight, Daeng. Could be our last campaign if it goes wrong."

"But what a way to go, eh?"

When Civilai awoke from a blissful, dream-ridden sleep, he had no idea where he was. It was pitch-dark, and he had a rice-whiskey headache. There wasn't so much as a firefly passing the window. He felt across the mattress for his wife, and when he didn't find her, he was certain she'd left him again. But then it came to him. The trip north. The Chinese invasion. The stash.

He reached under the bed. It wasn't there. Madame Daeng hadn't told them where she'd hidden it. Where could you hide twenty kilograms of heroin? Just as well he didn't know, perhaps. But wouldn't it have been fun just to . . . to try a little? He was a virgin. He lived in the center of the opium universe and had never sampled heroin. Opium, of course. Dull. Morphine, of course for medical procedures. But never heroin. After dedicating his life to the cause, wasn't he due a little recreational drug use?

He had no recollection of the geography of the bedroom, so he climbed uncomfortably to his feet and felt his way around the wall until he reached what resembled a door. He opened it, and a distant glow led him to the veranda. There, Siri and Daeng sat on opposite sides of the table, staring at an assortment of objects lit by a candle. They looked up when he appeared.

"Good morning, Brother Civilai," said Daeng.

"What time is it?" he asked.

"Three."

"What are you drinking there?" he asked.

"Johnny Black."

"At three A.M.?"

"We couldn't sleep," Siri told him.

Civilai sat on the spare chair and stared at the bottle. "Have you won the lottery?"

"You can get almost anything from China," said Daeng.

"Okay," said Civilai. "Pour me a glass or two and remind me where the latrine is."

"You'd best not use the latrine," Daeng reminded him. "There's a flashlight on the wall inside the door. Go find yourself a bush."

"Very well."

He took the light and staggered off into the early morning. When he got back, there was a glass waiting for him with . . .

"Oh, my word," he said. "Is that soda?"

"It is," said Siri.

"And is this ice?"

"Yes."

"How can a place without electricity produce ice?"

"Antarctica does it all the time," said Siri. "You'd be surprised what you can find in Muang Sing if you have the right connections."

"I don't want to know what you've been up to all night," said Civilai.

"Are you sure?" Siri asked. "You'd be really impressed."

"I'm certain. How are we doing with the treasure hunt?"

"We've reached a point where we need your magnificent mind," said Daeng. "We have all the parts but no whole. Or perhaps we have it, but we can't see it."

Civilai took a large draft of his whiskey and smiled. "Do you suppose three A.M. is too early to start drinking?" he asked. "It's all right. Don't answer that. Tell me what you've deduced."

"Well," said Siri, "we have the handwritten sheets our

friend in Un Mai translated for us." He flattened them out on the table. "The first is a work order for a Chinese maintenance team. These are the boys who go out and fix the mistakes the main teams have made. From the list, it looks like most of the time was spent clearing landslides and repairing subsidences. The next list is a requisition order for equipment to be used on jobs where the road was washed out. It's for concrete pipe segments, cement and replacement blacktop.

"The last sheets are role and salary lists for the workers on the maintenance crews. They cover the second half of 1976. The workers' names are written phonetically in Chinese characters even though the names are all Thai Lu. Mrs. Kew said that the Lu workers would be hired in China and brought over to work in Thai Lu areas in Laos. Perhaps they thought they weren't so likely to be homesick and leave. Who knows? When he collects his pay, the worker makes his mark here in the receipt column. But here's the odd thing. It seems that every month, apart from one or two exceptions, there's a new maintenance crew. Look at this. You'd think they'd train one crew to do the job well and hang on to them. But they had some sort of rotation policy. Mostly new names from one month to the next."

"Perhaps being on the maintenance crew was some sort of incentive," said Civilai. "If you work well on the road crew, you get a month on maintenance and earn a bit extra."

"You might be right," said Daeng. "In fact, it looks like the maintenance boys got six dollars a day more than they would have as a corvée laborer. That would have been one hell of an incentive back then. You'd expect to find more names repeating—good workers coming back to the crew—but they don't."

"Do any of the objects relate to the lists?" Civilai asked.

"Apart from the fact the finger had laterite under the nail, no," said Siri. "I suppose the *yuan* banknote might refer to salaries. The pipe stem might be . . . a pipe."

"Brilliant," said Civilai. "You didn't need me at all."

"What do you make of the requisition order?" Daeng asked.

"You know, the more I drink, the more insightful I become," said Civilai.

They topped him up. There were two ice cubes in the bucket, and they gave him both. He refused the cool water in which they'd been floating. "Give me a moment," he said.

He slid the documents closer to the yellow glow of the candle and pored over them. Siri and Daeng held hands and enjoyed the warmth of the blankets they were wrapped in. Siri's cough had become a permanent wheeze.

"Very well," said Civilai, at last, holding out his glass like a fortune teller who refused to divulge the future without having his palm crossed with gold. They topped him up again. "We have inconsistencies," he said.

"Good," said Daeng.

"It occurs to me that the volume of the order far exceeds the needs of the job."

"What do you mean?" Daeng asked.

"Well," said Civilai, "let's assume that a typical road is six meters wide. We'll give them the benefit of the doubt and say eight. And let's give them an extra meter on either side to help divert any water flow. That means they'd need maximum ten meters of concrete piping from one side to the other. Here, they've ordered twenty meters per job."

"Couldn't they have laid two lanes of piping?" Siri asked.

"Of course they could, little brother. But did you notice any double lanes of piping on any of the roads we've been on this past week?"

"You're joking."

"You did?"

"No, I mean, you're joking if you think I might have noticed pipes on our road trip."

"I don't think he's joking, Siri," said Daeng.

"Civilai?"

"Observation," said the old politburo man. "When you balance budgets, you have to keep an eye on where the money's going. Things like public address systems and paving stones and pipes. You have to keep your eyes open. If you don't, there'll always be someone waiting to rip you off. Look at how much cement they put in for. There's enough to build a full-size replica of the Taj Mahal."

"So you're saying that they over-ordered so they could sell the surplus?" said Daeng.

"Given the Neanderthal conditions up here in 1976, I'd say buyers for stolen building supplies would have been few and far between," said Civilai. "But let's keep that as one option."

"Then perhaps that's why the team leader changed personnel so often," said Daeng. "So nobody would notice the oversupply."

"So let's look at the two names on the worker list that are ever present," said Civilai. "And assume that they're the ones in on the scam. The top one here—Gwan Jin—would have to be the team leader. This other one—Gwan To—has the same surname, so he might be a relative."

"Gwan Jin is on the same salary as the others," said Daeng. "Wouldn't the team leader be on a higher rate?"

"The Chinese reds like to give the impression everyone's equal. Bosses and bottom-feeders on the same salary. The foreman wouldn't complain if he was milking the project and banking the profits."

"I don't buy any of this," said Siri. "Back then, the Chinese had checkpoints all the way to the border. The only roads in and out were the ones they were building or maintaining.

They're not going to let their road crews drive through with truckloads of pilfered building supplies."

"I agree," said Civilai. "I think the only way to sort this out would be to go to one of the sites."

"The bullet could be a warning for us not to get too close," said Daeng.

"I think it's too late for that," said Civilai. "What the . . . ?"

Out of the darkness came a figure riding a bicycle. He was carrying a bucket. He let the bike drop to the ground and dragged his feet up to the balcony, then stood in front of them as if awaiting instructions. Daeng and Siri ignored him.

"What do you want?" Civilai asked. "Wait! I recognize . . . My God. It's him."

"More ice," said Daeng, who nodded at the evil-eyed man. He stepped up and put the fresh ice bucket on the table in front of them. He carried himself like an inflatable paddling pool with a fast leak.

"How on earth . . . ?"

"Be back here at seven sharp," Siri told the man, who returned to the bicycle and vanished back into the darkness.

"How did that happen?" asked Civilai, too stunned to put ice in his glass.

"You said you didn't want to know," Daeng reminded him.

"What I didn't want to know was how he died. Not how he became an indentured servant ice-bringer. Last time I saw him, he was tied to a post and spitting at me."

"It was quite simple," said Daeng.

"I doubt that."

"It was Siri's idea. We took our prisoner to the front steps of the clinic, chained him up and let him watch while I cut open the twenty bags and scattered the heroin over the dry clay in front of the building."

"You never did," said Civilai, moribund.

"Yes," said Daeng. "Then Siri and I did a sort of restrained waltz to tread the powder well into the ground until there was nothing left to snort, inject or serve with lemonade. The thug watched open-mouthed as half a million dollars' worth of dope was rendered useless."

"We said to him, 'Do you understand what just happened?'" said Siri. "He couldn't bring himself to speak. 'We just danced your stash into the dust,' I said. 'Do you know what that means?' He shook his head. 'It means two things. One, that you now have to account to your boss for the loss of twenty kilos of pure heroin. Your boss will assume that you and your partner stole it, and he'll kill you. If you run away, he'll find you because there's nowhere to run to that you can't be found. But of course, you know that. Do you know what else it tells you?' He shook his head again. All the cocky bravado was gone. 'It tells you that twenty kilograms of heroin is small change to people like us. Don't let appearances fool you. In a day, we produce a hundred kilograms. We have direct markets in France. We don't have to torture and kill people because we are a business conglomerate and we pay our employees very handsomely. Our network is bigger than you could imagine. We know all about your boss and his insignificant operation. We'll be dealing with him soon enough, if you know what I mean. You're a small-time courier and collection agent. But that isn't to say we don't have positions for people such as yourself. I'm giving you a chance to come over to us. You'd start at the bottom, of course. Rock bottom. But in a year, maybe two, you'd likely be heading a district drug cartel. We reward good employees.'"

"In fact we probably didn't need to go into all that detail," said Daeng. "I think we had his undivided attention once he'd watched all that heroin destroyed. He became very docile after that."

"I must admit it's a better result than I expected," said Civilai. "But it doesn't actually explain the whiskey or the ice."

"Well," said Daeng, "when you went to bed so early, we decided to take a stroll over to see our friends Lola and Bobby. They'd told us all about their overloaded larder, full of ingredients that would be invaluable in a San Francisco kitchen but which have absolutely no use at all here."

"Like fifty kilograms of baking powder and no oven to bake anything in," said Siri. "So we told them we could find a home for it to benefit the rural poor. Lola packed twenty kilograms of it in Jiffy bags for us."

"We replaced the flour in the canvas bag and hid the stash," said Siri.

"That's a relief," said Civilai. "My nest egg is safe."

"While we were there, Bobby showed us his latest invention," said Daeng. "A refrigerator powered by a motorcycle engine. It was no larger than a toaster oven because it had in fact once been a toaster oven, but it really did freeze. He is something of a genius. He hasn't yet worked out how to stop everything in the fridge turning to ice, but that too will come. Meanwhile, he has ice."

"I joked that with all that ice, it was a pity we didn't have anything to put it in," said Siri. "And Bobby said, 'Oh, man, Siri. You'd be shocked how many donors in the old country consider alcohol to be somewhere near the top of Maslow's hierarchy of needs.' And he opened a cupboard, and there was a regiment of full bottles. 'Take 'em all,' Bobby said. 'Me and Lola don't drink.' We could have stocked up for a month, but we decided we needed our wits about us to deal with this drug lord and his honchos. Another drink?"

11
Nobodies

The Chinese invasion of Vietnam was in its third week. For reasons observers failed to understand, the Chinese didn't launch an offensive through Laos along the road to Dien Bieng Phu even though this would have given them a tactical advantage. Instead they advanced on two fronts, continuing attacks on Lang Son, Sa Pha and Pang Tho. The Chinese were losing a lot of men in the fighting and were being held off in remote areas in which they'd expected to meet little resistance. The Vietnamese village militia was a potent defensive force.

As the Americans had demonstrated admirably in the Second Great War, friends and neighbors who happen to have been born in a country you're at war with suddenly join the ranks of the enemy. You send them off to camps, reclaim your lent lawn mower, grab their best LPs and start talking about them as "them." But Laos didn't have any camps, so a new wave of ethnic Chinese migrants found themselves on the night ferries to Thailand. Hundred-year-old businesses shut down. In Vietnam, second-generation Chinese who barely spoke their mother's language were paying gold for seats on fishing boats to Australia. Suddenly, everyone hated their

Chinese populations. Or perhaps they'd always hated them but had no excuse for doing so. How can you trust such a successful race?

Muang Sing was still quiet. The second thug hadn't shown up for his allotted 7 A.M. delivery; Siri assumed he'd taken to the hills. So our three intrepid explorers set off to visit the nearest site listed on the Chinese work roster: the village of Seuadaeng. It was the home of Auntie Kwa, the weaver they'd met at her stall at the morning market. It was the one location they had yet to visit. Some three kilometers before the village, they came to a small bridge that gave credence to Civilai's recollection of seeing a single pipeline bridge at every site. Nothing elaborate. Merely a conduit for the wet season waters, a slight incline with concrete posts to mark the pipeline.

"This is it," he said. "Kilometer seven. Right here on the work roster." He climbed down from the jeep and began to pace out the width of the empty road.

"See?" he said. "In the dry season, you'd have no idea the runoff from the rivers would come this far. No sign of a stream at all. But in the rains, the road would be washed out if it weren't for this simple little bridge. They've done a good job."

He went to the far edge of the road where a concrete pipe protruded less than a meter into the lowland beneath the verge. "There," he said. "Six meters. What did I tell you? What would they need twenty meters of piping for?"

"Water towers?" Daeng suggested.

"Do you see one?"

"No."

"And why build a water tower?" Civilai continued. "This is three days' work at the most."

Daeng looked around. There were no buildings to be seen. No cows in the dry fields. In fact, the only life was a girl coming in their direction on a bicycle.

"Maybe she . . . ?" Siri began.

"Let me," said Daeng. She limped along the road to greet the girl, who braked and looked like she considered turning around.

"Hello, little sister," Daeng shouted.

The girl didn't reply. She looked querulously at Daeng.

"Do you speak Lao?" Daeng asked.

"Little bit," said the girl, so quietly the rustling grass almost drowned out the sound.

"Do you know Auntie Kwa?" Daeng asked as she mimed the weaving process.

The girl let out a brief smile, then recaptured it. She nodded.

"She's my good friend," said Daeng. "We're going to visit her. Is she home?" She finally reached the girl.

"She at the market," said the girl. "I go now." She put her foot on the pedal, but Daeng leaned against the metal basket.

"Wait," said Daeng. "Let me rest first. Do you remember when the workmen came to fix this road?"

"I don't understand."

"Men. Chinamen. Thai Lu."

A bolt of anger passed across the girl's face. She remembered right enough, and it clearly wasn't a good memory.

"What happened?" Daeng asked.

The girl shook her head and tried again to push down on the pedal.

"Where was their camp?" Daeng asked. "Where did they sleep?"

The girl pointed to a dip beyond a copse of trees some fifty meters away. "Sleep there," said the girl. Then added the word, "Always."

She pushed past Daeng and cycled away at speed.

Daeng returned to join the men. "Something odd," she said, and told them what the girl had said.

"What's odd is that they'd pitch camp so far from the road and in a dip," said Civilai. "According to the roster, they were here in the rainy season. There's high ground there on the other side. Why wouldn't they pitch camp there?"

"Perhaps they didn't want to be seen doing whatever it was they were doing," said Daeng.

They walked across the crusty earth to a point beyond the trees. There were the remains of three bamboo sheds.

"Well, they were obviously here for longer than the three days," said Siri. "You don't bother to build a hut unless you're staying for a while. For just three days they'd use tents or sleep under the stars. They must have used this base for other work around Muang Sing."

"If they were here long enough, they might have used the pipe segments to line a well," said Daeng.

"Possible," said Civilai. "But they were here because there was too much water. I doubt they needed to dig for it."

"Look," said Siri.

He was crouching down. The others came over to look. There at the doctor's feet was a spent bullet, slightly buckled. There was another a few meters away. Over the next twenty minutes, they found five more.

"They're the same caliber as the one we found in the hem of the *sin*," said Daeng. "I wonder what they were shooting at."

"If they stayed for a while, they'd have to get permission from the headman in Seuadaeng," said Siri. "He might be the person to ask. Let's pay him a visit."

"Ah, yes," said the headman after handing Civilai back his well-used *laissez-passer*. He was the rosy brown of chestnuts. "I remember the crew. They were here for three weeks. They fixed our road, then went off on other day trips."

"Did you have any trouble with them?" asked Civilai.

"Trouble? No. Goodness me, no trouble at all. Very polite they were. You know, they were all Lu, like us. From China, but the same language. Same culture. We look after our brothers and sisters. It's like me, you see? I'm from a Lu village down south. Our beloved government transferred me up here to be headman. And look . . . I accepted immediately, no worries. I have great friends already and an industrious wife."

The wife looked up from her scrubbing, a baby strapped to her back and another at her feet. She looked drained as a result of her industry.

"Did anything . . . unusual . . . happen on the night they struck camp?" asked Daeng.

"Unusual in what way?"

"Did you hear any shots fired?"

"Shots? Well, of course they were hunting down there. There'd be rifle fire from time to time. But nothing out of the ordinary. What exactly is your purpose for being here, comrades?"

Civilai butted in. "The Chinese road program is being phased out," he said. "Our beloved government would like to identify workers who were particularly conscientious in their endeavors to assist us in the development of our nation. We have medals to give out."

"I see," said the headman. "Then you've come to the right place. You won't find anyone better than the man who ran that maintenance team. The Chinese recognized his diligence. He went from head of that small team to become the head foreman of the entire workforce."

"His name wouldn't be"—Siri looked at his paper—"Guan Jin, by any chance?"

"Yes, I believe that is his full name," said the headman. "A most helpful and intelligent man."

"Do you know whether he's still around these parts?" Daeng asked.

"Why, yes, comrade. In fact I saw him just yesterday. He'd be easy enough to find. Just ask anyone where you might find Goi."

"Goi?"

"That's right. It's his Lao nickname."

The visitors exchanged glances. Another piece had slotted into place. They gave their thanks and returned to the jeep. As they were climbing in, the industrious wife ran out with a basket of fruit. The headman looked on proudly from the doorway. The woman put the basket on Daeng's lap.

"Thank you," said Daeng.

"Thank you for visiting," said the woman. She kept a tight grip on Daeng's wrist. "The night they finish camp," she said hurriedly and with a tremor in her voice, "there are shooting and scream. Twenty-six shot. One—one—one—one, like that."

"So where to?" asked Civilai.

"Back to the camp," said Siri.

"Goi," said Daeng. "The little finger himself."

Goi was a common word for the smallest of the litter. As soon as the headman mentioned the foreman's nickname, they'd all remembered the severed pinky. Had the first clue been the identity of the perpetrator?

"You do realize the headman is, in some respect, in cahoots with this Goi?" asked Civilai.

"Yes. But he won't expect us to go back to the camp," said Siri. "He thinks we're after the foreman."

"There's just the one road. Anyone passing would see us parked."

With that the jeep veered across the road, careened down the embankment and began to bump over the dried paddy fields.

"Four-wheel drive," mouthed Siri into the rearview mirror.

"I believe Madame Daeng with her natural padding would be better placed on this backseat," said Civilai. "The springs have all but given up on me."

With that he took off, his head hitting the canvas roof.

"That will teach you not to insult a full-figured woman," said Daeng.

They parked behind the small oasis of vegetation and went back to the area where they'd found the bullets. They each sat on a slice of tree that had been placed around a hearth. For several minutes they sat still and contemplated. It was Daeng who spoke first.

"Twenty-six shots," she said. "Thirty-one names on the work roster."

"And not a gunfight," said Siri. "The shots were spaced out. An execution. What do you suppose happened that night?"

"We are reading quite a lot into a brief statement from a miserable woman," Civilai reminded them.

"She was shaking," said Daeng. "She was terrified. I get the feeling she was taking a chance to talk to us at all."

"Come on," said Siri. "We're all thinking the same thing."

"It's just so . . . so obscene," said Daeng.

"It would fit in with the missing supplies," said Siri. "Twenty-six bodies buried in soft earth would be found soon enough. Dogs or wild animals would dig them up. The floods would wash them out. If I were about to make twenty-six bodies disappear forever, I could think of no better way than to bury them in cement in concrete pipe segments."

"And they'd even dig their own graves," said Civilai. "None of them would question a foreman who told them to dig wells in the middle of nowhere. Probably think it was some long-term plan."

"But why?" Daeng asked.

"Money," said Civilai. "Eventually everything's about money."

"But these workers were earning peanuts. It would be like stealing rice from a beggar."

"On an individual basis, perhaps," said Civilai, "but look at the mathematics. You wipe out a maintenance team, and you collect twenty-six salaries. Add to this the earnings they have in their bedrolls or their money belts. It was 1976. There were no banks. No money transfer agencies. They wouldn't trust anyone to take the money home for them. They'd do a six-month stint in Laos and carry their salaries around with them until it was time to go home. They might even ask the paymaster to hang on to their money until they left the job. If you eliminated them after they'd been here for several months, you could make a nice little income."

"And there would be no accounting for losses," Siri added. "They'd been recruited by an agent on the Chinese side, brought to a remote area in a foreign country at a time when nobody knew who was in control. An illiterate foreign laborer disappears. The family back in China waits a year for him to come home. They make a complaint to their local cadre. A slow and indifferent inquiry is conducted, and the findings come out something like, 'Look, lady, your son ran away from the road crew. He found a local girl and married her.' End of story. This is outlaw country where people like Goi reign. Nobody cares."

"Somebody cares," said Daeng. "Someone's gone to a lot of trouble to get us involved. Whoever put together this chain of clues knows what happened here. They understand they can't tell the local authorities, and they'd be very unlikely to interest anyone in Vientiane. But someone knew about you, Siri. Perhaps they had dealings with you somewhere down the line. They knew you wouldn't be able to resist a mystery like this. You were their only hope."

"What can I do?" Siri asked.

"Collect enough evidence to bring Goi to justice," said Daeng.

"We don't even have any bodies," Siri reminded them.

"Then let's start digging," said Daeng.

"But let us dig intelligently," said Civilai. "I for one would prefer to use an implement rather than scratch around with my bare fingers."

"Fear not," said Siri. "We have a Willys."

Clamped to the underside of the jeep were a spade and a pick. Admittedly they were suitable for diggers of short stature, which under normal circumstances would have included Siri. But Daeng forbade him from physical labor.

"Look at you, Dr. Siri," she said. "You're in no fit state to stand up, let alone dig."

The normal Dr. Siri would have argued, but the unwell Siri recognized his limitations. He was ill. Very ill, and in need of rest. "In that case, I shall show you where to dig," he said, and climbed into the jeep.

The earth in the dell was soft from the seasonal floods, and Siri began to drive up and down the gully. Civilai and Daeng sat on the log sections and watched him for some ten minutes. The dirt sank beneath his wheels with every run, all but in two spots where slight mounds appeared.

"He exhibits signs of cleverness from time to time," said Civilai.

"He married me," said Daeng by way of confirmation.

Siri cut the engine and leaned back in the seat. "I'd have a go over there if I were you."

Civilai and Daeng did as they were told, but they were a meter down in one of the mounds and still had no evidence of a burial. They were about to give up and divert their attention to the other mound when Civilai's shovel hit something solid. Together they cleared away the dirt with their hands, and sure enough, there was a large round table of concrete beneath them. So slapdash was the finishing that the fingers of a human hand protruded from it at one corner. Only one finger was missing: the pinky of the left hand.

"Shit," said Daeng. "It's true." She sat back on her haunches and shook her head.

Siri left his seat and came over to see what they'd found. "I'd wager this isn't the only site," he said.

"How many times do you think they got away with this?" Daeng asked.

"How many *sins* were there?"

"Seven. You don't think . . . ?"

"I wouldn't be surprised if we found a burial ground like this at every site we visited," Siri said. "Everywhere Goi and his associates set up camp with his maintenance crew. I bet he massacred every last one of them and stole from them. That was his initial funding for bigger and worse things. I imagine the skeletons in our new friend's killing fields lay far and wide."

12

The Seventh Deadly Sin

There really was no other choice but to proceed to the site at the end of the loop, the Thai Lu village eleven kilometers down the Nam Tha River where the seventh *sin* was produced. It wasn't the type of place you'd have to search for because it sat quite boldly beside the road to Luang Nam Tha. The village straddled the river, but there was no bridge. Villagers had become used to wading the wide shallow water course to visit friends or shop or run to meet guests who stopped on the roadside high above.

"It would appear they're expecting us," said Civilai.

A throng of children had scaled the steep hill and were huddled around the jeep. "It's him," said one child, pointing at Siri as if he were a pop star.

There was a group "Ooh" and a lot of incomprehensible Lu, and the girl who had recognized Siri said in Lao, "This way, Grandfather. Follow us."

"This is peculiar," said Civilai.

By now, Siri barely had the strength to walk. Daeng and Civilai propped him up on either side. They followed the children down to the river valley, across the pleasantly cold water and up the far bank to the schoolroom. It was a bamboo-and-straw affair with a dirt floor. But there were enough decorations and flowers to suggest it was a well-loved building. A blackboard message shouted WELCOME, DR. SIRI AND OTHER RESPECTED GUESTS in chalk. Some of the children showed the guests to their benches, and others brought them cool drinks.

"Do you suppose they do this for anyone who happens to stop on the road?" Civilai asked.

They sipped at their drinks and watched through the large classroom window as a group of adults gathered downriver and began to walk up along the track. Most of them were women. It didn't take long before first one, then two others became recognizable. There was Nang Uma, the young woman who ran the riverside guesthouse in Luang Nam Tha. Beside her was Auntie Kwa, the grumpy weaver they'd met at the morning market in Muang Sing. But to their utter surprise, behind them, as neat and presentable as ever, came Madame Chanta from the Women's Union, the woman who'd first pointed them northward on their hunt for the source of the severed finger. They walked into the classroom and immediately went to their guests.

"Congratulations on uncovering all our clues," said Madame Chanta, walking from visitor to visitor and shaking their hands. "Dr. Siri, I have a letter here for you from your Nurse Dtui. Oh, my. What on earth is wrong with you?"

"Fear not," Siri said, taking the letter and ripping it open. "I'll live long enough to discover what this show is all about."

Madame Chanta called to a wine-bottle shaped woman and spoke to her in Lu. The woman ran off. "We're getting you something," Madame Chanta said. "Something natural."

Siri laughed as best he could. "I'm in this state because of local remedies," he said. "I'm being naturopathed to death. What I need is some good old chemical compounds in familiar wrappings. Something so far from the tree that no natural contents are even mentioned on the packet." Then he buried his mind in the thick wad that was Dtui's letter.

"You're Lu?" said Daeng, ignoring her husband.

"My father was," said Chanta. "My mother was Lao Loom. She was a buyer of *pha sins* for the royal family. I continue her work in a small way in projects for the Union. I train country girls to master the skills that a generation of wars has wiped out. Even here in the north, weaving is a dying art. On your journey you've seen what's left of a Thai Lu cottage industry that just thirty years ago boasted a hundred and eighty looms. Mothers and daughters working together. When I traveled around the north collecting *pha sins* and laying out the clues for you, I was shocked at how few Lu weavers remained."

"All right," said Civilai. "Very sad, but why did you set up this corny treasure hunt? Why couldn't you just stop off at the Minorities Committee and tell them what you suspected? The police department, even?"

"I lodged a complaint there a year ago, comrade," she said. "I went back every month to see what had been done about it. I'm always told it's pending. That there were more pressing matters. I think that means they didn't believe me."

"I understand that," said Daeng, "but at the very least, couldn't you have come to me and Siri and told us directly what you suspected?"

Chanta sat at a spare desk and smiled. "Sister Daeng," she said, "do you recall a visit you paid to the union earlier in the year? You were telling us about the delegations you received from the downtrodden, the victims of crime and abuse."

"I do recall that," Daeng said.

"And do you also remember telling us about the problem you had discerning fact from fiction? About the storytellers who engaged you both in fantastic flights of fancy? Of tales that were just too bizarre to be true?"

Daeng nodded.

"But in all those visits," Chanta continued, "did you ever hear of anything so farfetched as an ugly, small-statured man with no physical strength who was able to establish a reign of terror? Whose name made grown men tremble? Who had been able to fund a drug empire from the blood of hundreds of his own tribe? You don't know me very well, Sister Daeng. There was no reason for you to believe a story from me than from any other of your couriers of the implausible."

"And so, the mystery hunt."

"One day, Dr. Porn and I were discussing Dr. Siri's fascination with cinema and crime fiction. I had a script that I really wanted somebody to read, but you had a queue of needy. I had to pitch my screenplay in a way that would really . . ." She stopped for a minute as a noisy Chinese truck crawled past the village on the main road. ". . . that would really distinguish my story from all the others."

"And how could you fail to get my attention with a finger in a skirt hem and a tasty clue to its origin?" said Siri.

"I knew Madame Daeng would seek out an expert on *pha sin*s from the north, and that expert would naturally be me. The only mystery was the color of the cloth you showed me. I knew Auntie Kwa only used blue cloth, so I was shocked when you showed me the *sin* with the green hem in your garden that evening. But I was unable to contact Auntie for an explanation."

"I still don't get it," said Auntie Kwa. "I'd posted my blue material as Madame Chanta instructed me. I greased the paper so the frank stamp would be worn off in transit and didn't put a return address. I was expecting you to come and see me, but I had no idea why the cloth had changed color. So I just played along. Sent you on to the next clue."

Siri held up the letter in front of him. "I believe I can explain exactly how that happened."

"Well, that's a relief," said Auntie Kwa. "We've all been wondering."

"So you're all in on it?" said Civilai.

"We had to get you up here," said Chanta. "To get you personally involved. To meet the players. To understand why we little people can't do anything to stop the horror that has taken over our province."

"We suspected the worst at Seuadaeng when we heard the shots," said Auntie Kwa. "We went there hoping to reclaim the bodies and cremate them. But they were buried in concrete. All we could retrieve was one finger. We knew who was responsible, so the little finger was symbolic. For a number of years we preserved it in formalin and displayed it on our altar. We had no idea there would be other atrocities."

"How many maintenance teams were there?" asked Civilai.

"It went on for a year," Chanta told him. "All the workers who disappeared were Lu from the Chinese side. Foreman Goi assumed that because they were Chinese, the Lao Lu wouldn't particularly care what happened to them. He figured we were too self-centered and stupid to notice what was going on in our midst. But we're the same blood. Our ancestors lived and worked and fought alongside one another. We all heard the rumors, but it took us some time to believe them. None of us wanted to imagine that a man could be so despicable. Foreman Goi was smart. There's no denying that. He got the work done. He could communicate with both sides, keep the books straight, iron out little administrative bumps. His only problem was the unreliable Thai Lu workers who—according to him—ran off on payday to the nearest booze shop and were never seen again. Drunkards, every one of them. Philanderers. They felt sorry for him in Peking. They admired how he could be so efficient in the face of such an unreliable workforce. How he could always recruit new workers. He was their star."

She seemed exhausted from the telling of her story. The villagers standing around the room hung their heads as if desperation were too heavy a hat to bear.

"So, Dr. Siri," she said, "what were the Thai Lu to do? The complaints from families didn't come through the official bureaucracy. They arrived along traditional routes: word of mouth and familial ties. And where did the telling end? With a rare educated Lu woman in Vientiane who taught people how to weave. How else could she tell her tale other than through the cloths that bound our people together? I'm afraid not all of our weavers could join us here today; Madame Duang in Muang Xai apparently slipped back into some other dimension. And of course we lost our sister in Muang Long."

She squeezed the hand of the weaver standing beside her; the weaver bowed her head in respect.

"But her death was not in vain," Chanta continued, "because in that simple scene you were able to witness the natural escalation of Goi's empire. In that first year, he makes enough from robbing the dead to buy up a stock of opium. From there he brings in chemists from China to produce pure heroin. He has his mobile team passing the villages to pick up the stashes and send them back across what is a very porous border. With the latest events—the invasion and all—there's been a mad rush to pick up long-term stashes like the one in Muang Long and get them out before all the road teams are kicked out of the country."

"Do you think Goi's left already?" Daeng asked.

"No," said Civilai.

They all looked at him.

"It was part of the arrangement," he said. "We asked the maintenance team to stay and continue with their program to make all the roads passable. It was a sort of token gesture to let the Chinese know we're just bowing to international pressure. He's here somewhere."

"And I imagine he's stopped massacring his work crews," said Siri. "By now he'd have a loyal team, a sort of personal entourage of thugs to protect him. It's what all the tsars do."

Daeng looked at Siri and smiled. She knew this addendum was for her benefit. Drug lords did not take kindly to the theft of their hard-earned stashes or the murder of their henchmen.

The remainder of the day was something akin to a United Nations workshop, albeit with practical outcomes and a budget that ran to a few baskets of sticky rice. The weavers and the elders and the visitors from Vientiane split into groups and drew up a list of contingencies and resources and other considerations to successfully wage war with a drug baron. They skipped the *how will this make you feel?* part of the process because it was damned obvious they'd all feel a lot better knowing they weren't going to be murdered in their bedrolls at night.

One of the major components of the resulting plan was the immediate involvement of Inspector Phosy, who, the weavers were convinced by their visitors, would stop heaven and earth to capture a freak like Goi. Siri had been disappointed not to make contact with their friend while he was in the north, but a villager was dispatched to Luang Nam Tha post office to attempt to make contact with the inspector upon his return to Vientiane. Just that small hope seemed to make everyone feel much calmer about events.

The Lu prepared a huge meal for their saviors and talked confidently yet drunkenly of a grassroots militia that would turn the tide against the pervading drug politics in the north. Siri had retired early and was unconscious the second his head hit the pillow. Before retiring for the night, Madame Daeng walked Chanta to a bench in the little village square.

The path was lit by a vast ocean of stars. They held hands as they bathed in its glow.

"I imagine you're starting to panic around now," said Daeng.

"I haven't slept a night since it all started," Chanta confessed.

"You've done a great thing."

Chanta looked at her role model. "That sounds like one of those 'You've been a great asset to the company but . . .' introductions."

"Not at all. Well . . . perhaps a little," said Daeng. "You are unquestionably brilliant, but don't forget the best armies keep their generals way behind the front line. You shouldn't be up here. You can better fight this fight in Vientiane."

"You don't think we can win this battle, do you?"

Daeng laughed. "Well, let me just think. You're asking me whether I believe a small group of weavers can vanquish a tyrant who has enough money to buy half a country. I'll be honest. You cut off the head of the *naga*, and within seconds a new head grows out of the neck. And you can hack away all day and night, and at one stage you notice that there are two heads now growing out of the neck. All you get is a lot of blood and a sore arm."

"This isn't exactly an inspirational talk."

"It could be if you're inspired at the end of it to go back to Vientiane."

"Daeng, I've given these people hope."

"And that's enough. Now we go back to the capital and put together a strategy to overwhelm Goi. You don't beat people like him on the battlefield."

"Who are you?"

"What?"

"You aren't Madame Daeng. Madame Daeng has always

encouraged us to take up a weapon and make a stand. To attack."

"Oh, her. She's having the night off. I'm the rational, logical Daeng."

"No, she's here. But she's afraid she can't give her full attention to the war."

Daeng looked away, but Chanta leaned forward so she could see the face of the doctor's wife. She could see the old lady's eyes welling with tears. Her hands were trembling.

"She's here loving her husband," Chanta continued. "She's the Daeng who wants a hospital close by. A pharmacy. She's a Madame Daeng who's afraid of the end of a dream."

"Don't talk such utter rot. How dare you?" Daeng got clumsily to her feet, still not looking Chanta in the face. "I brought you here to compliment you," she said, "and you dare talk to me like this? Do you have no respect?" She hobbled off.

"It's nothing to be ashamed of," said Chanta. "He's lived a good life."

"Bitch!" was the last word she heard.

"You have to tell them, you know."

"I don't think it would help, Bpoo."

"They have a right."

"They'd just worry. Make it all messier."

"Then Daeng, at least. You owe her that."

"That's funny. You giving me advice on dying with dignity. There's only one way. Neat. Sudden. The world shocked that there's no more Siri in it, a brief intimate ceremony and we can get on with the next act."

Siri and Auntie Bpoo were sitting on a telephone wire, looking down at the Mekhong. They were on the Thai side, and they could see the sleepy village of Vientiane opposite. One red moon set over Bangkok to the south, and another, even redder, set beyond the Chinese border to the north. A flock of chickens flew beneath them, skimming the surface of the river and squealing with delight.

"This is another dream, I presume," said Siri.

"As opposed to . . . ?"

"Premature reincarnation."

"Are you in such a hurry to be dead?"

"I thought this might be—you know—orientation."

"You really want to come back as a blue tit?"

"The flying part appeals to me. Holding on to a live wire with my toes is a challenge. It hurts. And I mean, how does one balance? Birds have little heads and unusually cumbersome bodies. The fulcrum is somewhere around their bladder."

"For a dreaming person, you really are investing far too much time on details."

"Right."

"Have you tried them yet? The wings?"

"Should I?"

"No better time for a metaphor."

"I just . . . ?"

"Step off the wire, spread those glorious wings and trust to fate."

Siri threw caution and himself to the wind, shouted "Yee-haw!" and dropped like a turd. Nothing he attempted would keep him airborne. He sighed and landed with an inevitable scatological splat on his bedroll. He had the taste of his own feathers in his mouth. He had a hand around his throat. It didn't belong to him.

The hand that was not wrapped around Siri's throat held a machete that glinted gently in the starlight. To his right he could see that Daeng had a knife to her throat. They had a brief moment to exchange a *this could be worse, but just in case it couldn't, you know how much I love you* glance.

Daeng was sure that if her husband had been in better shape, she could take on her assailant and have faith that he could hold off his own attacker. They both knew that a machete was a poor tool for a midnight assassination. It needed a backswing, which always gave the victim a chance to defend himself. A short, sharp blade did the job far more economically. All of which assured Daeng that they were being abducted rather than murdered.

The invaders used powerful flashlights. There were numerous beams scything back and forth on both sides of the river. From the direction of the light, it appeared to Daeng that most of the villagers were being herded upstream. There were shouts at one stage, then gunshots and screams. Then . . . silence.

Only one or two beams converged onto the track along which she was being dragged. In front of her she could see Siri, a man on either side of him, his feet barely touching the ground.

When they arrived once more at the schoolroom, it was lit by lamps in four corners. An insignificant-looking man sat at the teacher's desk, poring over documents. He seemed too shabby to be a bookkeeper. Beside him stood a man whose bulk suggested an enormous sack of onions. The lamplight reflected off the sweat on his dome of a head.

Neither man looked up when the captives were dragged in and perched on the benches. Besides Siri and Daeng and Civilai, the invaders had singled out the village headman and every one of the adults who had attended the afternoon session. The insignificant man looked up from the sheets in front of him, and his smile was like an invitation into an unlit tunnel.

"I am Goi," he said.

Daeng was disappointed that a man with less style than a vagabond could be the scourge of the north. Even history's most evil men were not averse to grooming. With his money he could have bought himself some teeth, had a haircut, found clothes that fit. Then again, some people were naturally dirty.

Goi looked up at his henchman, who went to the window and turned his flashlight on and off three times. They all heard bloodcurdling cries from the distance. Then more silence.

"The sounds you just heard," Goi continued in Lao, "were those of your entire village community being beheaded. Or at least those whose throats weren't slashed in their beds."

The deputy headman had understood the words. He got to his feet and was shot dead before he could take a step. The bullet that killed him passed through the arm of a woman in the second row. She screamed, and there was a brief moment of panic amongst the prisoners. Goi rode it out.

Daeng knew that the guards had orders to kill anyone who moved, so she remained rigid in her seat, her eyes locked on the foreman. Across the room, Siri nodded drowsily, apparently unaware of what had just taken place. The Lu sat with their heads buried in their hands, tears washing their cheeks. The fire of that afternoon had been doused in their chests.

"See what a mess you old people have made of all this?" said Goi. "So much unnecessary violence. What a lot of mayhem you've caused in such a short period of time."

He looked down again at his notes. "So," he read, "it appears you are going to defeat me with the coordination of the police in Vientiane. This force will be led by one . . . Inspector Phosy."

Daeng closed her eyes. He was reading from her notes of the afternoon meeting. There was a spy in their midst. The foreman's network was indeed far-reaching.

"Problem is," said Goi, "Inspector Phosy had a small

drowning accident. He can't even coordinate shit to come out of his own arse anymore." He laughed at his joke.

An involuntary tic passed up Daeng's leg and caused her knee to hit the underside of the desk. Two gunmen raised their weapons but didn't know who to shoot. Daeng was sucked dry by the news of Phosy. Disaster was clawing at her from every direction, and she had no control. No plan. And already she feared for another of her friends. In a situation like this, Civilai would find it impossible to keep his stupid mouth shut. But for the moment, Goi's attention was focused on her.

"You, you old bag," said Goi. "What a riot you are. I was thinking some daring gang of bandits had stolen my product. But then I heard of this stoned old bird at the market who had clearly been sampling my wares. I sent idiots to retrieve the stash, and they got what they deserved. I take my hat off to you, grandma. If I'd known who you were, I'd have gone myself. Believe me, I would have cut that smirk off your ancient face. I probably will anyway. And you even managed to turn one of my most loyal workers. Remarkable. And there I was, thinking I was such a caring employer."

He called out again in Lu, and two guards escorted Daeng's thug into the room. He was howling with pain, staggering on their arms like a child taking its first steps. Tears carved channels down the dirt on his cheeks. He had no feet.

"He won't run away again," said Goi, and produced that obscene toothless laugh that made Daeng want to get just close enough to shut him up. She'd met lunatics aplenty, but nobody had ever matched this. The various mafiosi resorted to cruelty to establish dominion, yet few would take a pleasure in their necessary work. Goi was depraved. She could tell he loved the brutality. Who would wipe out an entire village to teach someone a lesson?

She knew the plan. She and Siri and Civilai and all but

two or three witnesses would be eliminated that night. The surviving witnesses would tell the tale, and Goi's reputation would be enhanced. And the worst part was that she could truly do nothing about it.

The escorts threw Daeng's thug on the dirt. Goi pulled a pistol from his belt and shot him in the throat. She knew it was all part of the show.

"One more small matter to clear up before we say good night," said Goi. He pointed at Civilai. "You are . . . ?"

"I'm what?" said Civilai. The old politician had come to the same conclusion as Daeng. Nothing mattered.

Goi pointed the pistol at him. "Your name," he said.

"Paul," said Civilai. "It's biblical. My mother worked with Mother Theresa."

Goi was uncertain how to react.

"So, Paul," he said, "you and that dying old man over there took a jeep to Muang Xai. You stopped at the post office. One of you used the telephone to call Vientiane. What did you say?"

"I said, 'Hello. Hello. Can you hear—'"

Goi shot the weaver from Muang Sing dead and leveled his gun at the next in the line.

Civilai began to shake. He put his hands together. Tears formed in the corners of his eyes. "I told them that in 1976, seven work crews were murdered in cold blood," he said, staring Goi directly in the face. Wondering whether he'd hear the shot before he felt it. Daeng lowered her head. "I told them the men were buried in pipe segments sealed with concrete. I told them that the men worked under a foreman by the name of Guan Jin, alias Goi. That they'd trusted him. They thought their lives and their savings were safe."

Civilai was addressing this directly to the guards who stood around the room. "But Goi had no respect for his fellow man," Civilai continued. "No respect for life. And as was his habit, he had his men killed."

Goi smiled.

"Now we're getting somewhere," he said. "I'm afraid it might not be so easy to turn my guards against me because they don't speak Lao. But now I know what you know. Except my instinct tells me you didn't work all that out until after your visit to the camp at Seuadaeng. That means you were still clueless when you last phoned Vientiane. So . . ."

He leveled his gun at Civilai, who smiled and shook his head.

"I am tempted to shoot you," said Goi, "but then I'd never get to enjoy the torture while we find out where you put my stash. We did check out the clinic, of course. Awful waste of baking powder, that. We have some fun ways of getting information up here. I was expecting a bit more fight from your doctor friend. No fun at all hammering nails into someone who can't feel it. What's wrong with him?"

He leveled the gun at the top of Siri's head.

"Jet lag," said Civilai, and stood up.

"Old age," said Daeng, and she too got to her feet.

The guards didn't know who to shoot first. Madame Chanta stood up. "He sleeps a lot," she said.

"Well, let's wake him up," said Goi. He closed one eye for effect and squeezed the trigger.

"No!" cried Daeng.

The sound of the shot seemed to disorient the guards. It was quieter than Goi's two previous kills, and the old doctor's hair was unruffled. There was no sign of a bullet hole. Instead it was the guard at the blackboard who fell. Goi looked at his weapon as if it might have misfired. But then there was a second shot, and a second guard dropped to the ground. The gunfire was not coming from the schoolroom but from outside.

"Get down," shouted Daeng. She waded through the tables, grabbed Siri by the waist and wrestled him to the ground, then lay on top of him. The chaos increased all around as first one, then another, of the lamps was shot out.

From then on everything happened in shadows. Distant flashlights sliced through the night. The gunfight had a feel of desperation with everyone shooting at ghosts. Guards ran away without knowing where "away" might be. All around were the sounds of death and the wails of those begging to be finished off.

But in the melee, Goi and his henchman had crawled through a blind gap in the bedlam and found themselves beyond it. They climbed a heavily vegetated rise behind the school. Silo walked in front, breaking branches to clear the way for his boss. "Are you hit?" asked Silo.

"No, I'm not hit, stupid," said Goi. "Shut up and run."

Silo made it to the top of the embankment and had broken off half a bush so Goi might climb to the summit. He stood mesmerized as he looked back down at the sight of all the huts set ablaze. It was hypnotic. There was less gunfire, fewer cries, and suddenly the hell from which they'd escaped had become a beautiful spectacle. He could feel the warmth from the fires, see the smoke curl up and vanish in the stars. So pretty.

Goi, wheezing and clutching at his chest with his left hand, reached out with his right. He had just a few more paces to go. "Come on, stupid," he spat.

But at that second, he witnessed a phenomenon that few men experience. He could clearly see the fires reflected in Silo's eyes, burning in stereo, full of life. Then a hole appeared like a Hindu tilak on the man's forehead, and the fire lights went out in his eyes. And he was dead. Even so, he took a step forward before tipping over onto the slope he'd just climbed. And there he lay at Goi's feet. Useless.

The foreman used him as a step to climb the final meter, then rested on a flat patch of grass to catch his breath. To regain his thoughts. He had escaped. Was free to rule again. But who? What rival band had launched this attack? Or by some freakish chance, had some gang chosen that night to raid the village? Whoever they were, he'd find them. Let their god help them when that happ—

He sucked in his breath and threw himself onto the grass. The image of Silo's death had replayed in his mind's eye. The bullet hole. The blood and debris on his forehead. An exit wound. An exit wound. He had been shot from. . .

Goi turned to see a single flashlight buried in the dirt some twenty meters away across the flat top of the hill. Its beam was directed toward the sky. He'd been holding his pistol all this time, and he rolled onto his stomach with both hands in front of him. He shimmied backward until he dropped beneath the rise. He lay there, breathing heavily, hiding behind his gun.

"Whatever you're earning, I can pay you ten times more," he shouted. "Money's no object. Let me pass, and your family's taken care of for the next five years. Think about that."

Silence but for the crack of burning bamboo from the gulley.

He tried the same line in Lu, and in a variety of local languages. He even threw in English for good measure.

Silence.

He looked at the black forest ahead of him. Left. Right. Once he was in the woods, he'd be safe. They'd never find him in there.

He took aim at the flashlight, and the bullet smashed it into hundreds of pieces. But it made no difference. The stars and the fires had turned late night into day. He scurried to his left behind the crest of the rise to be closer to the trees. All he needed was permission from the sniper.

"All right," he shouted. "What is it you want? Trust me. Whatever it is, I can make it happen."

Again he worked through his languages. Again he was met by silence.

He crawled up behind a patch of shrubs and had a view across the clearing. Nothing moved, but he was aware that whoever attacked the village might send men up to find stragglers. He didn't have all night.

A figure moved across the way. Goi fired three shots. He was certain two of them had found their target, but the figure didn't drop. The foreman squinted and realized his target had no head. It was a shirt on a wooden cross. Guttural marbles of laughter rolled across the clearing.

"That's a revolver," said a voice in Lao. There was something familiar in the tone. "Nice piece of equipment, but it only has six bullets. You're out. And for future reference, you really didn't need to scramble up here through the jungle. There's a path. Much easier."

"Good," said Goi. "Very good. I could learn a lot from a man like you. Seriously. Let me hire you. What are you earning?"

"Thirty-two dollars a month," came the voice.

"I'll pay you a thousand," said Goi.

"That's very generous."

"Is it a deal?"

"You just tried to kill me."

"That happens in the heat of battle. In times of stress. But you're an intelligent man. You understand that. We don't have any personal grudges."

"Are you sure about that?"

"Come out of the shadows there, brother. You'll see I'm a common man just like you. A soldier in a fight that's none of our business."

"You aren't. You aren't a common man, and you are nothing like me," said Inspector Phosy.

He took a few labored steps forward and was illuminated in the glow from the burning village.

Goi got to his knees. "No," he said. "Not possible."

"Then I must be a ghost," said Phosy. "Which would you prefer?"

"How could you . . . ?"

"I'm not a big one for making villains feel better about themselves by explaining things before I kill them. This is just a showdown. It's the moment I was waiting for—dreaming of in those hours spent in your tomb."

"So you'll shoot me?" said Goi. "How satisfying would that be after all that time of plotting revenge?"

"Not satisfying at all," said Phosy. He held up his gun and tossed it back over his shoulder.

Goi laughed and got to his feet. All his confidence had returned and he swaggered toward the swaying detective. "Look at you. You're broken and sick and probably riddled with disease. You can barely walk. What do you propose for our showdown? Checkers?"

"Look at yourself," said Phosy. "Without your money and your bodyguards, you're a toilet mop. Except toilet mops smell better."

"So! Hand to hand."

Goi tossed aside his pistol and strode up to the policeman. He laughed. "I'm told two days of lying in shit isn't the best preparation for battle."

Phosy stepped up and took a deep breath. His eyes seemed unable to focus. It took all his effort to remain standing.

Goi was cocky now, shadowboxing to taunt his weak opponent. "Come on, sick boy," he said. "You really should have kept the gun. You aren't half the man you think you are."

Phosy took one more step toward him and sank to one knee.

"Oh, poor policeman. You realize the only way you'll win

this fight is if you accidently collapse on top of me. But wait. That might not be such a bad idea after all, because look what I've just remembered."

Goi unclipped the leg pocket of his army fatigues and drew out a forty-centimeter blade with a wooden handle. "Surprise!" he said. "Nice, isn't it."

Armed now, he marched toward Phosy, swinging his blade left and right, swishing it through the air like a pirate's scabbard. Three meters from the confused detective. Two. One. Swish, swish.

"Bye," he said, and pulled back the blade to strike.

Phosy reached behind his back to his belt and produced a Browning nine-millimeter. He fired once into the foreman's knee and watched the man drop to the grass with an incredulous look on his face.

"Surprise," said Phosy.

The foreman's eyes asked a question, but his voice was gone.

"What you saw me throw away back there was a branch," said Phosy. "The quickness of the hand deceives the eye. Why the hell would I want to fight someone like you hand to hand?"

He pumped another bullet into Goi's left foot and enjoyed the scream.

"Please don't kill me," begged the foreman. "I'm sorry. I'm sorry for what I did. Honestly. I barely sleep. The ghosts haunt me every night. I'll do better. Give me one chance, and I'll atone."

"Oh, shut up," said Phosy, and fired one more round into Goi's outstretched hand. He screamed and cried and rolled into a ball on the ground.

"I think he has enough holes in him now," came a voice.

Phosy sagged to his knees and let go of the gun. He'd used the last of his strength. His body was shaking.

Comrade Xiu Long, the last Chinese trade delegate, came up behind him and put a hand on his shoulder. "We don't want him completely dead," he said in competent Lao.

A number of men, armed but not in uniform, came out of the tree line and lifted the still-screaming foreman. When he saw Xiu Long, he switched to Chinese. Pleading. Crying. Accusing.

In Lao Xiu Long said, "You're going home now, Comrade Goi. Kindly shut up."

13

The Tears of Madame Daeng

"And all the time he could speak Lao," said Phosy. "And I had no idea, you lovely devil. And you had a doctor with you, such a versatile man. And you—I mean, he—tended my wounds and gave me awful concoctions that would clear the inevitable infestations from my internal organs. So beautifully done."

Amongst the medications the doctor had given Phosy was a brew that not only helped him forget the state of his skin, but also made him overly amorous. It was a side effect all those present could handle, even now as he sat beside the older Chinese official, squeezing his thigh. The same doctor was currently pumping Siri full of pharmaceuticals that had yet to be recognized by a health department anywhere in the universe. He was resting beneath a tree under the watchful eye of Madame Daeng. For some reason, everyone felt confident now that Siri's health was in the hands of the new enemy.

"Of course he does," said Phosy, still rambling on. "Exactly what kind of policeman am I? Of course my best friend in the world speaks Lao. The Chinese selected him to run the trade mission in Udomxai for five years, didn't they? A man can pick up an awful lot of Lao language from pretty girls in five years. Right, Xiu Long?"

He squeezed the man's thigh again. Xiu Long made no objection. Phosy looked up at the audience. Before him sat Civilai, Madame Chanta and the Lu elders. The schoolroom was the last surviving building in the village, so this was their town hall.

"I find one learns far more from conversations one is supposed not to understand than by being proactive," said Xiu Long.

"See?" said Phosy. "He speaks better than me. Proactive? I mean, how does he know words like *proactive*? He's gorgeous."

"All right," said the Lao government's delegate for Chinese affairs, also known as Civilai to the illegal immigrant Chinese ex-head of trade. "So you first came down here with Phosy under the premise of observing an investigation into an altercation between two village heads."

"That is intrinsically correct," said Xiu Long. "In fact we'd been looking for an excuse to cross back into Laos for a long time. We'd been investigating Guan Jin, also known as Foreman Goi, for some years. We have what I suppose you might refer to as spies dotted here and there, so we were aware of the level of influence the foreman wielded."

"So you did care about the plight of your Lu laborers?"

"Of course. We care about anything that adversely affects our international trade balance."

"Right. Well, that's very caring of you."

"I was interested to see how your inspector fared against such a notorious villain," said Xiu Long.

"How did I fare?" grinned Phosy, taking the time for one more squeeze.

"You were exemplary."

"Exemplary. Did you hear that? He's so lovely."

"I cleared it with our people to coordinate with Inspector

Phosy to collect evidence against Guan Jin," said Xiu Long. "But our efforts were thwarted to some extent by the invasion of Vietnam, the expulsion of Chinese road crews from Laos and troop maneuvers along the Lao border."

"Maneuvers that spilled over onto our side," said Civilai.

"Pure hearsay," said Xiu Long with a smile. "By the time we'd worked through the horrendous mountain of paperwork that results from the wholesale movement of troops, we'd lost touch with the inspector. Our chief spy on the work crews had been sent back to China, and his replacement had trouble locating Inspector Phosy."

"I was underground lying in shit." Phosy smiled and squeezed the Chinese knee once again.

"Indeed you were, Inspector. And for that I apologize. We blinked at a very important second. Our new man was a skilled craftsman who secured a position on the remaining maintenance team. He'd also had experience on Goi's bodyguard detail in the past. He was there the day they pulled Phosy out of the warehouse and dragged him to the edge of the crevasse. The worker pushed him over the edge, and he fell thirty meters. Fortunately the cliff was at the edge of a sand quarry that had filled with water. Our man pulled him to the bank. The inspector was in a terrible condition, however. A lesser man would have succumbed to those injuries."

"Succumbed," said Phosy drowsily.

"Foreman Goi had apparently received important news at that moment," said Xiu Long. "He and his men leapt into their trucks and fled, leaving just the one guard at the warehouse. Our man had stayed behind and hidden in the bushes. He was able to overpower the guard, release the other prisoners and go to the aid of Inspector Phosy. The warehouse was located no more than twelve kilometers from the border, and as you know, Comrade Civilai, we happened to have a large number of men at our disposal. We brought in a unit with a medical team and cared for the victims and took photographs for evidence. Inspector Phosy still had the authority to approve a joint operation. We decided to go after Foreman Goi.

"We had heard all about you and Dr. Siri by then, of course, Comrade Civilai. The brave politburo man who drove into an invading army and prevented serious border transgressions. Quite a feat, Comrade. I had made a similar recommendation myself but had been ignored. Through our network and reports of sightings of your *laissez-passer* at checkpoints, we were able to trace your comings and goings during your stay here. It became clear that you were visiting Lu villages and investigating the construction sites along our new roads. If you were able to collect any evidence against the foreman, I would greatly appreciate your sharing it with us."

"I have enough evidence to make your noodles curl, comrade," said Civilai.

"Excellent. Excellent. When we heard of your meeting with the headman at Seuadaeng Village and your interest in Foreman Goi, we had someone follow you here. We were all in pursuit of the same prey. We weren't sure what to expect, of course. We arrived shortly after, and our men took up positions in the hills and waited. But not long after you arrived, a Chinese truck traveled along the road above the village. We knew the license plate. It contained Goi and his henchmen. They stopped two kilometers along the road, waited until nightfall and made their way back here. When they started to herd the villagers to one central point, it was evident what their plan was. We intervened. Goi's men had torched some huts, and we weren't in time to stop the spread of the fire, but we did save the lives of most of the villagers.

"The inspector had seen you frog-marched in the direction of the school, and we followed them with a dozen men. We surrounded the schoolhouse. Our men had no clear angle to get off shots at Goi, but when the shooting began inside, we had no choice but to take out the guards and create as much chaos as possible. One of our team reported sighting two enemies climbing the hill behind the school. When we entered the schoolroom and found no sign of Goi and Silo, we knew where they'd gone. We took the pathway to the hilltop, and—against my objections, it must be said—Inspector Phosy insisted on conducting the arrest himself. As we were merely visitors, we stood back as we were told. Fortunately, Foreman Goi survived his injuries from that encounter and is well enough to travel to Peking. There he will face trial for his crimes against nationals of the PRC. Like your good selves, we do not consider our ethnic minorities to be any less Chinese than ourselves, or any less deserving of justice. Once he wakes up, I shall extend a formal invitation to Inspector Phosy to attend the trial."

Phosy was snoring gently with his head on Xiu Long's shoulder.

They took it in turns to suck rice wine through straws from the ceremonial pot and dedicated their round to Phosy and to the demise of a tyrant who had made their lives a misery. It seemed that everything bad had been erased. That, after a long period when everyone lived in fear, life could continue. Even when the gathering became rowdy, Phosy did not wake up.

It was when the dregs in the pot had started to taste more of water than of spirit, and the fatigue of the night's events began to drag them down and lure them to bed, that Civilai looked to the open doorway and was immediately struck sober. He'd known Madame Daeng for a considerable time, but he'd never seen her cry. She leaned against the doorframe, and tears raced down her face.

"Daeng, what is it?" he shouted.

had fled. Crazy Rajhid brought a two-meter jasmine bush. Nobody objected.

Reluctantly, it seemed, ministries had sent along representatives to pay their respects to a man who had been a thorn in their arses for too many years. They sat in rickety cane chairs and stared into space as they listened to one of the few monks who could remember all the sutras. He had been imported from Mixai Temple across the way. There were no actual ministers or vice ministers in attendance because the Party line was still that religious ceremonies fell under the auspices of superstitious nonsense. Party members who were in need of a blessing for this or that had taken to smuggling in monks in the dead of night to perform secretly in their houses.

Judge Haeng, still aspiring to become a minister, had sent a note to say he was sorry he couldn't come, but he had been called to an urgent meeting down-country. Two of the mourners had seen him sipping cocktails at the Anou with a girl with what they politely referred to as "a remarkable set of breasts." But despite the lack of safari suits, the hall was far from empty. In fact, it was rocking. When word got out of Dr. Siri's demise, even though they faced a day of docked wages, the common folk had put a halo of red around the date on their calendars. Hay Sok Temple hadn't seen such a gathering since the old regime. Groups sat in the shade of banana trees playing cards. Others reminisced with their favorite Dr. Siri stories.

The body lay on a teak bench under a white silk shroud. The left arm was exposed, held out above a pewter bowl of blessed water. The white-clad mourners had formed an orderly queue, almost unimaginable in any other branch of Lao society, and were using an engraved cup to pour lustral water over the open palm. They laid sandalwood flowers and lilies across the shroud and shuffled on to enjoy the breakfast feast spread on tables beneath parasols outside.

14
Above and Beyond

Dr. Siri's funeral was conducted at Hay Sok Temple on Sethatirat Road. During his early years in Vientiane, Siri had lived in a single room that overlooked the dusty, underloved grounds. He'd watched as, one by one, the monks had left the order until there was only one full-time abbot. And Siri had never been too sure whether he was human or spirit.

Siri's single room and the old house that contained it had been blown to bits by a mortar. But Siri spoke fondly of his nights at his kitchen table looking down at the dirty stupa and watching nature slowly reclaim the altars and the spirit houses. Only the prayer hall remained unforested, and it was there that a large photograph of Dr. Siri sat on an easel in the entrance.

There had been few photographs of the doctor, so like his house, his passport photograph had been blown up until it was almost unrecognizable. The face was a blur, but the studio had kindly touched up his white hair and eyebrows and given him green eyes. Though it was an abstract Dr. Siri, visitors still laid flowers in front of it. There were no florists in 1979 Vientiane, so posies had been collected from the forests or stolen from the front garden of families who

"It's not a bad turnout, really," said Siri.

"Most respectable," said Auntie Bpoo.

"I thought being dead might be more . . . more depressing."

"Death's what you make of it."

"Yes. Nice. Really nice."

"Look at all those people. Some traveled overnight without *laissez-passer*s, took their chances avoiding military check-points, just so they could be here. They've camped outside in the grounds. Do you know them all?"

"Not half. There are those I've seen, but most, if I've ever met them, I've forgotten where and when."

"But they remember you. That's the important thing."

"I imagine most folks wouldn't have a chance to observe. There's something sort of angelic about sitting up here look-ing down on your own funeral. Oh, look. There's Madame Lah, the baguette woman. I almost married her, you know. I'm surprised she's here. I thought she hated me."

"She probably does. Funerals are good for muttering curses under your breath when your turn comes in the queue. When she gets to your hand, she'll probably break your finger."

"Don't be cruel."

"The dog's a nice touch, lying there beside his master. I should have had animals at mine."

"You did—pigs, goats, buffalo."

"They were grilled. I don't think that counts."

"Ugly's more than just a dog, anyway. He was somebody relevant in a previous life."

"Oh, don't. Once you start getting into all that mumbo jumbo, you'll be stepping around cockroaches in case they were your granny. He's a dog."

"No. Look at him. Don't you think he knows what he's doing? He's on duty. Vigilantly protecting me from evil."

"He's asleep."

The queue of mourners snaked past the body, some stopping to dribble a little water, others splashing as if they were bailing out the *Titanic*. But most passed as quickly as they could. Too much time spent with a dead body was like standing in the rain and hoping for pneumonia. There were lost spirits in temples looking for new souls to inhabit.

Mr. Geung and his fiancée, Tukda, had walked respectfully to the body, but when the lab assistant reached the outstretched hand, he grabbed it and fell to his knees. "No!" he cried. "Don't g-g-go, Comrade Doctor. I love you."

The prayer hall fell silent for a moment. Then the chatter and the chanting continued. Tukda pulled at his arm, and reluctantly, Mr. Geung got to his feet and walked on.

The guests of honor sat alone on chairs at the four compass points: Madame Daeng, all in white, north; Civilai, south; Inspector Phosy, east; and Dtui, west. This seating arrangement had nothing whatsoever to do with a Buddhist ceremony. The four nodded their respect to the mourners. Four traveling monks, their dark brown robes grubby from the road, left their alms bowls beside the photograph like restaurant diners checking their wet umbrellas at the door. They were weary and had obviously traveled far to attend this funeral.

"Should we expect some wise men from the East?" Bpoo asked. "Camels, perhaps?"

"What can I tell you?" said Siri. "My fame knows no bounds."

He looked at the faces of the monks. One was elderly, two middle-aged and muscular, the last young, tall and skinny. Siri didn't recognize them, but he'd treated many men in battle who later entered the monkhood in thanks for being given a second chance at life. The sutra soloist monk looked at them, perhaps hoping they might join him and give him a little break from his chanting, but they ignored him and joined the queue. When they reached the body, the younger monks muttered some words of praise and passed on. The older monk took the cup from the bowl in his left hand and gently held the wrist of the corpse in his right.

Siri saw Ugly's ears prick up and eyes spring open. He looked at the body and the monk, and at first, he saw nothing. But then he witnessed something quite bizarre. The monk was checking for a pulse.

"This one," he shouted.

The hand protruding from the shroud grabbed the wrist of the monk. The four guests of honor leapt from their chairs, each drawing weapons from beneath their baggy white shirts. The mourners gasped and ran for cover as Comrade Inthanet the puppet master—posing as the corpse—pulled the shroud from his body, pointed and shouted, "Aha!" All eyes turned to the lead monk, who froze for a few seconds, the cup still in his hand. Then he and his fellows reached for the hems of their robes. They were packing too.

Now, anyone who's ever engaged a monk in a gunfight will know a saffron body cloth does not lend itself to a fast draw. Only one was able to retrieve his Colt 45 in time, but before he could aim it, Nurse Dtui was on him, and he was flat on his back on the floor. Mourners charged the other monks. Mr. Geung dived at the ankles of the largest and brought him down. The residents of Siri's house soon had the younger of the monastic group bound. Only the elder monk still stood.

Comrade Noo, the Thai forest monk, arrived with a six-meter bamboo ladder and ran it up to the roof beams directly above the funeral table. A plywood partition that had been designed to look like a part of the ceiling structure was pulled aside, and to the amazement of everyone not involved in the subterfuge, Dr. Siri crawled out and began climbing down the ladder.

The elderly monk screamed and spat and swore and used all his strength to get away. But Daeng had a firm grip of his wrists behind his back, and of course, the old monk was not a man. The Lizard had reached that age when time sucks back one's skin to leave an asexual skull. She was slight but had a masculine jaw and ravaged skin, and few people would have looked twice at an elderly monk to check his gender. She drew on all her strength to break free but she was running on nostalgia. There was a time that she could have overpowered a strong man, but she was old now and had nothing but vengeance to hold herself together.

15
Side Effects

As, indirectly, the burning down of all his neighbors' houses
had been Siri's fault, he agreed to rebuild the entire block. A
relative in the refugee camp at Ban Vinai had died and left
him a small fortune. The Lao administration had reached
the stage where they preferred not to know where money
came from, as long as it came. The officials at ministries
whose duty it had been to trace the origins of donations and
investments were now taking a small fee for not looking too
closely. That Siri's windfall had not been deposited in the
Banque Pour Le Commerce Exterieur Lao was not a surprise,
as putting money there was often like dropping ink into a
pool and watching it dissolve.

Dollars arrived from somewhere every week to pay the
builders, and a good, solid row of shop houses was being
erected opposite the river. The spying Thais with their high-
powered binoculars could only look on in awe at the rate of
development.

Civilai too had seen a run of good fortune. He'd bought
a Toyota truck in Thailand, which they'd floated across the
river one night on a bamboo raft. The seller assured him
it had belonged to a deputy governor who was killed in an

accidental drive-by shooting. The official's own gun was still in the glove compartment, a sort of free gift. They sat, the three of them on their recliners on the bank of the river, but for once, they were not watching the syrupy Mekhong wend its way south. Instead, they were admiring brickwork over a glass of Glenfiddich. Only Ugly had his back turned to the building site.

"Do you suppose this is what capitalism feels like?" Civilai asked. He was twirling the Toyota key ring around his index finger.

"I'd rather like to imagine capitalists have to contribute a little bit of labor before amassing their fortunes," said Siri.

"I labored for mine," said Civilai.

"Really? What did you do, exactly?"

"I spent several days sitting in a jeep, the rear seat of which was packed with heroin. Given my propensity for hemorrhoids, that was a particularly painful endurance. Tell me the name of yours again."

"Schistosomiasis."

"I'll never remember that. Doesn't it have a friendly local name I can drop at cocktail receptions?"

"Try 'snail fever.'"

"Snail fever? You almost died of snail fever? How embarrassing. How do you avoid it? Keeping your distance from French restaurants?"

Siri and Daeng laughed. Daeng threw an ice cube at Civilai.

"It doesn't come from eating them," said Siri. "They deposit parasites on your skin when you're in the water. I probably picked it up that day we went to help the fisherwoman. It's not that uncommon. You find it often in children."

"And you, a qualified doctor, couldn't even diagnose your own snail fever?"

"I've never had it before. It presents a bit like malaria, so I was confused. I'd associated the cold as a symptom, but it was totally unrelated. We'd all just picked up the flu in Vientiane. Having the two at the same time meant my body was less able to fight it off. The local tonics I was taking weren't strong enough to cope. Snail fever's quite treatable if you have access to the right medication."

"Unlike arsenic poisoning," said Daeng.

"Exactly. If I'd been directly exposed to that, I'd be dead and gone by now. It helped no end that the first *pha sin* was kept in the plastic bag all the time. It reduced our exposure to it."

"And there was your little mitten habit," said Daeng.

"Right. That helped too. I always use plastic gloves when I'm handling evidence. It's a policy I've tried to ingrain in the idiots at police headquarters. But even with gloves I feel that if all the *sins* had been treated with Paris Green like the first one, the close proximity to them in my backpack would still have killed me. Of course we know now that it was only the original skirt that was treated. The Lizard had no idea about the treasure trail, nor did she know there was a finger hidden in the hem. She merely diverted the mail to see whether there was anything in there she could use against us. When she found the *sin*, she decided to bleach the bottom of it and redye it with Paris Green. She's the type who'd have such things lying around. That was the bleach we found traces of on the finger."

"Why didn't the finger turn green also?" Civilai asked.

"The compound is more like a paint than a dye," said Siri. "It didn't penetrate the thick cloth completely. She'd probably have applied it with a brush. When it was dry, she washed off the residue, dried it and had it redelivered to our house. Then she sat back and waited for it to kill us. Of course it would have been far simpler for her to knock on the door and shoot us to death, but that isn't her style. She needs people to know how clever she is."

"When did you first know about the poison?" asked Civilai.

"In the letter Dtui sent with Madame Chanta," said Siri. "The one I read to Daeng on my deathbed. That was the first I knew that the Lizard had survived and that she was out to get us."

"So that's when I decided to kill my husband," said Daeng. "The timing was perfect. He looked so awful."

"Thank you for sharing it with me there and then," said Civilai.

"We needed your reaction to be authentic," said Daeng. "You are quite a horrible actor."

"Perhaps not as melodramatic as Mr. Geung at the temple the other day," said Siri. "It was lucky he broke down before the monks arrived. They'd have known for sure it was a setup."

"We needed everyone at the Lu village to believe Siri was dead," said Daeng. "We only shared the truth with you and Phosy later. That's why we whisked the doctor away in the jeep so quickly. The Lizard has a network. She would have been able to trace back to see that Siri's condition was getting worse as the trip progressed. She would have assumed it was the effects of the poison. And of course, it helped that she'd been expecting one of us to die. But this was the Lizard. She's taken deviousness to a new level. And she knew we were capable of matching her cunning. She would have found it impossible to resist checking for herself that Siri was gone. We were certain she'd be there at the funeral."

"And we're certain she's . . . ?"

"No doubt about it," said Siri. "The military didn't take any chances. They were embarrassed to have lost her the first time around. They marched her directly in front of the firing squad. There are photos. The commander asked me if I'd like a couple for the album. I declined."

The moon had started to rise behind the new rafters on

the roof. Siri and Daeng walked Civilai to his truck. "Is this a bullet hole?" asked Daeng, twiddling her finger in a perfectly round puncture in the tailgate.

"Air vent," said Civilai.

"And what's next on Civilai's shopping list?" asked Siri.

"Ooh, I don't know. I was thinking of doing a bit of Robin Hooding like yourself. Handing over wads of cash to those less blessed by the gods of illicit drugs. But then I decided it would only make them miserable. We have to keep the poor content with what they have. Wasn't it Marx who said, 'An increase in wages arouses in the worker the same desire to get rich as in the capitalist, but he can only satisfy this desire by sacrificing his mind and body'? I wouldn't want to be responsible for that."

Siri laughed, slapped him on the back and said, "And wasn't it Irving Berlin who told us, 'The world would not be in such a snarl, had Marx been Groucho instead of Karl.'"

There was no roof on their new shop, but what of it? The nights were star-studded, and the second floor of the new building was complete apart from walls and windows and floor tiles. There was a mattress at the top of a wooden ladder that would soon be a flight of stairs. It was house enough for them. Daeng climbed the ladder with a spring in her steps.

Siri followed close behind. "So how are you feeling about it?"

"I told you," she said. "It's perfect. I love my new legs."

It had been two weeks since Madame Daeng drank the voodoo woman's concoction. Within a week, the ever-present aches had subdued. She could walk without a limp. She had turned her back on the opium.

"I didn't mean the arthritis," he said. "I meant the . . . side effect."

"It's . . . I don't know. I suppose I'm getting used to it."

"Do you think it's stopped growing?"

"It seems to have. And to be honest, I could tolerate it being as long as a king cobra rather than spending the last of my years a slave to rheumatism. No. It could have been much worse. What if it were a horn?"

"You'd have to wear a hat."

"A long pointed one." She lay back and admired the stars. "You don't mind it, do you?"

"Not at all. In fact I find it rather erotic."

"Siri, you would find a tin tea kettle erotic."

"If you were wearing it, my love."

"Thank you."

They heard the frenzied scurry of Ugly chasing a water rat in the road below. Then silence.

"And what of my affliction?" Siri asked.

"Hardly noticeable."

"That's good. Good night, Daeng."

"Good night, Siri."

She turned to kiss him good night.

He wasn't there.

ACKNOWLEDGMENTS

With great thanks to Carol C, Sut, Grant, Robert, Leila, Bryan, Chantavon, Bounlan, Kathy R, Martin, Kyoko, Governor X, Micky M, Lizzie, Dad, Rachel, Tony, Tang, Bambina and David.

In loving memory of Ethel Violet Victoria Cotterill, who never read these books but loved them still.

And in dedication to Sombath Somphone, who we all hope will return from the *phi bung bot* and rematerialize someday.